MAXIMUM
BOB

ELMORE LEONARD

MAXIMUM BOB

Delacorte
Press

Published by
Delacorte Press
Bantam Doubleday Dell Publishing Group, Inc.
666 Fifth Avenue
New York, New York 10103

Library of Congress Cataloging in Publication Data

Leonard, Elmore, 1925–
    Maximum Bob / Elmore Leonard.
        p. cm.
    ISBN 0-385-30142-1 : $20.00
    ISBN 0-385-30456-0 (Large-print edition) : $22.00
    ISBN 0-385-30493-5 (Limited edition) : $100.00
    I. Title.
  PS3562.E55M39   1991
  813'.54—dc20   91-6539
                                                   CIP

Manufactured in the United States of America

Published simultaneously in Canada

August 1991

10 9 8 7 6 5 4 3 2 1

BVG

For the Honorable
Marvin

1

Dale Crowe Junior told Kathy Baker, his probation officer, he didn't see where he had done anything wrong. He had gone to the go-go bar to meet a buddy of his, had one beer, that's all, while he was waiting, minding his own business and this go-go whore came up to his table and started giving him a private dance he never asked for.

"They move your knees apart to get in close," Dale Crowe said, "so they can put it right in your face. This one's name was Earlene. I told her I wasn't interested, she kept right on doing it, so I got up and left. The go-go whore starts yelling I owe her five bucks and this bouncer come running over. I give him a shove was all, go outside and there's a green-and-white parked by the front door waiting. The bouncer, he tries to get tough then, showing off, so I give him one, popped him good thinking the deputies would see he's the one started it. Shit, they cuff me, throw me in the squad car, won't even hear my side of it. Next thing, they punch me up on this little computer they have? The one deputy goes, 'Oh, well look it here. He's on probation. Hit a police officer.' Well, then they're just waiting for me to give 'em a hard time. And you don't think I wasn't set up?"

This morning Dale Crowe Junior was back in the Criminal Division of Palm Beach County Circuit Court. In a holding cell crowded with offenders wearing state-blue uniforms that were like hospital scrubs. Blue shapes standing around in the semi-dark. Kathy Baker recognized some of them. They'd step into the light to say hi through the wall of bars. Mostly black guys in there, they'd ask how she was doing. Kathy would shrug. Same old business, hanging out in bad company. She told Dale Crowe, holding open his case file, he must be in a hurry to do time. Two days out of jail he was back in.

"I haven't even had a chance to fill out your post-sentence sheet, you're in violation."

" 'Cause I went to a go-go joint? Nobody said I couldn't."

"When were you around to tell you anything? You were suppose to report to the Probation Office, Omar Road."

"They said I had seventy-two hours. I been going out to the sugar house, seeing how to get my job back." Dale turned his head to one side in the noise of voices and said, "Hey, we're trying to talk here."

The blue shapes in the dark paid no attention to him. Kathy moved closer to the bars. She could smell Dale now.

"The police report says you were drinking."

"One beer, that's all. I urine-tested clean."

"But you're underage. You broke the law and that violates your probation."

Dale Crowe Junior was twenty, a tall, bony-looking kid in his dark-blue scrubs. Dark hair uncombed, dumb eyes wandering, worried, but trying to look bored. Dale was from a family of offenders in and out of the system. His uncle, Elvin Crowe, had this week completed his prison time on a split sentence and was beginning his probation.

Kathy Diaz Baker was twenty-seven, a slim five-five in her off-white cotton shirtdress cinched with a belt. No makeup this morning, her dark hair permed and cut short in back, easy to manage. She spoke with a slight Hispanic accent, the Diaz part of her, that was comfortable, natural, though she could speak without a trace of it if she wanted. The Baker part of her was from a marriage that lasted fourteen months. She had met all kinds of Dale Crowes in her two years with the Florida Department of Corrections and knew what they could become. His uncle, Elvin Crowe, had recently been added to her caseload.

"I can go to jail but I can't have a beer?"

"Listen, I spoke to your lawyer—"

"You don't think I stop and have a few after work, driving a cane truck all day? I never get carded either, have to show any proof."

"You through?" Kathy watched him take the bars in his hands and try to shake them. "I had a talk with your lawyer."

"Little squirt, right? He's a public defender."

"Listen to me. He's going to plead you straight up, but try to make it sound like a minor violation. It's okay with the state attorney. She'll leave it up to the judge, as long as you plead guilty."

"Hey, shit, I didn't *do* nothing."

"Just listen for a minute, okay? You plead not-guilty

and ask for a trial, the judge won't like it. They'll find you guilty anyway and then he'll let you have it for wasting the court's time. You understand? You plead guilty and act like you're sorry, be polite. The judge might give you a break."

"Let me off?"

"He'll ask for recommendations. The state attorney will probably want you to do a little time."

" 'Cause I had a *beer*?"

"Maybe ask you to do some work release, out of the Stockade. Try to be cool, okay? Let me finish. Your lawyer will recommend reinstating your probation, say what a hardworking guy you are. He won't mention you got fired unless it comes up, but don't lie, okay? This judge," Kathy said, "I might as well tell you, is very weird. You never know for sure what he's going to do. Except if you act smart and he doesn't think you're sorry, kiss your mom and dad good-bye, you're gone."

"What one have I got?"

"Judge Gibbs."

It seemed to please him. "Bob Isom Gibbs, I know him, the one they call 'Big.' Election time you see his name on signs, 'THINK BIG.' He's famous, isn't he?"

"He makes himself known."

"He's the one sent my uncle Elvin away."

"Dale, he's put more offenders on death row than any judge in the state." That shut him up. "What I'm trying to tell you is be polite. Okay? With this judge you don't want to piss him off."

Dale was shaking his head, innocent. He said, "Man, I don't know," in a sigh, blowing out his breath, and Kathy turned her face away. "You gonna tell him how you see this?"

"When the judge asks for recommendations, yeah, I'll have to say something . . ."

"Well, that's good. Tell him I've been drinking since I was fourteen years old and I know how, no problem. Listen, and tell him I'm still working out the sugar house. Have a good job and don't want to lose it."

"Anything else?"

"That's all I can think of."

"Just lie for you?"

"It wouldn't hurt you none, would it? Say I'm working? Jesus."

"You think I'm on your side?"

"Well, aren't you?"

"Dale, I'm not your friend. I'm your probation officer."

She left the holding cell, the dark shapes, the noise, passed through locked doors to a well-lighted hallway and was back in the world among sport shirts and flowered dresses, people waiting for court sessions.

"What's the matter?"

Kathy looked up. It was Marialena Reyes with her fat briefcase, the assistant state attorney who would be prosecuting Dale Crowe in about ten minutes. She was a friend of Kathy's, a woman in her forties, unmarried, dedicated to her work, this morning in a brown linen suit that needed to be pressed.

"I just talked to him," Kathy said, and shook her head.

"What else is new?"

"Nothing changes. They look at me, I'm this girl who comes around with a clipboard checking up. Like a social worker."

"It's up to you. I've quit saying go back to school, get a law degree."

"I'm in court enough as it is. What will Dale get?"

"I think a year and a day. He'll only do ninety days, but it's state time. Maybe it'll scare him good."

"He's just a dumb kid, thinks he's tough."

"Sure, that's his problem. Look at the positive side. It's one less you'll have in your caseload."

"I'll still have seventy-three. I trade Dale for his uncle Elvin. He came in Saturday, this big guy from the swamp in a cowboy hat. He sits down, starts fooling with things on my desk. . . . He doesn't think it's fair he had to do ten years DOC time and now five years probation—listen to this—for shooting the wrong guy. Not the one he was after. He wants to tell me all about it sometime. His attitude, it's like okay, so he killed a man, what's the big deal? I can see Dale Crowe in about twenty years . . ."

"If he makes it," Marialena Reyes said. "Yeah, I think he'll get at least a year and a day. Although you never know about Gibbs. If he got laid last night he could be in a good mood. He'll ask you for a recommendation."

"I know, and there isn't much I can say."

"You get along with him? He must've noticed you by now."

"We've never spoken outside of court. He calls me Ms. Bacar."

"That's close. He thinks he's funny, so everyone humors him."

"But I'm not Ms. Bacar," Kathy said. "And I don't feel I have to smile for him."

"You don't see him practically every day. At least I don't have to go out with him," Marialena Reyes said, "he likes them young. You see he was up before the Qualifications Commission again?"

"I heard something about it. Asked a woman to take off her clothes?"

"In his chambers, a public defender, a new one. Asked her to, quote, 'show me your goodies.' He told her he was helping select contestants for the Miss Sugar Cane Pageant and said, 'I believe you have what it takes.'"

"And they let him off."

"With a reprimand. They ruled his behavior reflected a misguided sense of humor rather than social maladjustment."

"I'm surprised," Kathy said, "she filed a complaint."

"Yeah, not many do. The last one was a court reporter. Not his, some other judge's. Gibbs asked her if she wanted to play Carnival. She said she didn't know how to play it and Big said, 'You sit on my face and I guess your weight.'"

Kathy caught herself trying to picture it.

"Maybe he's crazy."

"It's possible," Marialena said. "What we know for sure, he's pretty horny for a guy his age, almost sixty."

There he was now, and to look at him he appeared harmless. About five-seven with a solemn, bony face, dark hair combed flat to his head. Maybe too dark, Kathy thought. He dyed it. A little guy in judicial robes that looked too big for him. Round-shouldered in a way that made him seem purposeful crossing to the bench. His bailiff, Robbie, a sheriff's deputy in a uniform sport coat, told everyone to rise. Kathy glanced around. There weren't more than a dozen spectators, friends or relatives of offenders sitting in the front row, the ones in state blue.

Everyone remained standing as Judge Bob Gibbs looked over his court, his gaze moving from the public defender, a young guy Kathy didn't know, to a county deputy removing Dale Crowe's handcuffs. Now he was looking this way, where Kathy stood at the prosecution table with Marialena Reyes.

He said, *"Buenos días,* ladies. I see we have the Latinas versus the Anglos today. Good luck, boys. You're gonna need it."

The young public defender smiled. Dale Crowe, standing next to him now, didn't smile. The judge turned as his court clerk, Mary Ellen, handed him a case folder. He glanced at it and then looked toward the court reporter relaxed behind his steno machine. "You want this one in English, don't you, Marty?"

Marty said, "Yes sir," without moving, as deadpan about it as the judge.

Looking this way again, Gibbs said, "Ladies, is that okay with you? We take it slow and talk Southern? Else I don't think it would be fair to the defense."

Marialena Reyes smiled and said, for the people of the state of Florida, "I would prefer it, Your Honor."

"Ms. Bacar, is it okay with you?"

The little bigot with his solemn face and dyed hair stared at her, waiting.

Kathy said, "It's Baker, Judge."

"Excuse me?"

"My name is Baker, not Bacar."

Gibbs looked down at the case file and up again.

"It was Bacar though, huh, before you changed it?"

"It was always Baker," Kathy said.

Let him figure it out.

* * *

The next time Kathy Baker had to speak was when Gibbs asked if the Department of Corrections was happy with Mr. Crowe entering a plea of guilty. She said, "Yes sir."

Gibbs said, "You know it means I can revoke his probation and sentence him on the original charge, battery of a police officer. That's a third-degree five-year felony."

Kathy said, "Yes sir," wondering why he was telling her instead of the defendant.

"I see by the Offense Report," Gibbs said, "this business took place in the parking lot of the Club Peekaboo on Lake Worth Road. The officers asked Mr. Crowe for his identification. . . . It says Mr. Crowe responded in a rude and belligerent manner." Gibbs looked up from the case file. "How is that Club Peekaboo, Mr. Crowe? They take care of you in there?"

Dale grinned. "They sure do."

"How about this other place, where you socked the guy?"

"I'd stay away from there, Judge."

Kathy noticed Dale moving now, shifting from one foot to the other, anxious, beginning to have hope.

"You have size on you for a young boy," Gibbs said. "Been working out at Glades Sugar the past year. . . . You're what, only a few months shy of the legal age. . . . So, I'm gonna overlook the beer drinking. Is that all right with you, Mr. Crowe?"

Dale said, "Yes sir," grinning.

Marialena Reyes said, "Excuse me, Your Honor, but Mr. Crowe is in violation of a trust we placed in him. I think if probation is to have any meaning, he should be given at least a nominal amount of county time."

"Hey, Marialena," Gibbs said, "you and I are on the

same side. We both work for the state and realize a sanction is in order here. Ms. Bacar, you do too, don't you?"

"It's Baker," Kathy said.

"Baker, that's right. You changed it."

"I think I said it was always Baker."

She stared back at this redneck judge who wanted everyone to talk Southern.

"You insist," Gibbs said, "I'm not gonna argue with you."

Kathy said, "Thank you," and saw his expression change, that hint of fun go out of his eyes.

He said, "Don't thank me yet," and Kathy wondered what he meant. Now he turned to Dale Crowe.

"I can overlook your beer drinking, but not the attitude you apparently have, that if someone gives you a hard time it's okay to take a sock at him. Was it your daddy put that idea in your head? The reason I ask, I've had Dale Crowe Senior before this court on several occasions in the past. Either caught poaching alligators or apprehended with quantities of marijuana in his boat, coming off the lake."

Dale said, "That's when I was a little kid."

"I imagine learning on your daddy's knee," Gibbs said, "the one the alligator didn't bite off. I've had your dad, I've had your uncle Elvin, an individual I think of as a model repeat offender. Smuggling, armed robbery, hitting people over the head for their coin . . . I almost forgot the big one, a capital felony. They ever erect a statue to memorialize convicts, Elvin could be the model. And I believe I've had other Crowes, all of them your kin." The judge's gaze shifted. "Marialena, just out of curiosity, have you ever known of any good Crowes?"

"Your Honor, I don't know that much about the family."

"You've heard of them though."

"I've heard the name, yes."

"Well, you see my point. Anyway," Gibbs said, "if there's nothing any of you wish to offer in bar, mitigation or aggravation of what I'm about to impose, then I adjudge you guilty, Mr. Crowe. It is the judgment, sentence, and order of the law that you be confined by the Department of Corrections for five years, with credit for time served. You have a right to appeal . . ."

Kathy Baker said, "Your Honor?" at the same time Dale was saying, "Five years for what, hitting a guy? What was I suppose to do? The guy was all over me."

The young public defender had his hand on Dale's arm now as Gibbs asked him, "Who was, Mr. Crowe?"

"The bouncer, as I was coming out of the bar."

"But I'm looking at the original charge, Mr. Crowe. Battery of a police officer, causing injury. That's what I'm passing sentence on, your indifference to, if not utter disregard of, the law. Further, I'm gonna recommend you be sent to FSP, the Florida State Prison, where your daddy and uncle served their time. You'll be carrying on the family tradition."

Kathy said, "Judge, I'd like to remind the court, the defendant was on probation only two days when he was arrested."

"That's a good point," Gibbs said. "It confirms what I'm saying. He doesn't stop and think, does he?"

"What I meant, he hasn't reported to the office yet. Find out about all the conditions he has to observe."

Gibbs said, "That's a violation right there, not reporting in."

"No, that part's okay. He still had time."

"You haven't talked to him before this?"

She began to see where this was going and wished she hadn't said anything. "I saw him this morning."

"Where, in the holding cell?"

"Yes sir."

"So what is it you're telling the court?"

"I don't think it's in the interest of the state to give him all that DOC time, five years, for something he drew probation on originally."

"You don't?" Gibbs said, frowning, trying to look concerned, then glancing over at his bailiff and his court clerk, his team, before looking this way again. "What would you give him?"

Playing with her. She should never have opened her mouth.

"It isn't my place to say, Judge."

"You think Mr. Crowe's probation should be reinstated?"

Kathy hesitated. She wasn't sure that would be a good idea, let him off entirely. "I just think five years—he'll do about twenty months? That seems like a heavy sentence."

"I asked you what you'd give him, you haven't told us."

"I would consider, well, a year and a day, if you think he should do DOC time."

"You're basing this judgment on your appraisal of his character. . . . What else?"

"Well, his age, the offense . . ."

"Having talked to him," Gibbs said, "what, about ten minutes in the holding cell? Through bars, in all that noise and confusion? I'd be interested to know what you talked about."

"I told him his lawyer was right, he should plead guilty."

"And what did Mr. Crowe tell *you?*"

"I'm not sure I know what you mean."

"If you want I can put it hypothetically," Gibbs said. "What I'm getting at, how does an offender looking at five years get a pretty little probation officer to sympathize with his plight? What does he say to get you on his side?"

Kathy started shaking her head before Gibbs had finished. "Judge, I'm not on his side, I even told him that."

"He never said a word to you."

"Well, yes, he spoke . . ."

"I won't tell the court what I'm thinking and have it go in the record," Gibbs said. "But if you're curious—Ms. Baker, is it? If you'd like to know what I suspect, stop in my chambers after we're through here. In the meantime," Gibbs said, making a notation in the case file before looking up again, "the decision of the court stands."

Kathy kept watching Gibbs. The public defender was requesting Mr. Crowe be allowed time on the street, seven days to get his affairs in order. She watched Gibbs appear to think it over and finally rule okay, as long as the defendant reported to Probation on a daily basis. Now he was looking this way again, asking Kathy if she wouldn't mind keeping an eye on her boy. She was thinking, You don't have to smile. You don't even have to answer. Or she could say, Who do you mean by my boy, Judge, the defendant? She heard Dale's voice then, raised, and looked over, Dale saying to Gibbs, "Hey, Judge? I'm gonna see about this deal. You think you're through with me, Judge, you're fulla shit. Hear?" She saw Gibbs leaving the courtroom past two deputies who were moving quickly toward Dale

Crowe with handcuffs and shackles. It surprised her the judge didn't say something to Dale, hold him in contempt.

Marialena Reyes touched Kathy's arm.

"You going to see him?"

"I don't know."

"I think you'd better."

"He didn't say I had to."

"No, but I think it would be a good idea."

Kathy said, "I have to smile, too?"

Marialena stared at her for a moment. She said, "Do what you want," and walked away.

2

Out of his robes Judge Bob Gibbs became someone else, pleasant, almost a regular guy, saying he didn't mean to put her on the spot in there. No, what it was, he had a feeling young Mr. Crowe might have tried a sad story on her, he was sick or his mama needed him at home or he knew it would kill him to be locked up, the prey of older, lascivious convicts. . . . "I said at one point, 'Don't thank me yet.' Remember? Well, you can thank me now if you want."

"For what, Judge?"

"Sending young Mr. Crowe away. Taking him off your hands. If I'd reinstated his probation like you wanted, he'd be in violation again before you know it and you'd have egg all over your pretty face. What're you, Cuban?"

"Born in Miami," Kathy said. "I don't think I asked you to reinstate him."

"You didn't come right out and request it. I could tell,

though, he'd been working on you. I was gonna say, you don't look especially Latin."

Like he was paying her a compliment. If she wanted she could say, And you don't look like a judge.

What he looked like now, sitting behind his desk, was a farmer. The top of his forehead, where it disappeared into the dyed hair, was lighter than the rest of his face. A farmer or an Okeechobee fishing guide dressed for town in a short-sleeve white shirt and red patterned tie. He even had the cracker sound of those boys from the country. Old Bob Isom Gibbs, known as "Big" to his buddies. He sat with his hands behind his head, leaning back in his chair. From deep in the office sofa facing the desk, all Kathy could see of the judge were his raised arms, elbows sticking out, and his head, his hair shining in fluorescent light. On the wall behind him were framed photos of the judge posing with several different men holding strings of bass and what looked like speckled perch. No doubt taken at a fishing camp on the lake. In another picture the judge was standing in an airboat holding a two-foot alligator in each hand, by the tail.

"Don't feel sorry for him, he was due," Bob Gibbs said, "being a Crowe. You've heard the expression 'Born to raise hell'? That's young Mr. Crowe's belief. Mine's 'Hard time makes the boy the man.' He'll come out of jail therapy with a brand-new attitude, or else we'll send him back, won't we?"

"I thought you might hold him in contempt," Kathy said, "when he threatened you."

"Was that a threat? What'd he say, he's gonna get me? Sis, that's nothing, that's water off my back. You going with anybody?"

She had to take a moment to realize what he meant.

"Not anyone special."

"You date police officers?"

"I have, yes."

"Lawyers?"

"Once in a while."

"Married ones?"

"I won't do that."

"Why not?"

"I just won't."

"You want to have some dinner this evening?"

She said, "Judge, you're married, aren't you?"

He kept staring at her before he said, "You are too, aren't you? Or I mean you *were*. Why didn't I think of that?"

"Married and divorced," Kathy said.

"Sure, and that's where you got your name. I *knew* it. What's your maiden name?"

"Diaz."

He seemed relieved. "Sure, Cuban, but born and raised here. What's your dad do? Man, you people started coming—when was it, fifty-nine? You've just about taken over."

"My dad was a police officer in Miami," Kathy said. "Retired now on a disability. He was shot."

"Oh, I'm sorry to hear that."

"My two brothers are cops, also in Miami. One with DEA, the other Metro-Dade. My sister's married to an assistant state attorney."

"And here you are a probation officer. I'd call that a law enforcement family. How long you been with Corrections?"

"Almost two years. I went to Florida Atlantic . . ."

"Got married when you were in school?"

"After I got out. While I was working in screening at South County Mental Health."

That seemed to interest him, the way his eyebrows went up.

"I was working on my master's in psychology, but changed my mind. Those seventy-hour weeks were too much."

"So you're familiar with mental patients, how they act."

"At South County we had 'consumers.' They're not patients till they're admitted somewhere for treatment, or we sent them to detox. Most of the ones we saw were on drugs or alcohol, or both."

"You quit there to work for Corrections?" the judge said. "All you did was trade crackheads for fuckups. You like dealing with misfits, huh, losers?"

"My ex-husband used to ask me that."

"He was after you to quit?"

"If I could find a job that paid more. I was supporting him. He was in medical school when we got married, a first-year resident when we divorced. No, the problem, he was a superior being, but I didn't find it out till after we were married." Bad, talking too much about her personal life and the judge liked it, grinning. She got back to her job. "Working for DOC at least I'm outside most of the time. I have close to eighty-thousand miles on my car." If he wanted they could talk about her VW she'd bought secondhand that needed new tires again, a battery . . .

"You're in the wrong profession, the Probation Office? A bright, attractive girl like you? It's a dead-end street. Where do you go? Isn't there something you want to be?"

"When I grow up? I don't know," Kathy said, "I'll

probably get married again someday. I'd like to have kids."

"You already tried that. You have any offenders on Community Control? Wear the anklet, can't leave the house?"

"In the office. I don't handle any myself."

"Sometimes you call it house arrest? Like being in jail at home. Or married to the wrong person. Am I right?"

Kathy said, "I guess you could look at it that way," wanting to get out of here. Next thing he'd be telling her his wife didn't understand him, they were married in name only, had separate bedrooms, and that was why he saw other women occasionally and it would be okay if they had dinner together.

But he didn't. He said, "You studied psychology, you were at South County awhile . . . I can see you're a person who naturally feels sympathy for others, their problems."

He was back on the track, coming at her.

"What would you do if you're having a conversation with someone and all of a sudden she becomes a different person?"

He had to be talking about his wife.

"Like a mood swing," Kathy said.

He leaned close over the desk to shake his head at her. "I'm not talking about a change of mood or tone of voice." The judge speaking now, laying down the law. "I'm telling you she becomes somebody else, in voice and manner and what she says."

"Your wife," Kathy said.

"Leanne," the judge said. "Originally from Ohio."

Chronically undifferentiated popped into Kathy's head, but she wasn't that sure it applied and didn't want to get too far into this anyway. She tried to pass it off saying, "You're different now, Judge, than you were in court. Don't you think?"

"You can call me Bob, or Big, if you like."

No she couldn't. She said, "I'm different from time to time . . ."

"How different?"

"Well, like if something's bothering me, or I don't feel too good."

Or like right now. Wanting to get out of here.

In the next moment he was Bob Gibbs again, this farmer-looking guy, his voice quiet, confiding. He said, "But have you ever been so different you became a twelve-year-old colored girl who lived a hundred and thirty-five years ago in Clinch County, Georgia? A slave girl by the name of Wanda Grace?"

Kathy Baker said, "Your wife might need help."

"One of us does," the judge said.

3

The first time Bob Gibbs saw his wife she was performing sixteen feet beneath the surface of Weeki Wachee Spring, in a mermaid outfit.

He watched her through the glass wall of the underwater theater. Saw her gold lamé tail undulating, saw her long golden hair moving slow motion, Leanne smiling, showing her perfect teeth in that clear springwater before taking the tip of the air hose in her mouth, making a delicate, feminine gesture of it.

Bob Gibbs, already a judge, saw the purity of this healthy girl suspended in crystal water, air bubbles rising out of her, carrying her breath to the sunlight way above. Young enough to be his daughter, but that didn't matter. The man inside the judge said, "Oh, my," lured by a mermaid, taken with the idea of landing her.

He saw her outside after, pink shorts molded to her cute butt, hair still wet, turning wide-eyed and no doubt apprehensive, a man coming up to her in a dark suit and necktie. Introducing himself as a circuit court judge didn't exactly warm her up, but she did start to relax once he expressed how much he enjoyed the show and began asking her questions. He learned that her name was Leanne Lancaster, that she was from Luna Pier, Ohio, and had been at Weeki Wachee—this was her third year and she loved it, even if it wasn't doing her hair a lot of good. That their changing room was down underneath "where we zip up our tails," smiling at him by now. There were three mermaids named Kim in the show, out of thirteen, and last year there were four, *really*, all named Kim. He learned that a hundred thousand gallons of pure water a minute rose from the depths of the spring, up through cracks way way down there, and that he ought to catch the Birds of Prey Show and then take the jungle river cruise, see pelicans, raccoons, sometimes even alligators. Leanne hunched her shoulders and gave him a cute shudder as she mentioned gators. She said they could swim into the spring from the river but hardly ever did 'cause the water was so cold, hunching her little shoulders again as she said, Brrrr. . . . Bob Gibbs said, "Why don't we sit down and have a Coca-Cola?"

He told her he was from right here in Hernando County originally, born and raised, but had never seen the mermaid show before today. "You imagine that? The show's been here what, forty years and this is my first time?" He told Leanne he had returned home to attend a funeral but came here instead, acting on some impulse. Strange? He didn't mention being hung over from partying the night before, unable this morning to bear sitting through a Baptist eulogy. "And I used to work for the deceased when he was Hernando County state attorney, back before I moved to West Palm as a prosecutor, ran for judge of circuit court and have been presiding ever since."

Leanne had kept staring at him, nodding very slowly as he spoke.

She said, "I have been visited by a wise man," her look becoming strange, trancelike. "You're famous, aren't you? Sure, I saw you on the cover of a magazine."

"That's right. It was *Newsweek*."

Nodding again. "But I don't recall it had your name."

"On the cover? No, it said, 'In Florida Maximum Bob Throws the Book.' It was a story about the courts getting tough on drug traffickers."

"Just a while ago."

"Yeah, what they did, they made a big to-do over my giving a drug dealer thirty years, plus a two-hundred-and-fifty-thousand-dollar fine, when the state attorney was willing to let him off with probation."

"I wish I'd read it."

"I might have a copy lying around somewhere I'll give you. It's accurate—what I object to is the tone of the article, like I'm ac*cused* of throwing the book at defendants. I said, 'What is the book for if you don't go by it and, yes, occasionally throw it at a criminal offender.' They put that in. Then they cite how I reject pleas of leniency. I said, 'I send people to prison when they kill somebody. I see that as my job.' They mention that many of my rulings have not been popular and quote my saying, 'I'm not *in* a popularity contest.' When I sentence a man to death by electrocution, it's because I think he deserves the shock of his life." Bob Gibbs smiled at her. "Now you got me started."

Leanne smiled back saying, "This is interesting," hunching her shoulders and giving them a little shake.

"Listen, I've even been accused of having a low opinion of women. Which I'm here to tell you is a lie," Bob Gibbs said, and grinned.

"Why would they say that?"

"Oh, one time, sentencing a defendant for wife-beating, I happened to say, 'You can't live with them, you can't live without them,' injecting a note of levity at a serious moment, that's all, and the media and different women's groups jumped all over me."

She said now, surprising him, "What's your sign?"

Bob Gibbs wasn't sure. he told her he was born on the second of December without giving the year.

"Sagittarius, the Time Traveler," Leanne said, "I thought as much. You like to explore and have a highly developed sixth sense that guides you even when you don't exactly understand where it is you're going. You *do* know. It's just that you aren't in touch yet with your inner self."

"That must be it," Bob Gibbs said, and saw her expression change.

"Oh, my Lord," her eyes going wide. Now she brought her hand to her mouth and seemed embarrassed.

"What's wrong?"

"I just had a feeling. . . . Don't laugh, okay?"

"I won't."

"You promise?"

"On a stack of Bibles. What?"

"All of a sudden it hit me, that I may have been your mother in a previous life."

Bob Gibbs smiled, he couldn't help it.

"You said you wouldn't laugh."

"I'm not. It's just— I'll tell you, you don't look anything like my old mother."

"I'm talking about way before," Leanne said. "It could've been hundreds or even thousands of years ago when we were both somebody else. You understand? In our past lives."

She kept staring at him in what he thought of at the time as a cute way she had about her. So serious. This healthy girl, good-looking even with wet hair. She said, "You don't believe in reincarnation, do you?"

"The metaphysical is out of my jurisdiction," Bob Gibbs said, "but I do keep an open mind as evidence is presented." Actually believing this.

"But you're not too good at being told something and just accepting it. You like to do what you want, huh? I mean even though you're a judge, you're not tied down by what people think, you're unconventional."

It seemed okay to smile at that. "I could tell you some stories, too."

She said, "Are you married?" and right away got that serious look, half closing her eyes. "No, you were for quite a few years, but now you're divorced."

"How'd you know that?"

"Your wife didn't like it in Palm Beach."

"You're right again. Rosellen, being from Ocala, had trouble adjusting to the life."

Now she was frowning, giving him a puzzled look.

"But you don't live right in Palm Beach, do you? I was there once, I loved it. All those big homes on the ocean?"

"No, my property is out in the country. All kinds of trees, flowers . . ."

"You love nature."

"I do, yes. I'll tell you, I like being married, too, and almost was again but changed my mind."

The reason being, you seldom ever married the woman your wife finds out about and divorces you over. It was another type of law, unwritten, he could have told

Leanne about that day at Weeki Wachee, trying to see into her tank top whenever she reached down to scratch at sand fleas biting her legs.

Putting on her serious look, no doubt thinking she was reading his mind, Leanne said, "With your sign, it could happen again when you least expect."

"I'm ready anytime," Bob Gibbs said. "How about having dinner with me tonight?"

That was how it began with them nearly seven years ago. Before Leanne had her Experience. Before she hung up her lamé tail, moved to Palm Beach and a few months later they were married.

For a time he continued to accept her strange behavior as part of the cute way she had about her.

Not anymore.

The way it was with them now, Leanne would say, "Big, do you know why you're not a happy person?"

Here we go.

"Why you drink so much?"

She had told him why enough times that it didn't matter what he said or if he answered at all. Leanne would maintain that serene, netherworld, airy-fairy expression on her face, one Bob Gibbs had come to believe was pure dumbness, and say, "You're not happy, Big, 'cause you let your negative ego control you. You haven't learned how to open your heart and you won't even try."

He might say to her, "How do you know my heart isn't open?"

"I can see it isn't."

"Yeah, how?"

"By your aura."

"I forgot, my aura. What's it look like today?"

"It's bright red."

"Maybe it's my high blood pressure. Ask me how come, I'll tell you."

"Your aura should be mostly blue. Yours is orangy red, Big, and way too wide. Doesn't it hurt?"

"Only when you bring it up," Bob Gibbs said.

Then she might get a scared look, eyes rolling up into her head before they closed and opened again and she'd say, in her squeaky little colored-girl voice, "She keep telling you, Judge, what you doing to yourself. She must've did a hundred times, you still don't never listen."

Sometimes he'd tell her, "Now quit that." Or he'd snap at her, "What're you talking to me like that for?"

Leanne might look surprised and say to him in her own voice, "Like what?" Claiming she had no idea what he was talking about. If someone had spoken to him, it was this other person occupying her body.

That was the first year or so of their marriage. Now Leanne claimed she could be present while the other person spoke, the other person occupying only her invisible etheric body, her spiritual self. See, while she remained in her actual body.

The one putting on weight.

Going on seven years of this, since the day she had her Experience.

The way Leanne thought of it, it began just after one in the afternoon of a gorgeous day.

She remembered rising from the underwater chamber behind the screen of air bubbles, their curtain for the show, and seeing the surface of the spring above shimmering in bright sunlight. She remembered flashes going off inside the glass front of the theater, families on vacation with cameras and little girls who wanted to be mermaids. She believed this was the way spirits might see our world, like looking at us through sparkly water and glass from over on the other side.

She remembered they were doing the magic show that day, one of the Kims working dry, playing the theme music and doing the narration topside. Another Kim went into the box they pierced with swords and came out with a few rolls and flutters, smiling, showing the kids she was okay. Leanne remembered swimming to her position, flipping her tail out in the mermaid crawl, holding the end of her air hose and the banana in the same hand. Her part in the show was to make the banana disappear. "How?" asked Kim the narrator. "By eating that banana, sixteen feet underwater!" Actually about twelve feet, closer to the surface than the other four mermaids in the magic show, Kim out of the sword box now getting ready to drink a Coke. "Yes, sixteen feet underwater!" the Kim working dry said. Leanne believed she might have been even a bit closer than twelve feet, because she felt herself rise just a little as she was peeling the banana.

She remembered placing herself in profile to the audience, so they would see what she was doing, raising her chin slightly as she took a bite, began to chew . . . This was the part that still gave her goose bumps. First, the shadow, or a feeling something was up there, right above her. Then looking up and seeing the alligator, its pale belly, its snout, its stubby legs moving in the water almost on top of her as she was swallowing the bite of banana, in that exact same moment, that's why she choked and it got caught in her throat and she gagged, swallowing the banana but also a lot of water. She didn't remember dropping her air hose until she realized she didn't have it, but did remember not knowing which way to go. She saw the alligator's tail fanning in the water as it turned and came back, so she started to dive, coughing now, knowing she couldn't make it all the way to the air lock chamber, not without her hose. She remembered twisting frantically in that sheath of lamé binding her legs. She remembered the swirl of bubbles and sounds, her breath rushing out of her lungs and a terrible pain pressing against her chest . . .

The next part she remembered even more clearly, because *it* was the actual experience.

Being underwater . . . okay, then just for like a few seconds seeing her body being pulled out of the water into a boat and the Kim who'd been working dry starting to give her mouth-to-mouth, seeing four mermaids in the water, their heads showing, seeing all this from way above looking down. Then it got dark and she was somewhere else that was *like* being underwater only she could breathe now.

Leanne was asked later on by different people if it was like that tunnel you hear about. The one with the bright golden light at the end?

No, because there wasn't any shape to where she was that she noticed, or any light, just kind of a soft fuzzy glow. Like being way up in the sky as dusk turns to night except there was no wind as you might expect and it wasn't cold, it was nice. Leanne said she was moving, but not swimming now or doing the mermaid crawl, she was standing upright and sort of gliding through this huge expanse of nothing without moving her legs. Until all of a sudden she saw the little girl appear out of the mist, a little black girl raising her hand, and something stopped her. The little black girl had on a simple white dress and stood, oh, about twenty feet away, though not actually standing on anything, she was just *there.* She put her hand down and said, "Go on back, Leanne." She did, she called her by name. Said, "Go on back, Leanne. You cain't come here yet."

Leanne would tell about it many many times later on in psychic workshops and seminars in Florida, Georgia, and as far north as Ohio, get to the part, "You cain't come here yet," and there would be a chill in the room you could feel, people in the audience holding their arms.

The room where she opened her eyes that day was a different story. She said, "Where am I?" A nurse told her she was at Lykes Memorial in Brooksville, brought here close to death but now seemed to be doing okay. The nurse not too sympathetic or sensitive. So Leanne waited till Big came to visit. He was the first one she told.

"I had an out-of-body experience."

Big had hold of her hand lying on the covers, giving it pats.

"I did. I drowned, but it wasn't time for me yet so I had to come back."

He said, "I want you to quit that job of yours."

Leanne said, "Don't worry."

"I have a brick ranch house in the country on five acres, an orange grove, all kinds of palm trees, laurel oaks that tell it's spring with chartreuse leaves, orchids growing everywhere, a big screen porch . . ."

Leanne said, "It sounds nice."

"You want to marry me I'll put in a swimming pool, you can be my little mermaid."

Leanne said, "We hardly know each other."

"I know you're what I want."

"Can I think about it? Right now there's so much on my mind."

"Have your own car. Go to big society parties in Palm Beach. . . . Get some rest, sweetheart."

Patting her hand, kissing her on the forehead.

He smelled nice of aftershave and wasn't too bad looking. He was mature. . . . She wouldn't have to worry about her hair anymore or work in the gift shop or do the Birds of Prey Show, those huge things shitting all over the place. She wondered what the wife of a judge was called.

It was the next day Leanne heard voices in the hall and saw the black family walking past her room, come to visit somebody. One of them, she was bringing up the rear, stopped in Leanne's doorway and stood there looking in at her. A little girl about twelve.

Later on Leanne would tell the psychic workshops and seminars from Florida to Ohio, "It was the same little girl I met in my out-of-body experience. She smiled and turned as if to go and I said, 'Wait, please.' She looked at me and said, 'You be jes fine now, Leanne. I be back when you wants me.' I said again, 'Wait,' but she was gone. I got out of bed, walked up and down the hall looking in every room. There was no sign of the little girl, or her family. As soon as I returned to bed I fell into a deep sleep. It was evening when I woke up, feeling completely refreshed and at peace for the first time since my drowning. But there was something else I felt, like a presence in the room. I looked around . . . it was on my bedside table. A crystal. It wasn't there before and when I asked the nurse, she said she didn't know anything about it or what it was. I didn't either, then. I didn't learn until later it was . . . Can you guess? Of course, a rose quartz. With its pink rays that focus on the heart chakra and usher in love, forgiveness, inner peace. But at the time I had no idea . . ."

At the time the judge hovering over her, his presence so close she could see the blood vessels in his nose afire, a glow over his face that wasn't healthy, Big saying:

" 'I be back when you *wants* me'?"

"That's what she said."

"And you think she's from the spirit world."

"She must be."

"Well, if she knows how to get here from the other side, wherever that is, how come she doesn't know how to speak good English? She looked like the same one as in your dream, that's all."

"It wasn't a dream."

"Listen, I have trouble telling one from the other myself, and I see them brought up before me every day of the year."

She said, "If you don't believe me . . ."

And he was all sweetness again.

"Honey, you're my little mermaid. I want to take care of you, buy you nice things, make you happy." He said, "Look," and showed her pictures of his home in the country, all the trees, the orange grove, the flower gardens and grounds maintained by work-release inmates.

Leanne said, "It looks so quiet and peaceful. A wonderful place to meditate, have a little dog to play with." The only thing she didn't like too much was that canal right next to the property, a wide ditch full of water. "Are there ever alligators in it?"

Big said, "Honey, you want it fenced off, I'll have it fenced off. You want a little doggie, you got it, anything you want. Come home with me."

4

Every morning, if he got up early enough, he'd see her in the yard meditating: out there with her tiny dog Pokey, between the pair of Cuban petticoat palms she thought of as two women who'd been turned into trees—telling him that—though she had never heard or read of such a thing in any of her books. Christ, dozens of books on spirit communication, psychic enlightenment, aura reading, crystal healing, getting in touch with your chakras, channeling—which was what Leanne did to get hold of the little colored girl she called her discarnate entity, or sometimes her spirit guide. Ask Leanne how she did it, she'd tell you.

"Easy as pie. I raise my energy level to resonate with Wanda's, see, then she's able to use my energy channel to manifest herself through me."

Oh.

"That's her name, Wanda?"

"Wanda Grace."

"How old is she?"

"Twelve."

"That's all? And she knows everything?"

"Age doesn't matter."

"But why her? Why not somebody more like yourself?"

"Wanda was killed by an alligator."

Ask a simple question . . .

The time he did he saw Leanne get that scared look for a second, saw her eyes close, her eyelids flutter and now she was speaking in her little colored-girl voice.

"The gator drug me into the swamp and spun me round and round and round till I was drowned. Then what he did, he took me down to his house and lef' me, didn' eat me till I turn ripe. Tha's the way they is, like you ripe."

Leanne opened her eyes.

She said, "Wanda Grace's little dog ran away. It was when she was down by the swamp looking for Pokey it happened. The same month, the same day and hour as my Experience, except Wanda passed over in the year 1855. She lived on a plantation in Clinch County, Georgia, as a slave."

"Maybe," the judge said, "you can get her to dust and do the windows."

Oh, you didn't kid about Wanda Grace. Leanne's face would turn to stone and the judge would have to act innocent.

"Honey, I thought she wanted us to open our hearts and be happy, have some fun in life."

Leanne said, "Your idea of fun is cruel. Sending people to prison, degrading those less fortunate. Wanda Grace was a *slave*. All her people died of the fever except she."

What happened to the healthy girl who used to wiggle

her tail and could smile underwater? Now she communicated with a spirit and played with crystals to improve her inner vision. Show you how much sense that made, she'd bury the crystals in the backyard every few days, in the *dirt,* she said to cleanse them and restore their energy. Get her in bed, she might just as well have her tail on. It was like doing it to a woman in a trance. Hey, where are you? He would never ask *who* are you, afraid she might answer in her little colored-girl voice. She never did it with the lights on or spoke while they were doing it.

When she did speak during the day, in her mild, airy tone, it was to pass on information.

"Big, Wanda says you need psychic counseling, maybe even alchemic hypnotherapy, have a specialist take a look at that negative ego."

"I will if you'll get your head examined."

"Wanda says you need a good psychic cleansing, you won't be so irritable."

"Is that right? She ever take a look at the kitchen? The dishes piling up in the sink . . ."

"Some things, Big, are more important than others. I'm trying to help you."

"Why don't you go someplace else and do it? Like back to Ohio."

"Wanda Grace says I have to keep trying, use my mediumistic gift to raise your vibration level and you'll come to know your Higher Self."

And on that note Bob Gibbs said, "Why don't you tell that little nigger to mind her own business."

So frustrated he was admitting her existence. Going on seven years of this because Leanne had been scared by an alligator.

He did get her a dog from the pound, a tiny brown-

and-white hyperactive mutt that yipped and jumped up on your lap, a cute little pup Leanne named Pokey after Wanda Grace's dog. ("I calls him Pokey 'cause he like to poke his little nose where it don't belong. I tells him he goin' poke it in the wrong place sometime. . . .") He got her a car, too, a Ford Escort she drove to health food stores and now and then to Winn-Dixie when he hollered for meat and potatoes.

"Big, how can you eat the flesh of once-living things?"

"Easy, I chew each bite forty times."

But he didn't fence off the canal or put in a swimming pool or take her to any Palm Beach society functions where she might start talking like the help and embarrass him.

Was that the sign of a negative ego?

If it was, then maybe he'd better start thinking positive. Instead of not doing anything that would make her want to stay, work on an idea that would get her to leave. Of her own free will, without any hassle, legal complications.

And thought of a way to do it that made him smile it was so simple, sometimes wheeze out loud with delight as he entertained the idea and refined it. But then for months he continued playing with it, taking his time, not quite ready to commit himself. . . .

Until this morning talking to the little-girl probation officer, Kathy Bacar, he realized she was the incentive he needed to get going. Kathy *Baker*.

He wasn't sure why at first, but this little girl raised his vibration level, got him feeling energized for the first time in almost a year, since his girlfriend Stephanie moved to Orlando and for a while there he enjoyed a few casual encounters. But, man, it was work getting them from drinks and dinner into the sack the same evening. One-nighters could kill you. It was better to have a girl right there you could count on. Like Stephanie.

The minute she appeared in his courtroom charged with indecent exposure, jogging topless in John D. MacArthur State Park, he knew this big redheaded girl would fill the bill. She'd said to him in court, "Your Honor, I was doing nothing lewd or indecent." No, but he'd bet she would if given the chance, a woman he decided then and there had to be full of fun. He fined her two hundred dollars—had to—waited a week, phoned her and said, "How about a couple of hundred-dollar dinners to make up for what I put you out?" Their first date he learned Stephanie loved to drink as well as expose herself. He said to her, "I know where you can jog topless through a garden to your heart's content, while my semi-estranged wife is at a seminar in Ohio." What a picture it turned out to be: this big redheaded nymph, his Nature Girl, ducking through the laurel oak and cabbage palms, not a stitch on, her buddy the judge waiting with a Jim Beam in each hand. Simple pleasures were the best kind. Fond memories to store away—while you work on a new set.

Kathy Baker was a different type of girl, more virginal even though she'd been married. He hadn't really noticed her till she spoke up in court and he decided to chew her out. But then talking to her after changed his mind, seeing this was a good-looking girl up close with a cute figure. She had spunk too. If she was Cuban, so be it; there was a lot of it going around. She might not want to run naked through his garden; still, the garden could be used to soften her up, thinking this little girl would be squirmy and fun in bed. There he was wondering how to get to her and she says she'd worked in mental health. Bingo. All he had to do after that was tell about Leanne, ask the little girl her opinion and act interested. Maybe a benign form of schizophrenia, huh? Yeah, I've thought about a psychiatric evaluation, but the idea of it—I have that done to criminals. Nodding, saying yes, uh-huh, and I hope we can talk about this some more. "I'll be in the bar at the Helen Wilkes Hotel, five o'clock, if you have time for a drink . . ."

Where he was now and every evening at five.

He didn't expect her, so wasn't surprised or disappointed when she didn't show up. The big kidney-shaped bar at the Helen Wilkes was a hangout for judges and lawyers, both sides, and some of the newspaper people. Knowing this, the little girl might prefer not to come rather than feel out of place. That was all right, he was cultivating patience. Trying to.

But three bourbon Manhattans later his vibration level had him out in the lobby at the pay phone, dialing a number in Belle Glade he'd looked up and memorized weeks ago. He said to the woman who answered, "I'd like to speak to Dicky Campau."

She said, "You want frogs, we don't have none."

This woman would have to be the frog gigger's wife, Inez. He had seen her once or twice out at the lake.

"What I want is to speak to the man of the house."

That got a sound from the woman Bob Gibbs couldn't identify. In a moment a male voice came on saying, "Yeah?"

"This is Judge Gibbs speaking. You know that hearing of yours coming up?"

"I believe it's next week, Judge."

"I'm moving it up to the day after tomorrow. How'd you like to do me a favor?"

There was silence on the line.

"Do I have a choice in the matter?"

Bob Gibbs said, "Why certainly," sounding surprised. "You can be let off with a warning or draw a five-hundred-dollar fine and a year in the Stockade. Take your pick."

5

They crossed the middle bridge over to Palm Beach, Dale Crowe Junior driving, his uncle Elvin sitting back to take in the sights, what had changed in the ten years he was out of circulation.

On Royal Palm Way, Dale said, "Over here, they see you driving around at night in a pickup truck they're liable to stop you. They don't even need a reason."

Elvin said, "I won't worry about it if you won't."

He was cool for a guy his age, close to fifty. He had on a straw cowboy hat he said was the Ox Bow model and three-hundred-fifty-dollar boots he said had once belonged to his big brother Roland, now dead. Went off to Miami and got himself shot by a woman. Elvin talked about his brother a lot, saying how Roland had worked for the Italians down there and was paid a good buck for his services, wore three-hundred-dollar boots and suits made in Taiwan China. This was while they'd stopped for pizza at a place on Dixie Highway and had two pitchers of beer. It was going on eight o'clock now, dark out.

Dale said, "I get stopped and have to take a Breathalyzer I'm fucked."

"What're you worried about," Elvin said, "they might put you in jail? Tell them you're about to do five years, have to catch you later."

"Shit," Dale said.

He had cooled down since yelling at the judge in court and they threatened to put cuffs and leg-irons on him, then let him go when the judge didn't make a case of it. He had seven days to think of what prison would be like. Elvin, eating pizza, said he'd give him some pointers on how to jail. Since they'd be together this week.

Dale had let his uncle move in while his two roommates were finishing up thirty days for criminal mischief. Got freaked on crack and kicked in a guy's windshield for no reason. Now Elvin was talking about staying on after Dale left. The house was in Delray Beach, a dump but only a few blocks from the ocean. Smell that salt air, Elvin said, it would clean the stink of prison off him. Dale said, well, his roommates were about to get their release, he believed either today or tomorrow. If Elvin wanted to stay he'd have to talk to them about it. Elvin said he'd had enough of roommates to last him. If he stayed, they'd have to leave. Like that, taking over. Dale had said, "You don't know my roommates." Elvin said, eating pizza, "And they don't know me, huh? You don't either."

That was a fact. Ten years old when his uncle was arrested for murder and stood trial, Dale knew him more from photographs than face-to-face. Elvin in his airboat. Elvin standing with Dale Senior, the oldest brother. Elvin with Roland, both big guys, twins to look at them, except Elvin was a few years younger. When Roland was shot dead and Elvin sent to prison for killing a man he thought was the one had got the woman to kill Roland, nobody in the family seemed surprised.

Elvin was saying now, "This is a pretty street, you know it? Look at those palm trees. Those are the tallest palm trees I ever saw." He said, "I wouldn't mind living over here. It sure beats the shit out of Delray Beach." He said, "Summer I'd go back to the Glades, though, get me an airboat." He said, "Not too much traffic now, huh? The snowbirds've all gone home. I don't know why anybody wants to live up north. I go even as far as the Georgia line I get a nosebleed." He said, "Go on over to Ocean Boulevard and turn south."

Now they were riding along next to the Atlantic Ocean, black out there all the way to the sky.

Elvin said, "Nice public beach but no place to park. So it becomes a private beach for all the rich people live along here behind their walls. It's interesting how rich people fuck you and you don't even know most of the time they're doing it, huh? I had a cellmate my last year at Starke name of Sonny? Cute boy, use to work for a rich doctor. He's still rich, only he isn't a doctor no more. They took his license away."

Dale said, "Right there's where Donald Trump lives."

Elvin said, "Is that right? Who's Donald Trump?"

Before they ate and were driving around West Palm, Dale had pointed out the building Barnett Bank was in, its shiny black glass rising above old structures around it, and said, "You know what they call that building? Darth Vader." And Elvin had said, "Who's Darth Vader?" Dale could see how he might not have heard of Donald Trump in prison, but everybody in the world knew who Darth Vader was. Either one, though, was hard to explain, so

Dale let it go. Elvin wasn't interested anyway. He wanted to drive down to Ocean Ridge.

"What for?"

"The doctor I mentioned?" Elvin said. "He lives there," and began telling about Dr. Tommy Vasco and Sonny, who was his cellmate up at FSP his last year.

"Actually it wasn't quite a year. Couple of weeks before my release I sold him for two hundred dollars. Sonny had this blond hair you could see clear across the yard. I could've got more, but I let a buddy of mine have him."

Dale stared at his headlight beams on the two-lane blacktop, trees now closing in on both sides. He could feel his uncle, the size of him, sitting there in that cowboy hat. Dale set his tone of voice to be casual, uncritical, saying, "Well, I ain't getting into any of that. I'll tell you right now."

Elvin said, "I know cons that remain virgins, I'm not telling you it can't be done."

Dale shook his head at the road. "I won't even talk to a queer."

"Listen to me," Elvin said. "I'm a person was never married on the outside. But you get in there, something happens to you. Soon as I was put in with the population I started looking for a wife. Generally speaking, you poke or get poked. They'll fight over your skinny butt or you'll fight to keep it your own. It's got nothing to do with being queer, it's how it is. Sonny come along toward the end there, I kicked out this puss I had and said that one's mine, the cute blond. Don't nobody even look at her. It was okay with Sonny. He's the type goes along with whatever . . . Is this Ocean Ridge?"

"Manalapan," Dale said. "Ocean Ridge is next."

"Anyway," Elvin said, "here's this boy has to do a

mandatory twenty-five on a life sentence and he's I mean depressed, doesn't think he can hack it. He needed somebody like me to cheer him up. See, he'd keep house, tend to my wants, and I'd take good care of him."

Dale said, "What'd he do?" watching the road, seeing condos and big homes now.

"He killed a woman. Beat her to death and got first-degree."

Dale said, "Was this in the newspaper?"

"It musta been, was about a year and a half ago. At the time, Sonny was living with this Dr. Tommy Vasco, being his little helper. Sonny'd get girls for the doctor and the doc'd write drug prescriptions using fake names and Sonny'd go out and sell the stuff, mostly Quaaludes and Xanax, make himself some money."

"He got girls?" Dale said. "Whyn't the doctor get his own girls?"

"He use to, when he was married and playing around. He was always drunk or stoned," Elvin said. "Till his daddy swore he'd cut him off if he didn't behave hisself. See, this Tommy Vasco was a fuckup all his life. His daddy sent him to medical school down on one of the islands, set him up after, bought him this big house. . . . His daddy use to be a doctor, owns all kinds of property down in Miami, a rich tightass kind of guy, real strict and he has this fuckup for a son. You get the picture?"

"Wants the old man to think he's a good boy," Dale said, "so he pulls the shades down and does all his partying at home."

"There you go. And has Sonny get the women and the dope, all different kinds. But now the women, that's something else. The doctor was partial to big blond women, no

Latins. They had to be big but not fat and have good-size titties on 'em."

Dale said, "How many women would he have at a time?"

"Oh, he'd have two or three there for a party. See, what Dr. Vasco liked was for Sonny to take movies of him and a couple women in bed doing it. Then after, they'd sit around drinking, doing the cocaine and watch themselves on TV. Well, this one night . . . I forgot to mention, the doctor's favorite was a woman name Pola from Lake Worth. Big woman almost six foot and built. Sonny said she was bigger'n he was and Sonny musta been, oh, five eight or nine and kinda chubby. I'd call him that sometime, 'Hey, Chubby, look at what I got for you.'"

Dale thinking, Jesus. Not wanting to hear about it.

"And I'd give him a candy bar for being a sweetie. Anyway," Elvin said, "this woman I mentioned, Pola, come by one night alone, no other women there. They have their party, chop some rails, put a movie on. This Pola says to the doctor she bets his daddy would just love to see one of these movies, kidding with him. Sonny thinks she didn't mean anything by it, but he says the doc started to go crazy at the idea. He slaps her and she hits him back. They get in a fistfight and pretty soon she's beating up on him. So the doc yells at Sonny to help him. But Sonny, not being a fighter, picks up a poker from the fireplace and hits her with it. This woman he says come at him like a tiger and he had to keep hitting her till he give her a good one over the head and it killed her. So then the doctor tells him what to do. Put her in her car and drive up to Lake Worth. The idea, leave the car on the street with her in it and it'll look like she was mugged and the guy went too far, so take her purse. Sonny does all this, he's getting out of her car, when who drives up shining a light on him . . ."

Dale was nodding. Man, he could see it.

"The police. Sonny was charged, he had her blood all over him, and convicted," Elvin said. "He tried to tell them it was Dr. Tommy Vasco made him do it. They looked into it but couldn't put nothing on the doc except the fake prescriptions he wrote. He got like six months and can't practice medicine no more, which he barely did anyway. Sonny got life, the mandatory twenty-five, and is now keeping house for this buddy of mine. Okay. You want to know something else?"

Dale said, "What?"

"The judge that convicted Sonny and the doc is the same one gave me ten years straight up, minimum, and gave you five on that dinky violating probation charge. Judge Bob Gibbs, he must be one busy son of a bitch."

Coming to Ocean Ridge they had to stop at a light on A1A, dark and quiet out there, quiet in the pickup now, Dale seeing Judge Gibbs leaving the courtroom as he yelled at him. The judge walked out and now Dale tried to imagine a blond-haired guy hitting a big blond woman with a fireplace poker. As the light turned green and they started up again, he said, "You want to take a look at this doctor's house, where it happened?"

"I want to see the doctor," Elvin said.

"What for?"

"Sonny asked me to."

It didn't make sense to Dale.

"Like you have a message for him?"

"In a way," Elvin said. "Sonny wants me to hurt him."

6

Kathy Baker sat in her secondhand VW, faded beige, 78,746 miles on the odometer and tires going bald, waiting for Dale Crowe Junior to show up. His house was dark. The Crisis Center, where she had worked when she was with South County, was only a few blocks down Swinton Avenue from here. It was weird telling the judge how she'd moved from public mental health to Corrections and he said she must like dealing with misfits, losers. Sounding exactly like Keith, her ex.

Pardon me. Dr. Baker.

The way Keith would say it, "No one with an ounce of ambition would work in public mental health." With his condescending tone. While she was supporting him, paying the bills. "Your willingness to deal with subhumans indicates a definite personality disorder. Your adjustment reaction to adulthood." Telling her she was unwilling to face the real world. A guy who locked his doors to drive through Little Havana, where she grew up.

Her mom said, "He's perfect. Marry him quick before

he gets away." Sure, it was what you did, got married and had children. Most of her school friends were already married to guys in trades, working construction. Keith was at the University of Miami studying to be a doctor.

Her brother Ray Diaz, with Drug Enforcement, said, "That's why you married him?"

She could talk to Ray because they were close and not just in age, two years apart. She had felt growing up that if she were a guy she would be Ray, just like him.

"I try to explain why I married him, it sounds dumb."

Ray said, "Accept it. You were."

"Gimme a break, I was twenty-three. Keith looked like he was sent from heaven. Coral Gables, good family, modeled for a sportswear catalogue . . ."

"You oughta be ashamed of yourself."

"He was quiet, had a nice smile, perfect manners . . ."

"No sense of humor," Ray said. "The guy didn't know shit except what was in books and you helped him with that. You know what the big problem was? He found out you're smarter than he is. But once he got his MD he was a doctor and you weren't. Ask Dad or Tony, they saw it."

Tony, her older brother, a uniform Metro-Dade cop. She'd bring Keith home to visit or have dinner, her dad and Tony would watch sports on TV, any sport. When Keith got his MD and went to North Broward as a first-year resident in psychiatry, Tony said, "That's all he is? I thought he was a fucking king at least." Ray said he acted superior so no one would know he was a moron.

She said to Ray, "I thought he was just playing doctor and would get over it. I guess he never will. Keith said my problem was I thrived on abusive situations. Boy, tell me about it. When I did lay into him I said all the wrong things. You wouldn't have made it through school without me. You wouldn't have eaten, had clean clothes to wear, all that. He'd go, 'Oh, did I force you? Make you work at that place?' One time when I blew up he said, 'I have to deal with emotional Latins all day and I come home to one.' In that superior tone of his. I said, 'For Christ sake, why did you marry me?' You know what he said, now that he's a doctor and doesn't need me? He said, 'That's a good question.'"

And the judge, in his chambers, said she didn't look especially Latin. Like he was paying her a compliment.

Oh, thank you, Your Honor. What she always wanted to hear from a redneck racist asshole old enough to be her father. So obvious, coming on with that business about his wife's mental condition, speaking in another voice. Oh, really? Going along with it instead of saying, Judge, married to you, no wonder she wants to be somebody else.

She was supposed to feel honored a judge wanted to sleep with her. Like she'd made it to the big time and could tell the lawyers who hit on her to kiss off. The lawyers in their nifty suits. "You're a bright little girl, I might be able to do something for you." Like what? "Oh, make your job easier." How? "Oh, put in a word here and there." She was supposed to see it as her big chance. Wow, get to go to bed with a lawyer.

At hospitals it would be, get to go to bed with a doctor. A nurse at North Broward had liked the idea. The one Keith visited evenings, an hour or so at a time.

It was her brother Ray, a surveillance expert, who found out. He said, "If he was clean I would never have told you. But he isn't, so there it is. You want, I'll have a talk with Keith, straighten him out." Kathy said, "No, I'll handle it."

A car rolled past, a dull shape, its exhaust rumbling, and stopped in front of Dale Crowe's house. Two young guys got out with grocery sacks, one tall enough to be Dale but built heavier, broad through the shoulders. They walked up to the house talking in loud voices, flying high this evening, and went inside. A light came on in the front room, the door still open.

There were lights in some of the homes along the street, single-story frame houses back among old trees and overgrown shrubs, a low-rent neighborhood no one cared about.

The house where the nurse lived in Pompano Beach was like one of these. Three years ago—she might still be there.

The two young guys seemed right at home. Maybe they'd know where Dale was, seven days before going to prison. She should have taken the time, had a talk with him after the hearing instead of going in to see the judge, sit there like a good little probation officer. Yes, Judge . . . Oh, really?

Kathy got out of her car and locked it, thinking about the night she drove up to the nurse's house, in the same car but didn't lock it that time. She had walked past Keith's Mustang convertible his parents had given him for graduation, went up to the door and rang the bell. She rang it six times and remembered thinking as she waited, they bought him a car but let her pay the rent, buy the groceries and she never said one goddamn word about it. The nurse opened the door frowning. A small blond nurse in a pink wrap and with a tiny white dog in her arm.

Kathy said, "There's something I'd like to tell my husband."

The blond nurse said, "Your *hus*band?"

Maybe she didn't know.

"The one in the bedroom," Kathy said, moving past her.

He was out of bed standing naked, about to put on a pair of pale-blue briefs she washed whenever they were in the hamper. He looked at her and said, "Would you mind waiting in the other room," in that tone of his.

"I guess I don't know how you're suppose to act," Kathy said, "you catch your husband fucking a nurse."

"Don't be crude."

"That isn't what you were doing?"

"Why don't you go home and wait for me. We'll talk about it later. All right?"

"I brought all your clothes, your books . . ."

"What do you mean?"

"I mean I brought all your clothes and books. What do you think I mean? All your stuff, it's in my car, loose, I didn't pack it. I'm going to take it out and put it in your car. If it's locked I'll lay the stuff on your car or throw it in the street, I don't know, whatever I feel like doing."

"You brought all my things?"

"Everything you own, your books, your catalogues, anything else you paid for, which isn't much. You can come out and help me if you want, or you can stay here and fuck your nurse or fuck the dog, I don't care, you're out of my life. And my apartment."

He made faces, frowns, standing there naked with his cute undies in his hand. He said, "I don't believe you're doing this."

"Hey, Keith, come on. We Latins are very emotional,

man. You know that." On her way out she said to the blond nurse still holding the dog, "He's all yours."

Elvin and Dale had to wait before the door was opened by a stocky little guy Elvin judged to be light-skinned colored, except he had a big honker on him and maybe was trying to pass. He looked out at Dale's pickup in the drive sucking at his teeth, giving the truck a careful inspection before saying, "What is it you want?" With just enough accent that Elvin had to change his appraisal. This was some kind of Hi-spanic booger with a big nose, Cuban-looking now. There was all kinds of them.

Elvin said, "Where's the doc at?"

The guy only had the door open a foot or so, peeking out at them. He had his hair greased back in a knot, a teeny stud earring in one ear, and was wearing one of those Cuban shirts that hang outside your pants. He said, "The doctor isn't in practice, he's retired."

Elvin shook his head. "I ain't sick, you dink. This is a social call. Tell the doc a friend of Sonny's is here."

The name didn't seem to mean anything. The guy said, "Wait here," and closed the door about a half inch from being shut.

Elvin said to Dale, "That ain't nice, leave us standing here with our thumbs up our ass," pushed the door open and walked in.

The Cuban-looking guy was already down the hall, clickity-clicking along the terrazzo floor in high-heel boots, turning into a doorway now. He never looked back, so didn't see them come in. Elvin motioned and Dale followed, Elvin taking his time to look in the living room—too dark to see anything—and inspect the weird paintings and statues they had in the hallway, Elvin frowning, stopping at a black shiny one he told Dale he believed was a bare-naked woman, but wouldn't swear to it.

They reached the doorway and there was the Cuban-looking dude standing with his back to them at a dinner table set with lit candles. Another Cuban-looking guy with slick hair was sitting by himself at the head of the table. This would be Dr. Tommy Vasco, having his supper. Elvin noticed another place set, another dinner somebody had been eating, and recalled the dude who'd opened the door sucking his teeth. But who was he?

He turned as Dr. Tommy looked this way and got up, holding a napkin to his silky shirt.

"I thought I told you to wait."

The guy serious, giving them a dirty look. Elvin said, "Hey, I'm waiting. Come on."

Then heard Dr. Tommy say, "It's all right, Hector." No doubt believing his guy was about to get knocked on his ass. Elvin could read guys like Dr. Tommy in a minute, the kind went through life scared and became sneaky. Born rich or he'd never be living in a place like this.

"I was hoping you might be showing your movies," Elvin said, getting right to the point. He saw the doctor had on pants like pajamas and shiny little black slippers with gold crests on the toes.

Dr. Tommy said, "Excuse me?"

"The movies Sonny took of you and your women."

Now the dink was trying to smile.

"Sonny, yes. How do you know him?"

"We jailed together. He said look you up, tell you he thinks about you all the time."

"Oh, I see," Dr. Tommy said, no doubt getting the picture. "You were with Sonny, uh?"

"He was with me. I'm Elvin Crowe? This here's my

nephew, Dale. Yeah, I took care of Sonny and he kept house for me."

The dink was nodding. No doubt thinking fast.

"He was suppose to keep up this house but wasn't too good at it. He had other things he liked to do better."

"Like sell dope," Elvin said.

"Yes, he was good at that."

Now the dink was shaking his head instead of nodding, keeping busy there.

"It was a shame what he did to that girl."

"He saved your butt, didn't he?"

The doc smiled. "He told you that?"

"You got in a fight with her and she was beating the shit outta you, so Sonny hit her with a fireplace poker."

Now the doc was shaking his head again.

"Sonny had his own reason for killing her. You want to know if I'm lying? Ask the police." Dr. Tommy gave Elvin a shrug. "They have the weapon he used, his fingerprints. What Sonny did, he tried to involve me because he was alone. You know, scared to death. I understand that. I don't hold it against him. Now it's too bad, he's paying for what he did." The doctor looked at his gold wristwatch and said, "Listen, I wish I could ask you to stay, but I have an appointment this evening. I'm very sorry."

Elvin said, "Yeah, I was hoping you might show me your movies."

There he was trying to smile again, act natural, sucking at his teeth. The other teeth-sucker—Hector?—stood there staring. Elvin couldn't tell from their plates what they'd been eating. Something with brown gravy all over it. It looked pretty good, whatever it was.

The doctor was saying, "No, I don't have those movies anymore, they're gone."

Elvin thinking, Bullshit, but said, "Well, I just wanted to tell you Sonny's doing fine, staying out of trouble."

"Listen, that's good to hear. I'm happy you stopped by."

"I bet you are," Elvin said. "Maybe if I'm over this way again and you're home . . ."

"Of course, anytime. If I'm here you're welcome," Dr. Tommy said, holding out his arm to mean either his house or pointing to the door.

His guy Hector moved past them to show the way out, Elvin telling him in the hall he knew the way and getting another dirty look over the dink's shoulder.

When they were in the pickup again heading out the drive, Dale said, "I thought you were gonna hurt him."

"I am," Elvin said.

"Well, when?"

"I haven't figured out how yet," Elvin said. "You hurt a guy for another guy, you want to see something in it for yourself, if you can."

The one guy tried to give Kathy a hard time.

When she asked if Dale was home and they invited her in, they were okay for about half a minute. Once they started goofing around, insisting she have a beer with them, she brought a wallet-size case out of her purse and held it open to show her ID and shield. See it?

No shit, a probation officer? Acting like they'd never heard of one before. They were both pretty ripped, their eyes shining like glass, and still drinking, a dozen or so longneck beer bottles on a wooden crate they used as a coffee table. One of the guys stumbled over to the sofa and fell into it. She was watching him when the other one grabbed the ID case out of her hand.

"Katherine *Baker*? You're Cuban, aren't you?"

Everyone interested in her nationality. "I'm Department of Corrections," Kathy said. "What are you?" A rockhead for one thing, no doubt lights popping in his brain.

She snatched her ID case back before he decided to keep it and he didn't like that one bit. Gave her a snarly look and tried to grab it again. He reached for the case and Kathy got hold of one of his fingers, the little one on his right hand, and bent it back enough to make him say "Owwww, hey," hunching his shoulders. He made a fist with his other hand, cocked it getting a mean look and she bent the finger some more. This time he yelled out, "Jesus Christ, let go, God damn it."

"If I do, you'll behave?"

"I'll bust you in the mouth if you don't."

She said, "You mean it?" giving the finger a twist. He was a big guy and that finger was thick.

He said, "Okay okay okay," trying not to move, his shoulders hunched up again.

It was a tough situation to get out of.

Sooner or later she would have to let go. Then what? If he wanted to hit her, he would. She had a pistol Tony, her Metro-Dade brother, had given her and was licensed to carry, but kept it in her apartment. Corrections said probation officers shouldn't get into situations like this, so there was no reason to pack. Walk away and call the cops. This had happened before and she wasn't hit when she let go. But those times it was different, the guys were on probation. She told them, "Don't ever touch me again, or even think about it," and they backed off, knowing she could violate them, maybe break a finger, too. But this guy wasn't on probation, that she knew of. If he hit her she could call the cops, get him for assault. Then have to appear against him in court, spend all that time . . .

"You know my name," Kathy said. "What's yours?"

He told her it was Ron, easing his shoulders down.

"You don't want to get in trouble, do you, Ron?"

"No, ma'am."

"You gonna behave?"

"Yes, ma'am. Anything you say."

She did not want to let go of that finger, but said, "Okay then," because she had to sometime and let go of it.

Before she could move he grabbed her by the shoulders, threw her down on the sofa next to the other one sitting up asleep, and got on top of her, got her neck bent against the cushion smelling of mildew, one of his knees between her legs, working it up tight against her.

He said, "You know I just got out of jail?"

Wanting to scare her if she wasn't scared already. Or maybe impress her, a guy his age.

"I know you're going back, you don't get off me."

"You like to broke my goddamn finger. I never even touched you."

"You're touching me now, Ron."

"Showing you I can be nice if I want."

Breathing his beer smell in her face. She turned her head enough to see bare dirty windows, a lamp without a shade, paint peeling from the stained walls and ceiling.

"You're a nice guy, then get up."

"But I like it here. I'm close to it, huh?"

"You think you're gonna have sex with me?"

"If I want, and I'm getting the urge. Feel it?"

She said, "Ron, I can break something else besides your finger." And heard the door bang open.

Ron started to turn his head.

Now she saw a cowboy hat up there above them and Ron was gone from her yelling "Hey, shit—" as he was yanked away, knocking longnecks off the crate they used for a coffee table and she saw who it was in the straw cowboy hat, Elvin Crowe, holding the young guy Ron by his belt and shirt collar in back. Kathy pushed up in the sofa to straighten her shirtdress, get it down over her bare thighs. She saw Elvin looking at her and saw Dale now, Dale moving out of the way as Elvin threw Ron out the door. Elvin came over and pulled the other one up from the sofa, grunted with the effort but didn't look at her now or say a word. She saw this one's eyes come open, startled out of sleep, no idea what was happening. Elvin dragged him to the door and now this one was gone, out into the night. She saw Elvin turn to her adjusting his cowboy hat, though it hadn't been touched, setting it straight again over his eyes.

He said to Kathy, "Now then, can I get you something? A cold drink?"

7

The alligator, a ten-foot female weighing about five hundred pounds, opened her eyes and, after several minutes, moved her head from side to side, drowsy, disoriented, not knowing where she was, not catching the scent of anything familiar other than grass and dry soil. No water close by. She raised her head and hissed in the night, in the sound of insects. The wind rose and with it came a scent she recognized as something she liked that she had smelled before sometime in her life and had eaten. After several more minutes she began to move in a sluggish sort of way as though half asleep, not entirely upright on her legs, brushing the grass with her tail. The scent she liked became stronger as she moved and kept moving until her snout touched something she had never smelled before. She sniffed and air came through it into her nostrils, bringing a strong scent of the thing she liked. Now she pushed and whatever it was in front of her bent against her weight until it gave way and the alligator walked through it and felt the ground cold now, smooth and hard. The scent she liked was here, though not enough in one place that it would become the thing itself she could fasten her jaws on and tear or take into her mouth whole. She settled on the cool ground, feeling it become warm beneath her as she went to sleep.

One time Leanne happened to mention that psychic power was at its highest level between the hours of two and four A.M., and thought she would never hear the end of it.

Big jumped on that, asking why she didn't go outside to meditate *then*. Was she afraid of the dark? She told him, "No, I'm not afraid of the dark. I don't get up in the middle of the night 'cause I don't have to. I can raise my cosmic consciousness anytime I want." She could, too.

He'd act innocent and ask her, oh, then why did she go outside every morning six o'clock on the dot if she could do it anytime? Her answer to that was "Because I love the morning. The world glistens and is clean."

He'd become crude in his anger saying, bullshit, it was because she was afraid of the dark, not letting go of that idea, until she would turn it around and remind him of what *he* actually was afraid of.

"You're scared to death of dying."

She knew he didn't like her saying that, but it was true. He could send people to death in the electric chair without giving it a second thought. But mention his own passing, like saying to him, "Big, you're gonna have a terrible time on the other side if you don't open your heart before you go." He'd become furious trying to think of something smart to say, something hurtful. She'd say to him, "Oh, my God," before he thought of a remark to pass, "you should see your aura," and that would usually end it.

He hated knowing he had an aura she could see and he couldn't. Sometimes she'd catch him standing in front of the full-length mirror on the bedroom closet door, looking at himself naked.

This morning he was looking out the kitchen window by the sink.

"Nice day, huh?"

Almost pleasant for a change.

He usually didn't get up till seven. By eight-fifteen he'd be in his pickup truck with a mug of coffee heading for the courthouse.

"We could use a cleanup, that blow we had. I'll call the Stockade for a crew. Those monkeys, if I could find one guy knew what he was doing. . . . Get me a Japanese gardener brought up on some charge, killed his wife, I'd have the son of a bitch confined out here. Lock him up in the pump house at night."

What Leanne could not understand was how a person who loved flowers could be so irritable. What happened to the soft-spoken gentleman who came to Weeki Wachee, bought her Coca-Colas, patted her hand in the hospital . . . made promises he never kept. That part was okay. She had Wanda Grace, she had Pokey, she had her crystals, she had gifts more valuable than any earthly goods. . . . Which reminded Leanne, as she gathered three white quartz forming a triangle on the kitchen table and dropped them in a leather bag, she had a window crystal buried out in the yard, returned to the earth to get its visionary power turned up. She'd dig it up this morning after meditation and a nice talk with Wanda. Leanne turned from the table.

"Pokey? Where are you? Here, Pokey! Come on, sweetheart." She stooped down as Pokey came skidding across the vinyl floor to hop up into her arms. "Her wants to play with Wanda's Pokey, don't her? Big, she hears that other Pokey bark and just about goes crazy, runs around in circles."

She heard Big, standing at the sink, mutter, "Jesus Christ." If she could ever get him to say that with reverence it would change his life. The old poop.

"You want, I'll fix your breakfast."

"No, you go on."

"There's oat bran, bananas . . ."

"Fine. Listen, you be careful."

Walking through the dining area and the living room with Pokey and her bag of crystals, Leanne was thinking, Careful of what? That was a strange thing for Big to say. Was he becoming human after all these years?

She slid open the glass door and stepped out on the porch, a concrete slab painted a pale gray that ran the length of the living room, across the front of the house. About to slide the door closed behind her, Leanne stopped. She saw the huge hole in the screen, the edges of it pushed inward. She heard a strange hissing. She turned her head toward the sound and saw the alligator, a giant alligator up on its legs looking at her, and she screamed and was back inside the house sliding the glass closed, locking it, before she realized she was no longer holding Pokey and her bag of crystals. She screamed again and kept screaming as Big came in a hurry from the kitchen.

He got to the glass door in time to see Pokey, for a moment, in the alligator's jaws before the alligator raised its head as if to look up at the tile ceiling and Pokey was gone, swallowed whole. In those moments all Bob Gibbs could do was stare, not believing an alligator was on his porch. It wasn't supposed to be there but it was. The next moment he was running into the bedroom to get his .38 revolver, knowing his shotgun wouldn't do the job. By the time he got back with the weapon Leanne was wailing and sobbing something awful, becoming hysterical on him and standing in the way. He had to push her aside to slide the glass door open enough to draw a clear bead on the gator, Jesus Christ, a big one he estimated to run ten or twelve feet. There were hollow-points in the revolver, given to him by a fishing buddy of his in the Sheriff's Office, Bill McKenna, in charge of all their criminal investigations. Bob Gibbs closed one eye, aimed at the alligator's head, a spot between its beady eyes that showed red when you shined a light on them at night, and fired—Christ, Leanne screaming again, throwing him off—and fired and fired again until the revolver clicked empty. The alligator didn't even shake its head. It hissed a couple of times, came over and smashed the glass door to pieces with one swipe of its tail.

When the first green-and-white arrived Leanne and Bob Gibbs were out in front by the gravel drive, on the side away from the porch. Both the uniformed deputies came bareheaded with their hands on their holstered revolvers. One of them asked where it was, sounding confident, used to this type of call. Bob Gibbs said, "It's in the goddamn house. In the living room."

By the time they had gone around to the yard by the porch and could see the alligator inside, another green-and-white arrived and two more deputies in dark green joined the group. Bob Gibbs told them he had put six hollow-points into the son of a bitch and it was in there eating his sofa. Leanne, still sobbing, told them it had eaten her dog. One of the deputies said, "Well, it's a fact, gators love dog." Leanne asked if somebody would get that leather bag, see, lying there on the porch? The deputy who mentioned gators loved dog checked the loads in his revolver and said, "Let's go do it."

The four deputies stood in the middle of the porch, about fifteen feet from the alligator in the living room. They fired their magnum revolvers through the shattered door frame with patience and deliberation until the alligator raised up, started to come at them and the deputies got out of there, hurrying out to the yard.

Now the alligator was once again on the porch. Leanne watched it nuzzle her bag of crystals with its snout, saw the jaws open and she began to scream even before the leather bag disappeared inside the alligator's mouth.

Gary Hammond came in an unmarked Dodge Aries, light gray. He was in the driveway on the other side of the house, out of the car putting on his suit coat when he heard the scream. So Gary arrived on the alligator scene in his dark-navy tropical suit, dressed to go to work.

He had been told what to find here, but was still surprised to see the judge and a woman who must be his wife, in a pink warm-up suit, and four deputies with drawn guns, all looking at a full-grown alligator on the porch, the gator not paying much attention to them. It twisted sideways as if to bite its own tail, jerked itself straight and that tail lashed out to send a metal table and chairs flying. Now it crawled around to see what all the noise was about and rested there with its back to them.

They had noticed Gary Hammond walk up, one of the deputies nodding to him; but now they were talking, the deputies and the judge, sounding like hunters.

"We musta hit him."

"Yeah, there's blood. See, on the cement there? Less he cut himself coming through the glass."

"No we hit him a good twelve times."

"More than that, boys. I put six in him before you got here."

This was the judge, in bedroom slippers and a sport shirt hanging out of his pants. Gary Hammond had appeared in his court to testify and have warrants signed, but had never been introduced to him.

"I know a fella has a gator skull on his microwave," a deputy said. "Looks like a hunk of rock."

"We need something heavy, a high-powered rifle."

"Hit him with an ax. That'll do him."

"I think we better get Game and Fish out here."

"Or some old boy from the Glades, Canal Point."

Gary Hammond said, "One of you better bring a car around here."

That got them looking at him. The deputies knew he was a sergeant in the Detective Bureau, worked Crimes Against Persons and was maybe a homicide star. Check the suit. They might know he'd transferred from Palm Beach PD, where he'd kept the island safe for millionaires, but that was about all these deputies would know of Gary Hammond.

One of them said, "Sir, what do we need a car for?"

A mild kind of put-on, polite in front of the judge and his wife.

"The gator walked in there," Gary said, "it can walk out. What do you do then?"

The deputy said, "I guess run like hell." With a grin to show he was kidding.

"I'd want a car to jump in," Gary said, "even if we didn't have Mrs. Gibbs to think of." She looked as though she might be in shock or some kind of trance. He saw her eyes half close and the lids flutter as he said, "You know an alligator can outrun a man?"

Gary turned toward the porch, see what the gator was doing, and just then heard a voice that sounded like a young black girl.

"You bes' hurry up get that car."

The one in *Gone With the Wind*, Butterfly McQueen.

That was who he thought of and turned back expecting to see the deputies grinning, one of them way out of line trying to be funny. But they seemed as surprised as he was, glancing at one another.

Now the judge said, "You heard him. Get a car."

Him? Meaning you, Gary thought, not the voice. The judge ignoring the voice.

Gary said, "Judge," and introduced himself. Bob Gibbs gave him sort of a nod, that's all. He seemed more concerned for his wife and took her aside now, whispering to her. One of the deputies walked off and then started to jog. The other three moved toward the porch, though didn't get too close, talking again, looking at the alligator.

Gary Hammond stood by himself in his neat navy-blue suit.

This morning a few minutes before seven Gary's boss, Colonel McKenna, had called him at home and said, "You're not doing anything, are you?" Gary's current assignment had him reviewing cold cases, homicides over a year old and still open. No, not something pressing, which McKenna knew. He told Gary about the alligator report and how to get to the judge's house, out Southern Boulevard about a mile this side of the Stockade, turn left. "It might be the gator wandered in," McKenna said, "a canal runs by his property. Or some idiot brought it as a joke. Or then again it wasn't meant to be funny. You understand? So look around good."

"What do I do about the alligator?"

"Call Game and Fish if you have to. What I'm concerned with is finding out how it got there."

So now, the next step. . . . He could call Game and Freshwater Fish, wait around for somebody to come out and kill the alligator. That was a fact, they weren't going to dress its wounds. Gary watched a green-and-white creeping toward them from the far end of the house, coming past sabal palms, dipping over the uneven ground in low gear. The judge seemed to have a tropical garden out here, orchids hanging from trees. . . . He was taking his wife by the arm toward the squad car. The three deputies were looking that way now.

They could spend half the day waiting for a Game man to get here. Then stand around some more, watching. Gary thought about taking his suit coat off. No, he'd leave it on, he was comfortable in it. He drew the Beretta holstered on his right hip.

Walking past the deputies Gary racked the slide to put a nine-millimeter load in the chamber. They turned as one at the familiar sound it made. Gary kept going, his eyes holding on the gator as he opened the screen door, closed it quietly, walked up to stand over the gator and stare at its head. You could crouch low and shoot it through an eye or into its ear to find its tiny brain. Or you could stand close and aim at a spot directly behind the animal's skull, drive the bullet straight down to cut its spine. He had seen Game men and contract nuisance hunters kill this way. A shame even when it had to be done. Poachers hit them with an ax or a sledge looking at forty-seven dollars a foot for the hide to make belts and shoes for snappy dressers.

Someone, Gary believed, had brought this gator. It did not know where the hell it was or want to be here lying on a cement floor. There were nicks in its hide, a mark on its skull, a dent, it looked like, where someone had given it a good lick. He aimed the Beretta at the spot behind the skull, the muzzle a foot away, and fired one shot. The gator flattened and lay still.

The deputies waited for him to come out to the yard before they filed in, each one giving him a look before approaching the gator to poke it with a toe.

"I think it was brought here," Gary said, standing with his back to the kitchen sink. "It could be malicious mischief we're looking at, criminal negligence, or it could be more serious."

The judge had come into the kitchen dressed for business in a gray suit and maroon tie. He said, "Wait," got a glass from one cupboard, a bottle of Jim Beam from another, and poured himself a good one, eight o'clock in the morning. He went to the refrigerator for ice, then moved Gary out of the way to add a splash of water. Now he took a couple of deep pulls on his highball, raised the glass and said, "Ahhh, that's better. It's been quite a day. An alligator walks into my house and my wife walks out. She says, 'That's it, I'm leaving.' "

"I could see she was scared," Gary said. "But she'll get over it. I mean, you don't think she'll actually move out, do you?"

"That's what she says."

Gary watched the judge sip his drink. He didn't seem too upset.

"This is the second time it's happened to her. She isn't going for three, I know."

"You had one here before?"

"No, it was up at Weeki Wachee, years ago. My wife was a mermaid at the time I met her. An alligator swam into her act one day and she hasn't been the same since." The judge paused to take a drink. "It did something to her, I don't know what. See, then another one comes along, the poor woman can't handle it. I said, 'Well, hon, it's up to you.' At least she can go someplace there aren't any alligators. Maybe in time . . . I don't know, people do have phobias. Some are scared to death of cats. A cat walks in the room, they're petrified."

There was something here Gary didn't understand. He said, "Yeah, but everybody's afraid of alligators. You'd better be. I mean it's normal."

The judge had turned and was gazing out the window, at deputies appearing out of the trees, poking through his plants.

"What're they looking for?"

Gary edged up behind the judge to look over his shoulder. He said, "I think the alligator was brought here." Then had to step back when the judge turned to face him.

"Why?"

"Well, I did notice driving in, there's a canal over on the other side of your property where it might've come from . . ."

The judge said, "I don't see there's any question about it. That canal hooks into a network of canals. One or the other will take you right up to Okeechobee."

"I know," Gary said, "but I can't see a gator that size climbing the spoil bank and coming all this distance through your orange grove away from water."

"You're an alligator expert," the judge said. "You didn't tell me that."

"No sir," Gary said, "but I do know they live in water and never go too far away from it. That's why I think it was brought here. And if it was, its mouth would've been taped shut and its legs bent up behind its back and taped together. The legs hinge in a way you can do that. So I wondered, when they got here and pulled the tape off, if they might not've just thrown it aside."

The judge half turned toward the window again.

"That's what they're looking for, tape?"

"Duct tape or electrical tape. Either one."

"You find any?"

"Not yet."

The judge nodded and took a sip of his drink.

Gary said, "You didn't hear anything last night?"

"Not a sound."

"I was thinking if they drove in with it, came past the house . . . Maybe your wife heard something."

"No, she didn't either."

"Could I speak to her?"

"You're asking me, can you have a conversation with her about *al*ligators? In her condition?"

"I wondered if she might've heard a truck."

"Jesus Christ, but you keep beating on it. I just told you she didn't hear a thing. Now we're through here. I'm going to work."

Gary said, "Yes sir," and paused and said, "Can I ask you something else? It's unrelated. Well, in a way it is." The judge, with the glass raised to finish his drink, didn't answer. "When I first got here," Gary said, "I told one of the deputies to go get a car. In case the gator came out after us." The judge lowered the glass and was looking directly at him now. "Right after I said it, I heard a voice that sounded to me like a young black female, you know, kind of a high voice? Repeating pretty much what I said."

Gary waited.

The judge stared at him.

Gary didn't care for his expression. Ice-cold.

The judge said, "What's your name again?"

"It's Sergeant Gary Hammond."

"You like detective work?"

"Yes sir, very much."

"Better than driving a squad car."

"Yes sir."

"Did you know Colonel McKenna was a buddy of mine?"

"No sir, I didn't."

The judge said, "Well, you do now, boy. When I tell you we're through here, it means we're through, you don't ask any more questions. You understand?"

"Yes sir."

"The alligator wasn't brought here as a prank or otherwise, to cause anybody harm. It came out of that canal all by itself. So there's no need of you to write up an Offense Report."

Gary said, "I still have to tell Colonel McKenna what happened."

"That's all right," the judge said, "long as you don't color it." He smiled then, his mouth did while his eyes remained cold. "Tell Bill for me he should've sent the dogcatcher."

Gary said, "Yes sir, I will," paused a few seconds wanting to bite his tongue, but had to ask it. "Judge, has your life ever been threatened?"

8

There was a judge friend of Bob Gibbs, now
retired from the bench, who described Palm Beach as "an
island off the coast of the United States." Bob Gibbs
agreed one hundred percent. Cross Lake Worth east and
you were in a different country, the top end of the Gold
Coast where the rich and famous lived. But you know
what? Go the other way, drive west out beyond Twenty
Mile Bend and, man, you were in a different *world*, the
Glades, bottomland America with a smell of muck and
fish and half a million acres of sugarcane off on the left
side of the road there. He liked Palm Beach, enjoyed being an honored guest at the balls and functions, eating
free. But never felt the kick that coming out to the Glades
gave him. Why was that? His judge friend who'd retired
and moved up to the Panhandle said, " 'Cause you're a
redneck at heart. Why do you think? If you'd been born
here you'd be moonlighting gators for hides and meat instead of sitting on the bench, an ill-tempered judge."

Recalling that got Bob Gibbs in touch with his feelings, as Leanne would say, aware of a different kind of kick this trip. One right in the gut. Anger mixed with a foreboding something messy could come of this alligator business. What in the hell was Dicky Campau thinking that he delivered it alive?

They were to meet this evening at Slim's Fish Camp on Torry Island. Cross the bridge over the rim canal and you were there, in the marshy lower end of Lake Okeechobee, not too far from Belle Glade. Bob Gibbs found the frog gigger inside Slim's visiting with friends and pulled him out into the dark, over by the Coca-Cola machine.

"How many times did I tell you. It was suppose to be a dead one?"

"It was, when I left it." Dicky looking bewildered at the thought of its having come alive. "Judge, me and my wife took the truck, figure to run along the dike. We spot her in the canal right there by the cleaning dock eating on some softshell turtle. I thought we might have to go clear to Canal Point, but there she was. I shine a light on her, see about eight ten inches between the eyes? I know she's a big'n."

Bob Gibbs said, "What was our deal? Deliver the son of a bitch *dead.*" He couldn't say it enough.

"Judge, it *was.* Ask my wife. I used a snatch hook on a quarter-inch line. I caught her clean, one throw, tied off around my trailer ball and pulled her out of there. I don't mean she come willing, she fought it, pretty near tore the trailer hitch clean off my truck. I said to my wife, 'We got us one.' Next, I hit that gator over the head with a ten-pound sledge. One stroke, she let out her air and never made another sound."

"It came back to life," Bob Gibbs said. "Walked through my screen porch and into my house."

"Prob'ly smelled your dog."

"It *ate* the dog."

"Judge, I told you when you called, I hunt frog. Outside of that gator they arrested me for I ain't trapped one in years."

Bob Gibbs thought a minute, hearing insects in the night and the sound of country music coming from Slim's.

"You know that canal by my place? I'm saying that's what it came out of."

"It could've."

"I want to know for sure."

"It's possible she swum down there."

"And came into my yard."

"I guess. Listen, Judge? You know my wife's pretty good at estimating. She looked at that gator and saw about four hundred dollars in the hide. She figured the meat, five bucks a pound, could bring another hundred. What I'm saying, that was part of the deal, Judge. You call me to pick her up afterwards and she's mine. Am I right?"

"And nobody would know about it but us," Bob Gibbs said. "That's right too, isn't it?"

"Yes sir."

"I stopped by the Helen Wilkes after court this evening? Everybody in the entire goddamn place knew about it. They're even speculating it was put there to get me. And you know why? 'Cause the son of a bitch was *alive.* 'Cause I had to call the sheriff to come *kill* it."

Dicky Campau said, "So you don't have it no more, huh?"

9

Kathy Baker was here because the detective, Sergeant Gary Hammond, had called the office wanting to talk to her about Dale Crowe Junior. She told him she was just walking out the door, but had to be at the Detention Center this afternoon and could stop by later. The county jail was right behind the sheriff's building. He said fine. She had met Gary Hammond once before, but he didn't seem to remember.

Louis Falco, a sergeant with the TAC unit, was also here. Kathy knew him slightly from the Polo Lounge, an after-work hangout off Military Trail, but had never seen Gary Hammond there. She had a feeling he didn't drink or smoke and went to a Protestant church on Sunday. But a neat-looking guy, lean build, no ring. White button-down shirt and print burgundy necktie, very nice. She wondered if cop groupies out at the Polo Lounge would go for Gary Hammond or think he was impersonating a police officer. He looked more like a lawyer than a guy in law enforcement. Mid-thirties, say, but no ring. The only thing that marred his neat image, but a nice touch, his hair was kind of long, dark brown, down over the collar of his shirt.

Gary Hammond was telling them, "If you ran the names of all the bad guys convicted by Judge Gibbs who are back on the street and wouldn't mind taking a whack at him, you could paper this room with the printouts."

Kathy let her gaze wander from Gary's desk to take in the size of the squad room with its rows of desks, walls and ceiling a dull yellow. But with those glass-front offices all around the four sides, there wasn't a whole lot of wall space. How many names was he actually talking about? Kathy didn't ask. The guy liked his wallpaper analogy and was trying to make a point.

He liked it so much he was taking it next door to Sex Crimes saying, "If it was possible to count all the bad guys still *in* doing a hard fall, but have friends on the outside they could get to pay the judge back, we'd have to use the walls in there too."

Kathy didn't know about the walls in Sex Crimes. She did recall they had lamps on the desks and artificial flowers. Part of that squad room was Child Abuse.

Gary Hammond moved on saying, "If you consider just the wackos and rockheads that pass through Gibbs's courtroom every day of the week. Or it could be a guy never had even a parking ticket, all of a sudden he draws time on a DUI manslaughter, got drunk and killed somebody with his car. The guy loses his job, his family, his life is ruined and it's all this judge's fault."

What he was actually saying, Kathy decided, it could be anybody. Including Dale Crowe, for some reason singled out or she wouldn't be here. Though she still didn't see what Dale had to do with the alligator.

Lou Falco didn't know why he was here either, asking, "What do you want *me* to do about it?"

Kathy wondered that too. This didn't seem to be a job for TAC. The Tactical unit specialized in undercover work, surveillance, narcotics investigations . . . But also dignitary protection. That could be it.

Gary said he was looking down the road, trying to anticipate what might happen next. "I'm wondering if the judge shouldn't have a watch put on him. Nothing elaborate, park a green-and-white at his house, drive him to court . . ."

Falco said, "In case another alligator gets after him? You don't even know it was put there."

"I'm ninety-five percent sure."

"Even if it was, you can't call it attempted homicide. People get alligators in their swimming pools all the time, they don't call TAC. You play golf, don't you? Any course around here, walk in the rough you're liable to step on an alligator. Listen, I don't want to tell you your business, but at this point the only lead you can get is from the judge. What's he say about it? Anybody threaten him lately?"

"I asked him and he threw me out," Gary said. "We're no longer on speaking terms. All I got from the judge, nothing happened during the night they were aware of. He wouldn't let me talk to his wife."

Kathy said, "Did you see her?"

"Yeah, but that's all."

"What's she look like?"

"Attractive, blond, thirties, putting on weight. Scared to death of alligators, according to the judge. So afraid one might come back, she left." His gaze moved to Falco.

"But there's no reason to think it was meant for the wife. Not when you have a highly qualified potential victim like Judge Gibbs."

So much for the wife. Kathy said, "You know where she went?" Gary was looking at her again. "You said she left."

"I have no idea."

"You could ask him."

Now he shook his head. "Not a chance."

She wanted to talk some more about the wife, a woman who believed she was a twelve-year-old black girl. Bring it up for whatever it was worth. . . .

But now Gary was saying, "The judge tells McKenna it came out of the canal. He doesn't want to hear any more about it. McKenna says fine. But then he pulls my squad off cold homicides and tells me to look into it. Only, he says, don't make a big deal out of it."

"You tell him," Falco said, "about papering the walls?"

"We're starting out with the most recent ones that seem likely. Offenders the judge sent away who got their release in the past couple of months." Gary's hand touched a file folder on the neat desk, everything in place. "DOC sent us a list this morning we're checking out. The reason Ms. Baker's here, she has a probation violator who threatened the judge. When was it? The day before yesterday."

Kathy said, "What are you talking about?"

Gary was looking at her until Falco got up from his chair, ready to leave, saying, "You want my opinion, Gary? You're way ahead of yourself. McKenna says don't make a big deal out of it? That should tell you he doesn't see it as a hit. But he has to put somebody on it to cover his ass, just in case. So you go through the motions, take McKenna at his word and don't strain yourself."

Gary was shaking his head. "McKenna said that because the judge didn't want any publicity. But you saw the *Post* this morning? Gibbs's picture on the front page?"

"And I saw how they played it," Falco said, "called him gator bait, right? How'd they put it?"

" 'Has Judge Become "Gator Bait"?' " Kathy said.

Gary was looking at her again. "You read it?" She nodded and he said, "A reporter, guy I've known all my life, calls me, wants to know what happened. I told him we have no idea how the alligator got there, if it was delivered or came on its own. They put in the paper, 'Investigators speculate whether sentence has been passed on Judge Gibbs.' I didn't even say well, it's a possibility. But they want to believe it was an attempt on his life."

"They're having fun with it, that's all," Falco said, " 'cause the guy's an asshole. Think about it. You want to do somebody, there better ways'n with an alligator. I'll see you."

Gary told her his friend at the *Post* asked if he could get a picture of the alligator, wanting to know what happened to it. Kathy had the feeling he would keep talking about the alligator if she let him. But then listening to him she thought of a question and asked, "Who killed it?"

"I did."

"You shot it?"

He nodded, didn't say another word about the alligator and now she asked him, "Where did you hear Dale Crowe threatened Gibbs?"

"I was told by a deputy who got it from Gibbs's bailiff.

Crowe said, 'You'll see me again.' Or, 'You'll get yours.' Something like that."

"You haven't seen a transcript?"

"They're getting me one."

"Dale said, 'If you think you're through with me you're full of shit.' Is that a threat?"

"It could be."

"How many shots did it take, to kill the alligator?"

"One."

Kathy stared at him and he stared back at her. "What did you use?"

He leaned to one side to touch his hip. "This."

She paused before saying, "Dale was mad. He got state time and doesn't deserve it."

"Battery on a police officer, that's a third-degree five-year felony, any way you look at it."

"You like sending people away?"

"It's what I do."

"Yeah, but do you like it?"

He took his time, maybe thinking about it. He didn't look like a guy who shot alligators or collared offenders. He looked like . . . a nice guy. He said, "If I didn't like it I wouldn't be here." And asked her, "You know where Dale was the night before last?"

"With his uncle. They got home about nine."

It seemed to surprise him. "You sure?"

"I was there. You know his uncle, Elvin Crowe?"

She watched Gary stare at her as though the name was familiar, one he'd seen or heard recently. He had nice eyes. She liked blue eyes after seeing brown ones most of her life. His were a deep blue. She didn't care too much for those pale, light-blue ones, killer eyes, the kind Keith had. Gary had a file folder open now, reading a Department of Corrections printout that listed the names of offenders who'd recently gotten their release. The one he had mentioned. The list went all the way down the page, names coming out of the forty prisons and correctional facilities in the state of Florida.

The other night at Dale's house Elvin offered her a beer. If she wanted something else he'd send Dale to the store for it. Elvin polite, talking Southern to her in that syrupy way, Dale not saying a word. She told Elvin no thanks. No socializing with probationers. She told Dale she'd see him tomorrow and got out of there. Stopped by yesterday, he wasn't home and hadn't called the office. She had spent most of today looking for him, asking around.

"Elvin Crowe," Gary said. "I remember Elvin, shot a guy out on the Turnpike. He's one of yours?"

"One of seventy-three or seventy-four."

"If Gibbs sent him up . . ."

"He did," Kathy said.

"Then he fits the profile. Both of them, Dale and Elvin."

"Everybody fits your profile," Kathy said.

He smiled and it surprised her. She had him down as an achiever, a guy who took his work very seriously. He was so neat. Look at his desk. But the smile was real.

He said, "I try to keep an open mind. Everyone's dirty till they prove they aren't."

No smile now, playing with her. He was quite a nice-looking guy. She liked his eyes, she liked his mouth too, his hair . . . She said, "You'll love Elvin. Wait till you meet him."

"I like them both. You know where they went that night?"

"They said they took a ride."

"Out to the Glades by any chance?"

"Palm Beach."

"No alligators in Palm Beach. Or not the kind I have in mind. I still like your two guys. When do you see them again?"

"I have to check on Dale every day. Four to go."

"He's behaving himself?"

Kathy hesitated. "I haven't seen him since the other night."

"That puts him in violation, doesn't it?"

"He's already facing five years."

Gary raised both hands. "He's yours. You don't want to violate him, don't."

"I leave here, I'll stop by their house."

"Elvin lives there too?" Gary looked down at his sheet. "I have a Belle Glade address for him. If he's from out there, I imagine he knows something about alligators."

"I have to go," Kathy said, and got up.

"I wouldn't mind tagging along, but I have to be somewhere at five."

She didn't want him along anyway, not if she got a chance to sit down with Dale, find out what he was thinking. Still, she said, "That's too bad. You might've had a chance to meet Elvin."

He smiled, just a little. "You want to see if I can handle him, don't you?"

Kathy shrugged, trying to look innocent. "Why would it be a problem?"

He got up from the desk saying he'd walk her out.

He did have a gun and had shot an alligator. She saw the Beretta as he slipped on the jacket of his navy-blue suit, his shield pinned to his belt. Now the gun was hidden and he could be a young slim-cut executive. He put on sunglasses. She said, "Pretty cool," and meant it, head to toe.

Walking along wide yellow hallways he became a tour guide talking in a quiet tone about forensics, serology, the use of lasers in latent-print detection, not his areas but he knew things and was probably a very good cop. She mentioned her brothers, Tony and Ray, into Miami street life and dope busts. Freeze, motherfuckers. Do you ever say that? He said, I think I have. What was she trying to do, talking like that? They passed a workout room and he asked if she was into aerobics, any of that. She said no, but my ex-husband ran five miles every other day while I cleaned the bathroom. He smiled but didn't ask any questions or say if he was married or not. Or if he worked out. In the lobby a uniformed captain, crew cut, white body-shirt stretched over his belly, said, "Sergeant?" almost past them and they stopped. "I believe you could use a haircut there."

Gary said, "Yes sir, I'm getting one today. You know I always try to meet your expectations."

Was he serious?

Kathy wasn't sure. Maybe the captain wasn't either the way he stared at Gary, not saying a word. Then gave them a nod, walked on, and they went through the entrance, Gary holding the door for her. They stopped on the walk leading to the parking area and he said, "Well," facing the sun behind Kathy and squinting a little.

She said, "Were you putting him on?"

"Who, the captain?"

"You always want to live up to his expectations."

"He believed me."

"Sure, what's he going to say? Listen, you want a haircut, I'll give you one."

"You know how?"

"I used to cut my brothers' hair all the time. I could do yours easy."

"Yeah, when?"

"Call me at the Omar Road office, make an appointment."

He was smiling again. "I'm glad we got a chance to meet."

"You don't remember the other time?"

Look at his face. He had no idea what she meant.

"Last August in Riviera Beach, by the projects. You were driving that unmarked Dodge everybody knows is a cop car. I'm walking along . . ."

He was smiling now.

"You pull over and stop me, want to know if I'm looking for crack or already bought some. You ask to see my ID . . ."

Now he was nodding. "Your hair was different."

"It was long then. You couldn't believe I'd go in that neighborhood alone, to check on one of my guys."

He said, *"That's* where it was. I've been racking my brain."

"I could see that," Kathy said, beginning to realize it was hard to tell with this guy when he was sincere and when he was laying a line on you. Maybe not so different from her brothers. "Well, it's been nice."

No ring. Which didn't mean anything. Maybe divorced and took his kids to the beach on weekends. There were all kinds of those around. Walking away she turned back and said to him, still in the same place watching her, "You didn't tell me, do you work out?"

"Once in a while." He raised his hand and said, "I'll see you."

Yeah, but when?

10

Leanne had said to Bob Gibbs, "When you get home from court today I'll be gone. I'll call one of my dear friends"—meaning some nitwit from one of her psychic workshops—"to drive me to the bus station."

That was the extent of her intelligence, to leave here you took a bus. He told her, trying hard to sound dejected, to take the car if she wanted. Long as he had his pickup.

She said, "Don't ask if I'm going to the Spring or back to my roots, Luna Pier, Ohio, because I won't tell you." She said, "I may not ever speak to you again, Big, for what you did. I hope someday I will have it in my heart to forgive you, but I can't promise."

Bob Gibbs said wait now, curious, forgive him for what?

She said, "Having that alligator brought to our house."

He worked himself up protesting. How could she accuse him of something like that? What would be his reason?

Leanne said, "I don't believe it was to see me dead, you pass that sentence in court and keep your hands clean. But I know now you want to see me leave, so I will."

He couldn't argue with that. Still, he told her she should try opening her heart. Get in touch with her spirit guide and seek her guidance in looking at this situation.

Leanne said, "Wanda Grace is the one told me you had the alligator brought."

There was no way he was going to argue through Leanne with a twelve-year-old colored girl dead 135 years and hope to come out ahead. He helped Leanne with her suitcases full of rocks and books, and put them in her car.

That was forty-eight hours ago and he hadn't heard a word from her since. So Bob Gibbs was feeling new life this afternoon in court. He had two sentencing hearings, one of them Dicky Campau up for alligator poaching . . . but no probation violations, damn it, no chance of the little girl making an appearance. Marialena Reyes was prosecuting. He asked her if she happened to see Kathy Baker in the courthouse. Marialena said no, not today. Bob Gibbs left the bench, everyone rising, stepped into his chambers and told his JA to call the Probation Office and ask for Katherine Baker, he wanted to see her about a matter. Then had a fit when she wasn't there. "Well, where is she?" His judicial assistant, another Bob, who'd been with him ever since coming to the bench, said, "If they don't know, Judge, how'm I suppose to know?" Bob Gibbs returned to the courtroom. This time as everyone rose his mood was taking a downward turn.

The first hearing didn't help any.

It started out looking simple enough. The defendant, a repeat offender, had previously been given ninety days on a burglary of a conveyance, but before going to jail had been allowed thirty days on the street. During this time he was arrested again, twice, on a grand theft auto and a petty theft, stealing a pack of cigarettes. Marialena Reyes said they were dropping the grand theft auto, since they didn't have much of a case, and would recommend enhancing the defendant's sentence from ninety days to nine months in the county jail. But the defendant wanted state prison time so he could get his glasses and his teeth fixed, which the police broke when they arrested him on the grand theft auto, now dropped. Marialena Reyes said okay, then she was recommending twenty-seven months DOC time. The defendant said that wasn't fair, twenty-seven months for stealing a pack of cigarettes? Marialena explained to him he would only do nine of the twenty-seven months; it would be the same as county jail time except he would have a chance to get his teeth and his glasses fixed. The defendant said no, originally he was going to do six months in the Stockade on the burglary of a conveyance and it was reduced to ninety days. So how about giving him eighteen months DOC time and he'd do six? How did that sound?

Up on the bench Bob Gibbs pictured Kathy Baker out at his place, strolling about in a white dress and a straw sunhat as he showed her his flowers, his orchids blooming in trees, watched her expression as she realized what a sensitive man he was, in close touch with nature. He could daydream and still follow Marialena and the defendant—okay, but that was enough. Time to end it. Bob Gibbs banged his fist down hard. He said, "What is going on here?" And to the defendant, "Keep arguing, you'll do the entire twenty-seven months." The defendant said,

Judge, that wasn't fair. And Bob Gibbs said, *"Fair?* What's fair got to do with it?"

They showed utter contempt of the law but expected the system to be fair, which to them meant lenient.

There was Dicky Campau and his wife, Inez, a big ugly woman, in the first row behind the defense table, Dicky expecting his hearing to turn out fair. Get off for doing a favor. Except he hadn't done the favor the way he was supposed to.

Leaving the bench Bob Gibbs told his clerk he'd be right back. In his chambers he said to his JA, "Call the probation office and get her home address and phone number for me, Katherine Baker."

"I'm way ahead of you," his JA said, and handed him a sheet of note paper. "She lives in Delray."

Bob Gibbs, not caring for anyone to be way ahead of him, said, "Call them back. What I want is for her to phone *me*, at home if not before I leave here."

"Give them your unlisted number?"

Be fair with the hired help too, show patience.

Bob Gibbs said, "Think about it. How would she call me otherwise?"

The allegation against Dicky Campau was that he had taken a young alligator from the Palm Beach Canal, approximately fifty yards south of Summit Boulevard, killed it and was skinning the tail when apprehended by a sheriff's deputy. Someone in the neighborhood had called 911 upon hearing gunshots about fifteen minutes earlier.

Dicky Campau had told at his arraignment, he was on his way to Charley's Crab with a load of fresh froglegs when he saw the gator on the spoil bank, not in the canal, and it was already dead when he stopped and checked. He said he would plead guilty to skinning the tail for meat before it turned as anybody would do that saw it laying there, but he had not killed the gator, a young male just under six feet. That was Dicky Campau's story. As long as no one had seen him pull the gator out of the water with his snatch hook and hit it over the head with a tire iron, he was sticking to it.

What messed up Dicky Campau's story, the deputy at the arraignment had testified there was a .22 rifle in Dicky's pickup and because gunshots were reported he assumed this was the weapon used. Dicky swore that even those couple of times before when he'd been arrested for poaching, he never used a rifle. He testified the deputy had smelled the .22 and *knew* it hadn't been fired. It must've been somebody else saw the gator before he did and shot it for sport. The deputy had said he was not a ballistics expert and Dicky had said, "He's got a nose, don't he?"

It was too late now to check the rifle, determine if it had been fired—this had happened over two months ago. They didn't even know for sure what had killed the gator. But the prosecutor, a Latin woman, kept bringing up the .22 saying we know shots were fired and the defendant was found with a dead alligator and a rifle. What other conclusion can be drawn.

That was the case against him. Like saying the only way to kill a gator was to shoot it. That deputy hadn't even looked at his tire iron.

Now Dicky Campau waited for Judge Gibbs to come through. Maybe say something about it being unfair to convict a man when all we know he did was cut some tail meat. The judge was looking right at him now.

"In that the defendant understands and appreciates

the findings of these proceedings and is capable of entering into a plea . . . admitting he was in the process of
skinning the alligator when apprehended, I have to agree
with the state, at least in substance. But, I'm gonna go
easy on you, Mr. Campau."

Dicky liked the sound of that last part.

"I understand you're a hardworking man with a wife
to support. So I'm not gonna give you jail time, deprive
you of your means of making a living. Instead, this court
fines you five hundred dollars and places you on probation for a period of one year."

There were legal words after that Dicky Campau
didn't understand, in fact barely heard, even staring right
at the judge, who was coming off the bench now, everybody getting up as he left the courtroom. Dicky felt somebody take hold of his arm and knew it was his wife.

Inez said, "Do him a favor and he'll do you one. That
was some deal you made."

Dicky walked away to get fingerprinted and sign
some papers. It gave him time to think, wonder how he
was going to raise five hundred dollars without killing
another gator. It gave his wife time to think too, because
when they were out in the hall and he mentioned it, she
said, "That ain't the way to do it. They catch you now, you
go to jail."

He asked her, "How, then?"

Inez said, "Get it off the judge."

come about. Convicts, they'd sit around talking about jobs, banks they'd held up, argue about how to blow a safe. Now you got *in*mates instead of cons and these guys are crazy. All they think about is getting dope and getting laid, looking to see who they can turn. See, once you get turned you're pussy. *In*mates, they'll snitch you for smoking a joint, anything, to get in good with the turnkeys."

Dale said, "You want another beer?"

Elvin said, "Sit still when I'm talking to you."

Dale eased back in the sofa, Elvin staring at him.

"What you have to learn is how to ride the rap, do your own time, but get salty quick as you can. You're in the population you don't have to be good-looking, you're a new punk coming in and that'll get you elected. The first one comes at you and you back down, you're pussy. What you have to do is boo him up. A nigger, you have to stick him. See, if a nigger has a white boy, even one's ugly, he thinks he's a big man. What you do is buy yourself a shank. You can get anything you want in there but a woman. Some pretty good shine we call buck, made of rice or orange juice with some yeast and sugar. We'd have some poor asshole keep it in his cell while it set up." Elvin paused. "I better show you how to make a shank. I could use a spoon. . . . The easiest kind of weapon to make, you melt the end of a toothbrush and stick a razor blade to it. I cut a dink one time looked at me funny, he's got a scar now from sixty-five stitches in his face. You won't kill a person with a toothbrush, but he'll stay wide of you. Let's see . . . Yeah, what you might do till things settle down, stick a book in your pants under your shirt, one in front, one in back, so your belt holds 'em there? It'll give you some protection in case a dink tries to shank *you*. He comes in high on you, going for the throat or the heart, the books won't do you no good. But most times it goes down is in a crowd and the dink will stay low so as not be seen. There was a boy one time, they're hurrying him to the infirmary and this one holding the stretcher drops his end and stabs the boy again. So don't trust nobody till you find out who's with who, how they hang out together in the yard. Understand? They send you to Starke write me and I'll give you the names of people can do you some good. It'll cost you, nothing's free. But it's nice to have friends, huh? Listen, where your keys at? I have to go someplace."

"I have to go someplace too," Dale said. He wasn't sure where, but knew he had to get out of here. Out of this house, out of Delray and keep going. He'd been to Orlando to Disney World and Daytona Beach a lot of times, but he'd never been past the Georgia line or to places he'd like to see like California.

"Dale? Where your keys at?"

It was quicker to shoot over to Dr. Tommy's house from Delray than coming down from Palm Beach sightseeing, like the other night. Elvin took Dale's pickup north on 95 to Boynton Beach, cut over to Ocean Ridge and it didn't take him fifteen minutes.

From a dump full of palmetto bugs, called roaches other places, to what Elvin believed was the slickest house he'd ever seen. And yet a little sneak like Dr. Tommy owned it. The house was light-gray brick with white trim and shutters and a white tile roof. It didn't look to have any size till you went up the drive through palm trees and sea grape and saw it was built into high ground, a lot more house on the ocean side where it had a big flagstone patio, a swimming pool but no diving board—shit—and all kinds of shrubs and palm trees dressing up the grounds. Elvin found this out by walking around the outside of the house and there was Dr. Tommy on his patio reading the paper, a tall drink on the table next to him, the whole patio in shade with the sun off on the other side of Florida.

Elvin said, "How we doing today?"

He didn't see the Cuban guy—what was his name? Hector. Dr. Tommy was also a Cuban but hard to tell. Neither one of them had what you'd call that true greaser look. This doctor was a shifty booger though. Look at him. Shorts and no shirt, tan and skinny, squirming to sit up straight, putting his nice face on. Some newspapers slid off his lap to fall on the flagstone. Dr. Tommy didn't seem to notice.

"Well," he said. "I didn't expect you so soon. No, I should say I expected you, yes, but didn't think it would be this soon."

Getting his meaning straightened out. Elvin didn't see it changed anything. He pulled a chair away from the glasstop table, a heavy wrought-iron patio set, nothing but the best, settled into the chair's maroon cushions, then had to turn his head to look up at the house this close. Two floors with an upper deck across the back and stairs coming down from it.

"Being put out of business hasn't seemed to hurt you none," Elvin said. "What kind of doctor were you?"

"I still am," Dr. Tommy said. "Dermatologist." He raised a finger to his cheekbone. "Those brown spots you have right here should be looked at."

"You're looking at 'em, aren't you?"

"I mean tested. You have to be careful, you let it go, it could be melanoma."

"Now you're trying to scare me."

"If you don't worry about skin cancer . . ."

"I been outside all my life."

"That's why you have those spots. But you wear a hat, that's sensible. What else you want to know?"

Dr. Tommy didn't seem as nervous talking about skin as he did movies the other night. Elvin put his hat down on his eyes a little more. "I been thinking about what Sonny told me."

"Oh, the movies?" Dr. Tommy said. "I can hear Sonny. Told you if you got your hands on them, even one, you could make a lot of money. Is that right?"

Smiling now—look at that. Not a bit nervous.

"That was Sonny's idea, threaten to show my father unless I paid him. But he didn't have the nerve to do it himself, so he tried to get a young lady to help him. She would do all the work, keep him out of it. But she came to me instead, told me everything. So then I accused Sonny in front of the young lady. He called her a liar and she hit him with her fist, a big woman. Sonny had to protect himself, so he hit her with that iron thing, the poker."

Dr. Tommy paused to take a sip of his drink right in front of Elvin, not bothering to ask if he wanted one. Elvin wondering, What's going on here?

Putting the glass down the doctor said, "Okay, he told you a different story. And you believe him because Sonny is a beautiful liar. Am I right?"

Elvin had to readjust his hat on that one, set it looser on his head. "You catch him," Elvin said, "he'd like roll over on his back with his paws in the air. Give you this sad look so you won't hurt him too much."

"You know him," Dr. Tommy said, "and you don't know whose story to believe? I'm talking about why that young lady was killed. But really, what difference does it make? You're more interested in those movies than the truth. I tell you they're gone, you don't believe me. It's why you came back. What were you in for, in prison?"

Shifting his gears all of a sudden.

"I shot a guy," Elvin said.

"You kill him?"

"Course I killed him."

"I thought something like that. Okay, so now you come to work a deal on me. But there aren't any movies, so what do you do now? You want to search my house if you think I'm lying?"

Here was this dink talking right up to him. It took Elvin a moment to adjust, resetting his hat again where it would stick to his forehead.

He said, "Well, we sure got a lot cleared up there, didn't we?" and looked toward the house.

The doc's boy, Hector, was out on the upper deck now in his Cuban shirt, leaning on the rail watching them. He had shoulders on him for a little guy, short in the legs but maybe worked out, knew some tricks. He acted like a girl and was an ugly fucker, reminding Elvin of sneaky types he'd known up at Starke.

"If I was to take you up on that," Elvin said, "look around your place . . ."

"Yes, if it pleases you, do it."

"He won't try and stop me?"

"Who, Hector? What does he care? It's not his house."

"What's he do for you?"

"Oh, the laundry, cleans the bathrooms, makes my drinks." Dr. Tommy looked up at the deck. "He wants to know what you do for me."

Elvin saw the guy up there hunch his shoulders, still

leaning on the rail. He said something in Spanish. Now the doctor said something back to him and Elvin looked over to see him smiling.

"What're you talking about?"

"He said if we have to serve time, this is the place to do it, that's all. A private joke."

"Guy like him, if he wasn't so fuckin' ugly he'd do okay in the joint."

"Hector loves me," Dr. Tommy said. "I could ask him to shoot you, I believe he would, yes. Hector is very emotional."

Elvin said, "Convicted felon, you have a gun in the house? That could get you in trouble."

All it did was get the doctor smiling again.

"You're still looking for a way to work some kind of deal on me," Dr. Tommy said. "Okay, you want, call the police. Tell them I have a rifle my father gave me. I was fourteen years old and he took me to hunt wild pigs. You know what happened? He caught me shooting flamingos. From that time when I was a boy he started watching me."

Maybe this guy was a retard. Elvin said, "What'd you shoot flamingos for? You can't eat 'em, I don't think."

"Why? What difference does it make? Fuck the flamingos. Fuck you, too. You want to call the police, tell them I have a rifle? Uh, tough guy?"

Elvin said, "What's wrong with you?" The guy acting strange, his eyes getting a funny look, while his voice was fairly calm.

"Or would you like to use it?" Dr. Tommy said. "You have the experience, uh? You're looking for a score . . . I'm serious now. You listening?"

"Yeah, I'm listening."

"I'll pay you to kill a man. What do you say?"

What Elvin said was, "How much?"

And it got Dr. Tommy smiling again, the dink easy to tickle, saying now, "You're my man, Elvin," becoming pals all of a sudden. "I knew it as soon as you walked in the other night. You don't care who, only how much."

"If the price ain't right," Elvin said, "what's there to talk about?"

The doctor nodded his head, his smile gone but his eyes shining as he gave the figure.

"Ten thousand."

That didn't sound too bad. Get half up front.

"To kill the man," Dr. Tommy said, "who ruined my life."

It didn't look too ruined to Elvin.

"I can't work, I have to sell my possessions to live. My paintings, works of art . . ."

Getting a good buck, too, if he had ten grand laying around the house. "We talking cash for this job?"

"Yes, of course."

"You been thinking about it long?"

"More than thinking, finding out about him. Where he lives, where he goes to drink, the women he sees. Hector is my eyes while I'm a prisoner."

Whatever that meant. Elvin said, "Well, shit, you ought to know where he lives."

"But it could be too late," Dr. Tommy said. He bent over in his chair and started gathering up the newspapers he'd dropped, Elvin noticing he had *The Miami Herald,* the *Sun-Sentinel* . . . The doctor handed him one saying, "Here, on the front page of the *Post.* You must have seen it."

Elvin took the newspaper. The second he spotted the picture, that bony face grinning out of the page, he said,

"Jesus Christ, this is the guy we're talking about? Judge Gibbs? I thought you meant your daddy."

"He's already dead."

Elvin said, "And didn't leave you nothing, huh? On account of you shot that flamingo and been generally fucking up all your life. I forgot for a minute there it was Gibbs convicted Sonny and nailed you on the dope charge. He's the same one sent me up." This was getting good, realizing he had his own pay-back motive now besides money. Why hadn't he thought of it? "The other day this same judge give my young nephew five years for nothing. You met him, Dale Crowe Junior?"

Dr. Tommy was waiting, staring up at him.

"Have you read the paper? I ask that assuming you can read."

Elvin gave him a look, narrowing his eyes. "You think I don't know how?"

"Well, for Christ sake do it, will you?"

Elvin found the column, read partway into the story that asked if the judge was gator bait and stopped.

"There's somebody already tried for him?"

"That's the question, why I wonder if it's too late," Dr. Tommy said. "If I thought of it, how many others have too? Are thinking about it right now?"

"Shit," Elvin said, "you want Bob Gibbs you might have to get in line, huh?"

12

One time Kathy said to her brothers, "You guys are lucky. You go after offenders you know are dirty, get a conviction and you have a sense of accomplishment, huh? You've done something. I think it's like a game with you. High-risk but it pays off and it's fun. You know what I do? Paperwork. I check up on people who wish I'd leave them alone and then I fill out forms. I don't get anything out of it because I never finish. It's always the same losers, one after another."

The latest one, Dale Crowe Junior. She stopped by his house, didn't see his pickup but knocked on the door. No answer, so she walked around the house looking in windows, hoping Dale hadn't run off. Her brother Tony, with Metro-Dade, said, "You don't like it, quit. Do what you want. You're smart, for a girl. You think we have fun, apply to Palm Beach PD. That'd be pretty light duty, nothing you can't handle up there."

Her brother Ray, her buddy, said, "You know how to find people, you know how to talk to offenders. I think you'd make a good investigator. Why not?" Yeah, but have to drive a radio car first, do street work. Meet the same kinds of people she did now but on a different basis. Confront them armed. Perhaps some time or other have to use the gun.

She thought of it looking in Dale's windows and right now wished she had the .38 snubnose Tony had given her. In case Elvin was home and got funny. Maybe asleep when she knocked on the door. But all she saw through the windows was trash, low-class living, discarded stuff, cans, longnecks, empty pizza cartons. . . . She wished now Gary Hammond had come with her. Talk, get to know more about him.

Driving home she wondered where he lived. She was still in the apartment off West Atlantic in Delray Beach. No more Keith with his attitude and his sporty outfits she used to gather from the floor. Finding out about the blond nurse hadn't bothered her as much as picking up after him. The blond nurse gave her a quick way out. She couldn't imagine Gary Hammond leaving his clothes lying around, or the top off the toothpaste. But maybe she wouldn't care if he did. Little things became irritations when you weren't getting along. The last she had heard of the major irritation, Keith—excuse me, Dr. Baker—he had switched his specialty from psychiatry to anesthesiology. It was Ray who told her about it. He still didn't trust Keith. She said, "I've almost forgotten him."

Except now he was popping into her mind again when she thought about Gary Hammond, in a way comparing them. She had never caught Keith looking at her unless he wanted something. Looking just to look. In the shower she wondered what Gary Hammond saw when he looked at her with his nice eyes. The phone rang as she was getting out.

"This is Bob Gibbs."

Kathy stood at her desk in the living room, felt the towel slip and held it with an arm across her breasts. She said, "Yes, Judge," as if he called her all the time.

"You get my message at work?"

"I wasn't in this afternoon."

"You were supposed to call me."

"No, I'm sorry."

"How's your boy Dale Crowe doing?"

"I'm going to stop by his house this evening."

"Good. I want you to come by here after. I'm at home. Be a good chance for us to talk."

"Judge? . . ."

"Mainly about my wife's condition."

"How is she?" Kathy said, stalling. It wasn't the question she wanted to ask.

"You mean is she normal? Hell no, I told you that."

"Is she home?"

That was the question. It got a moment of silence.

"I suppose you heard about the alligator business."

"It was in the paper."

"I know it was. I didn't want Leanne to get mixed up in it, her mind the way it is. I sent her to Orlando for a few days, visit friends she has there. You have a pencil? I'll give you directions."

"Judge, I'm not the least bit qualified."

"Hon, let me decide that, okay? You want to help me, don't you?"

She wanted to say, Look, I'm not going to bed with you. You mind? So leave me alone. If she could say that . . . But then wondered, what if she could learn something? If they did talk about his wife . . . Something Gary didn't know about. Maybe help him. Get to see him again . . .

"Judge, it might be late."

"That's okay, hon. Long as I know you're coming."

Kathy put on jeans and a polo shirt, opened a can of beer and made herself a tunafish sandwich. Now she was *hon*. What was she supposed to call him, Big?

Dale's junkyard pickup was in front of the house when Kathy returned, almost six-thirty, starting to get dark. But it was Elvin in his cowboy hat and boots who opened the door.

"Well, look it who's here. You come to check my wee-wee?"

"I want to talk to Dale."

"Come on in." She moved past him into the dim living room and Elvin called out, "Dale? Where are you, boy?" He paused, listening, and said, "I guess he ain't home. I just got back myself from a business deal."

Sounding like the judge. Both with that country-boy way of talking.

"You have a job?"

"One's been offered me. A good'n too."

"What kind of work?"

That got a smile.

"One that gives you peace a mind. Makes you feel good."

"What does that mean?"

"Oh, nothing."

Playing with her. If he had a job he'd tell her.

"You know where Dale might be?"

"I 'magine he's in town hunting beaver. Get himself some of the real thing 'fore he goes away."

Kathy turned to leave. He reached out to take her arm and she pulled it away saying, "Don't touch me, Elvin. You try it again you're in trouble."

That got another smile. Elvin holding his hands up, innocent. "I saved your butt the other night and you act like we're strangers." He moved past her, hands still raised. "Come on, sit down a minute. Remember I said I'd tell you about this dink I wanted to shoot?" Elvin eased his big frame into the sofa. "The time I got the wrong guy?"

Kathy said, "Will it take long?" Interested, but not wanting to show it.

"Lemme ask you one. How many people you take care of ever killed anybody?"

She came over to sit at the opposite end, not answering, on the edge of the sofa that smelled of mildew, aware of the stained walls, the bare light bulb in the lamp without a shade. It was behind Elvin's cowboy hat as she looked at him, waiting.

"I'm the only one, huh? I'm your star you get for five years, if you make it. How long you been with Probation?"

"You want to tell me about someone you didn't shoot or someone you did, or what?"

"Both," Elvin said, smiling just a little. "You heard of my brother Roland?"

"Is he in prison?"

Elvin took his hat off saying, "He's dead," and put it back on. "Roland was working for the Eyetalians down in Miami when a woman shot him, said he broke into her house. See, the woman was married to an Eyetalian guy that died. Good-looking woman, wore sunglasses all the time, this hat with a big wide brim on it. Roland was taking care of her needs and this dink come along and edged his way in with her. On account of, see, she's got all kinds of money. It was her pulled the trigger, yeah, but was this dink set it up. He *knew* it was Roland in the house and told the woman it was somebody broke in. 'Cause he didn't have the nerve to do it hisself. Understand?"

Kathy moved to get up. "I have to go."

"I'll cut it short, get to the good part where I find him tending bar and living in a two-bit motel on Dixie, up in Lake Park. That's all Niggerville there now and wasn't much better then. You know where I mean?"

She said, "Elvin, listen—"

He held up his hand. "I'm there now, wait. I'm watching him, I know it's the guy. I'm deciding when to hit him when he takes off on me. I follow him, before I know it we're out on the Turnpike heading north and I'm thinking, shit, I could end up touring the country after this boy. Well, he turns in at the first plaza, you know, the rest stop? There wasn't hardly anybody there, it was late at night. I spot him going in the men's room, so I take a minute to check this .38 revolver I got on me. Now there's two doors to the men's, so I go in the one he did that takes you in where the toilets are . . . Wait, I forgot to mention, there was a Greyhound bus pulling up as I come inside, so I know I don't have more than a half a minute."

Elvin squinted now, acting surprised, adjusting his hat.

"I look around, there's nobody in the men's. I'm thinking, What's going on here? Till I notice, looking at the doors to the toilets, I see feet under one of 'em. So I walk over and bang on his door, start yelling, 'Come on out of there quick. The place is on fire.' I hear him, this voice saying, 'What? What?' and then I hear the toilet flush." Elvin grinning now. "Far as he knows the place is burning up and he's in there flushing the toilet. I step back. Soon as the door starts to open I'm squeezing that trigger, *wham, wham.* See, I want him standing, but I want him to fall in there, not out in the open. I shot him four times in the heart."

"Someone you never saw before," Kathy said.

"Wait now. I didn't see him good *then* was the trouble. I run out, here's all these people coming off the bus. Five of 'em ID'd me."

"They caught you right away?"

"Still on the Turnpike. Florida Highway Patrol ran me down. They take me in, want to know what I got against Ignacio Nieves. I said, 'Who's Ignacio Nieves?' Anyway that was the guy's name. The only thing I can figure," Elvin said, "this dink knew I was on him. I follow him in that one men's room door to the toilets and he come out the other side from the washroom, giving me the slip. Don't matter killing the guy was an accident. I pled to second-degree, best deal I could make with a semi-smoking gun and this judge, the son of a bitch, gives me ten to twenty-five with probation. You like my story?"

"I'm not sure," Kathy said, "why you told me."

He looked surprised. "I want you to see I'm not some ordinary two-bit fuckup you got on your list."

"What do you call shooting the wrong guy?"

"Anybody could've made that mistake. I'm talking about now. If we're gonna be seeing each other the next five years . . ."

"Once a month," Kathy said, getting up from the sofa. "We're not going steady."

Elvin was next to her by the time she reached the

door. "Yeah, but there's no reason we can't get along." He put his hand on the door as she started to open it.

"Touch me, Elvin, you're back doing the twenty-five."

"Listen, okay? I just want to mention, I had a girl write me when I was in the joint? One I never met in my life but seen my picture in the paper and read about me. She'd send these letters, say she knows in her heart I'm the kind of fella, all I need to straighten me out is some tender loving care." Elvin grinned. "My cellmate sure liked to smell those letters. But what I was wondering, if that's how little girl probation officers see us bad boys."

"Yeah, what I do," Kathy said, "is devote my life to making fuckups and losers happy. I'll see you." She pulled the door open and went out.

"You saying I'm a *loser*?" Sounding surprised to hear it. "Hey, there things I could tell you . . ."

"Next month, at the office."

Going down the front steps to the walk she heard him say from the doorway, "How 'bout tomorrow? You still need to see Dale, don't you?"

He watched her drive off in her little Volkswagen. Ms. Touchy, that was a good name for her, asking did he have a job. He had felt like saying he was leaving for work directly and she'd read about it in the paper the next day or so. That would've been good. See her face after calling him a loser. Losers didn't make ten thousand dollars for a night's work.

The gun Dr. Tommy had given him was in the fridge, in a box a pizza had come in Elvin recalled as being piss-poor. The idea he had was to go up to the judge's house with the pizza box, knock on the door. . . . If there was cops around he'd say he must have the wrong address and do it another time.

Dr. Tommy's boy Hector was a sketch coming out with the rifle first, this little pump-action .22. Elvin had looked at it and said, "Doc, I ain't going after flamingos. I'm gonna shoot a full-size judge."

Dr. Tommy thought he meant he wanted a heavier rifle. Well, let's see, he had a Savage, a Remington, both thirty-ought-sixes.

Elvin said, "Doc, I ain't gonna sit in a blind neither, waiting on a buck to come past. What I want is a gun I can stick in my pants and walk up to the man." When Dr. Tommy looked like he had to think that one over, Elvin said, "I know a person like you, one time in the dope business, wouldn't go to bed without a pistol in the drawer next to it. I bet chrome plate with a pearl grip."

The one Hector brought out, once Dr. Tommy gave him the sign, was stainless but with a walnut grip, a Ruger Speed-Six .357. Not the gun he'd pick if he had a choice, but she'd do the job.

"Okay, and where's my half down?"

This was where he ran into a wall.

"How do I know," Dr. Tommy said, "you won't take the five thousand and I never see you again?"

"'Cause this is my kind of work," Elvin said. "Why would I settle for half?"

Dr. Tommy's offer was "Two grand when you tell me how you're going to do it. The rest *if* you do it."

Elvin didn't like that *if*. He said, "I'm gonna knock on his door and shoot him when he opens it."

"That's your plan?"

"It's how I do it."

"I want to know when and where."

"Tonight. How's that? Out to his house."

"Yes, but how do you know he'll be home?"

Dr. Tommy dragging his feet. It got Elvin mad.

"You want this done or not?"

"I want to be sure."

"So do I," Elvin said. "What I'll do is shoot him and you pay up after, the whole thing, or I shoot you too. How's that sound?"

The doctor gave him a shrug. "You kill him and I read it in the paper, we have no problem."

Nothing to it, since he wasn't doing a goddamn thing. Elvin hated a person talking to him like that. Little booger sitting there on his patio . . . If he had ten thousand cash to pay out he'd have more where it came from, in the house. Something to look into after.

Not two minutes, from when Ms. Touchy had left, Elvin was in Dale's pickup heading out, the pizza box on the seat next to him. He took 95 up to West Palm and turned left on Southern Boulevard, following Dr. Tommy's directions. He'd said it would take about a half hour. Elvin said, "If you're a pokey driver it might." He knew this road, repaved since he used to travel it, lined with reflectors that popped in his headlights. Keep going, it took you out to the Stockade and the Loxahatchee Road Prison for dinks, drunks and short-timers. Either place you could walk out the front gate. Beyond there you were heading for the Glades. This trip he was going only as far as the first stoplight past the Florida Turnpike.

It turned red as Elvin approached and he had to pull up behind cars in the inside lane. The directions said you turned left here, followed the road to a dead end, turned left and then left again on a dirt road that went along a canal before it veered through woods and took you up to the house. One-story red brick, sitting by itself. Fine. He'd drive up fairly close and make his delivery.

The light turned green. Elvin got ready.

He watched the first car in the lane ease out and then wait for a car to pass from the other direction. The next two cars in front of him continued straight ahead. Elvin didn't move, still watching the first car as it made its turn. A light-colored Volkswagen. He said, "Jesus Christ," out loud. If that car wasn't Ms. Touchy's it was one just like it.

13

Bob Gibbs was outside waiting for her, standing in the beam of a spotlight mounted on the house. He motioned her to nose in toward the open garage and stop right there in the drive, behind the blue Ford pickup that had a cap with windows mounted on the bed.

"You have any trouble finding the place?"

"Not a bit," Kathy said. She almost told Gibbs, helping her out of the car, to take his hands off her. A reflex, or not seeing that much difference between this judge and a criminal offender.

He brought her into the kitchen through the garage, told her to make herself at home while he fixed her a Jim Beam and water, not asking if she wanted one, and freshened his own. Both of their glasses were enclosed in orangey red holders—to keep the drinks cold or your hand dry—the word *Gators* printed on them. "In honor of the University of Florida football team," Gibbs said, "not that visitation the other night." He took Kathy out to the porch to show where the alligator had entered, the screen back in place but torn and sprung, held down with a length of two-by-four. "Smashed the glass door; I had it replaced, but I'm still waiting on the screen man. Look in there at the sofa how it's all chewed up."

"Your wife saw the alligator?"

"She pretty near stepped on it."

"No wonder it scared her. She went up to Orlando, uh?"

"For a while. Come on outside." He picked up a flashlight from the metal table.

They went out to a yard full of dark shapes, the judge stopping to sniff the air. "You smell it? Night-blooming jasmine." Kathy sniffed, looking at Australian pines, a scraggly mahogany tree against the sky.

"You like tropical plants and flowers?"

"When I can see them."

"Look it here." The judge flashed his light over foliage, vines, identifying bird's-nest fern, staghorn, Vanda orchids. "See the bloom spikes?" Here, a white Cattleya with a yellow throat. The lavender orchid was Dendrobium. He had orchids climbing trees and hanging from moss pots. "I deal with ugliness all day long and come home to beauty."

Why was he telling her this? Or why had Elvin told her about killing a man? The judge and the ex-convict both trying to impress her. The judge showing what a sensitive guy he really was.

"Your wife work in the garden?"

"She plays with rocks."

"She does? What kind of rocks?"

"Quartz crystals. She buries them in the dirt to clean them, restore their—whatever magic they're suppose to have. This is called African Shield. My wife thinks those two petticoat palms were once women who were turned into trees. See what I mean? Look up there. Bougainvillea growing out of that cabbage palm."

"Where do you think it came from? The alligator."

"Canal over there, the other side of the house. Here, take this in your hand, crush it up good and smell it. Wild bayleaf."

"What if someone brought the alligator?"

"As a joke? That's a lot of trouble to go to."

"I was thinking," Kathy said, "more as a threat to your life."

Bob Gibbs said, "Why?" and sounded surprised. "Because I hand out tough sentences? I never exceed the guidelines, I can't. My rulings are fair, my convictions are appealed and sometimes reversed, but not too often. Look it up."

Kathy said, "Yeah, but if some guy doesn't see it as fair . . . There're some crazy people in the world." Thinking of Elvin again. "Or sociopaths, with no respect for human life . . ."

"You're not kidding, honey, and there's plenty of them. This is the vanilla orchid, the only one I know of with food value."

Elvin came out of the dark with his pizza box into the spotlight shine looking at the Volkswagen parked there by the open garage. She was here, no doubt about it, and that was too bad. Ms. Touchy, she was a salty little thing for being as cute as she was. Spoke right up to you. He reached the front door thinking if she was in the toilet or someplace away from the judge he could do the job and she might never see him. Man, but it would have to be her birthday to get that lucky. He rang the doorbell. If she saw him he wouldn't have any choice in the matter. He rang it again. Get right down to it, there was no way he could take a chance on her not seeing him, even if he didn't see her when he shot the judge. No, he'd have to find her. Tell her, well, it's too bad, but you shouldn't have been here. He pressed the doorbell again, held it and could hear it buzzing inside the house. He let go and tried the door. It was locked. He walked along the house looking in windows at dark bedrooms till he came to the attached garage, saw a door in there, stepped in and tried it. The door opened in his hand. Now he had to quick put the pizza box under his arm and pull the Speed-Six revolver from his belt, underneath his shirt hanging out, before stepping inside.

The ceiling light was on in the kitchen. Elvin stood listening for sounds, voices, till he noticed the bottle of Jim Beam there by the sink. He stepped over to it, laid the pizza box on the counter and had himself a taste of the bourbon. Mmmmm, for pleasure only, not the least nervous. Okay, they weren't in the bedrooms he'd looked in the windows at. They weren't in the dining area, dark in there. A lamp was on in the living room, but it was about all Elvin could see from the kitchen. He held the Speed-Six in front of him moving from bright light to dark to soft light in the living room, nobody here either. But, hey, the glass door to the porch was slid open and a lamp was on out there. He saw a round metal table, some chairs. He saw where the screen was ripped and pushed in and felt himself jump as a beam of light came on outside and flashed around in the trees. That's where they were, out in the yard. He saw the light beam move and touch the little girl, saw her face white in the dark . . . He'd been looking to have some fun with her, but that was not going to work out. The judge had the flashlight. The hell was he showing her? Elvin watched for a minute. It made sense to wait for them to come inside, be able to see them good. He might even have time, sure, for another taste of that Jim Beam.

The judge showed her a plant called monstera delici-osa saying, "It looks like a big green weenie, huh? It turns ripe you can eat it." This guy was too much. She was pretty sure he winked at her in the dark.

They walked back toward the house, the judge holding on to her arm now above the elbow, fingering her bare skin, telling how he liked to go down around Immokalee in the Everglades every once in a while, wade in the swamp with an onion sack and a hunting knife looking for wild orchids. Plenty of them down there. He asked if she liked to camp out, but didn't wait for an answer. He said she ought to go with him sometime, it was an experience. You could not get closer to nature than in the Everglades.

Kathy said she didn't care too much for snakes.

Or alligators. She wanted to get back to the alligator on the porch, ask if it might have been meant for his wife. Find out if she was coming back or not.

They were near the house, walking past the kitchen toward the screened porch. The judge said he had two prize orchids in there he wanted to show her. He'd freshen their drinks and they'd sit down, get comfortable . . . the judge speaking when the pane of glass in the kitchen window shattered with the hard sound of a gunshot. Kathy turned toward the window, saw the light on inside, white cupboards, saw . . . something else as the second pane shattered and again heard that hard crack of sound out in the dark she knew was rifle fire. She dropped to the ground dragging the judge with her as another pane shattered and another and heard a final gunshot without glass breaking, the report echoing, coming from somewhere in the back part of the yard.

Neither of them moved lying face-to-face in coarse grass, one of his legs over hers, Kathy listening. There were no sounds now, not even insects. She tried to concentrate and picture exactly what she saw in the window as the second pane of glass exploded: a glimpse of movement that could have been a man, there for part of a moment and gone.

She heard the judge say, "Jesus Christ," in a whisper and saw the stunned expression in his eyes. "Somebody's trying to kill me."

What Elvin did was lose his concentration for a minute sipping the Jim Beam, comparing it to what he used to drink at Starke, the shine they called "buck" and wasn't any stronger than wine, about fourteen percent, tasted awful but did the job. That recalled the smells and noise living in a cellblock, the same dirty walls in your face all the time, and he stepped to the kitchen window not thinking till he saw them outside, right there, through his own reflection and the glass broke, *Jesus*, as he looked at it, woke up and ducked aside as the glass kept breaking, glass flying, *Jesus, somebody shooting at him!*

Elvin left the way he had come, ran down the gravel drive crunching under his boots to Dale's pickup and drove out of there, none of it making sense till he was back on familiar ground, on Southern Boulevard heading east and had time to think.

To realize, no, it couldn't have been the judge shooting, it was somebody else back in the yard shooting at the *judge*, not him. And thought of what he'd said to Dr. Tommy about having to get in line. Like a Canal Point turkey shoot, load up and wait your turn.

And if all the shots did was hit the window, then the judge was still game. That was a relief.

Coming to Military Trail, Elvin saw the lights of the Polo Lounge off to the left. Last time he was in there it was called Flounders. He bet though they'd still pour you a Jim Beam if you asked.

14

All Kathy had to tell the 911 operator, it was Judge Gibbs's house and the first green-and-white arrived within five minutes. After that they kept coming, more green-and-whites at first and a road patrol sergeant who spoke to Kathy and told her to stick around. The judge wasn't saying much at this point, still dazed, having another drink. Pretty soon unmarked cars began arriving, the recognizable ones from the Detective Division and Technical Services, then different makes and models, people from TAC, some Sheriff's Office brass and the sheriff himself, Gene B. Givens, a man about fifty with a slight build. He wore a straw cattleman's hat and seemed quiet, nodding as detectives told him what had happened. By now every light in the house was on, the backyard was bright with squad-car headlights and spots and farther out flashlights were moving around in the dark. In the kitchen evidence techs were looking for the bullets. Kathy noticed the pizza carton and thought it strange they'd bring food with them.

She settled into a lawn chair on the porch, she thought out of the way. But now the judge came out with his drink, Sheriff Gene Givens, who looked like a sheriff, and a heavyset middle-aged guy wearing glasses they called Bill or Colonel McKenna. The judge had phoned him directly. They were followed by four detectives, one of them Gary Hammond in his navy-blue suit and tie but still no haircut. Kathy waited for him to notice her. He smiled, turning it on and off, standing with the others as Gibbs, McKenna, and Sheriff Gene Givens sat down at the round metal table. She saw Lou Falco now. With him was another guy from TAC she had met at the Polo Lounge. Falco looked over and nodded. He said something to the guy with him and he glanced over as they went outside.

Get a look at the girl who was with the judge. They'd all been doing that. Another point of interest, the hole the alligator had made.

A deputy came in with the glasses they'd dropped in the yard, holding them upside down, his fingers inside. Gibbs said, "All you'll get off of them are my prints. And hers, Ms. Baker's." Acknowledging Kathy for the first time.

McKenna said, "You were outside?"

"I've been trying to tell you, the guy was shooting at the house, not at me."

Changing his tune. Lying flat on the ground he believed someone was trying to kill him. But since then he'd had a few more drinks.

Sheriff Gene Givens said, "Bob might have a point."

"Some nut trying to scare me," Gibbs said. "Ms. Baker and I were talking about people like that earlier. She came out to discuss a probation violator she's been having trouble with. Boy I sentenced the other day to five years. Dale Crowe, that name familiar?"

Gary Hammond said, "Judge, he threatened you, didn't he, in court?"

That got everyone's attention. McKenna asked what exactly Dale Crowe had said. Kathy watched Gary Hammond stare at the wall to get the words right in his mind. He looked over at her and she stared back at him. He gave it a try then. "I think Dale said, 'I'm gonna see about this deal.' And, 'You're not through with me yet.' Something like that."

"He said, 'If you think you're through with me,'" Kathy said, and they were all looking at her again, "'you're full of shit.'"

They kept looking at her till McKenna said to Gibbs, "He's out? You didn't cite him for contempt?"

"I didn't hear it as a threat."

Or maybe, Kathy was thinking, he didn't hear it at all.

"What else is it," McKenna said, "'I'm not through with you,' but a threat? And you let him off on a bond?"

"I gave him seven days to settle his affairs."

"I think you're one of 'em he plans to settle," McKenna said. "This guy's a Crowe? Lives out in Belle Glade?"

Kathy listened to them putting two and two together, seeing a nexus in shots fired at the house and the alligator brought here the other night, by people who would know how to do it. No question about it now, the gator was brought here, a live ten-footer, and when it didn't do the job then Dale or one of the other Crowes came with a gun. Not to scare you, Judge, to kill you. This would go down as an attempted homicide. The first thing they had to do was locate Dale Crowe Junior. They all looked over at

Kathy again as McKenna asked when she had last seen him.

"Two nights ago."

"I recall," Gibbs said, "he was suppose to report to you every day."

"He didn't," Kathy said, "and I don't know where he is." Sounding dumb, but what else could she say.

"You checked his house?"

Kathy nodded. "And I've been looking for him."

"So you came out here," McKenna said, "to get a warrant signed? That's all you can do, have him picked up."

Kathy watched McKenna turn to his detectives now, finished with her. He told one of them to call Belle Glade, have Dale picked up, his dad and any other Crowes that might be around. He said to the table, "I think we have a chance to close this one before it's barely open. Save us going to the computer for suspects."

Gary Hammond said, "Colonel?" and Kathy thought he was going to mention papering the walls with names. He didn't, he said, "Dale Crowe lives in Delray Beach with his uncle, Elvin Crowe. Ms. Baker was going over there this evening, I believe." Looking at her again.

"Elvin was there," Kathy said. "I asked him where Dale was, he said he was around someplace."

"Elvin Crowe," Sheriff Gene Givens said. "I haven't heard that name in a while. If I was making up a list I'd put Elvin Crowe right at the top."

"Well, let's get started," McKenna said. "Crimes Persons has the investigation. We'll have TAC surveil the suspect's house, starting with Dale Junior. And, Big," McKenna said, turning to Gibbs, "you're gonna be in TAC's care till we close this one."

Sheriff Gene Givens said, "You'll have to change your routine, Judge."

"You won't be going to the Helen Wilkes after work every day," McKenna said. "It's gonna play hell with your social life, Big, but you'll just have to put up with it, a while anyway."

Kathy watched Gibbs. He didn't seem too happy. Sends his wife away, he's free to fool around all he wants, and now he'll have TAC living with him, driving him to the courthouse. She began thinking, What if he planned to send her away? . . .

McKenna was saying this would go in the log and become public knowledge. "In other words the newspaper and TV people are gonna come after you. You'll be glad to have TAC around to keep them off your back."

Sheriff Gene Givens said, "The trouble with this kind of case, once it's known, it can bring out the copycats. Give people ideas. That's why we want to close it fast."

"Before the lunatics get into it and somebody sends you a letter bomb," McKenna said. "We'd keep it under our hat, but you can't hide dignitary protection, the news people will find out. The advantage, it'll be talked about and maybe one of our informants will hear something."

"I'm not opening any mail," Bob Gibbs said.

Looking to get a laugh, maybe beginning to like the attention. Kathy wasn't sure. Or he was feeling no pain, all he had to drink.

"We'll check your mail," McKenna said, "and most likely put a wire on your phone, here and at court."

An evidence tech came out from the living room holding up a glass that rattled as he shook it. He said, "Sheriff, four .22 longs," placing the glass on the table. "They went through two of the cupboard doors and were in the wall, inside."

McKenna said to Gibbs, "Is that how many you heard, four shots?"

"I believe so."

Gibbs looked over and Kathy hesitated. She said, "There were five, but only four hit the window."

That got them looking at her again, McKenna saying, "You sure?"

"I heard five."

"From how far away, would you guess?"

"Somewhere in the back part of the yard."

"Were the shots hurried or evenly spaced?"

Kathy paused. She could hear the rifle shots and saw the window again, a glass pane shattering and a glimpse of someone or *some*thing in that part of a moment. Thinking she should tell them. But what did she see? She was certain of the five shots, evenly spaced. Tell them that. But now Gibbs was talking.

"Ms. Baker was pretty scared, as you can imagine. I believe I threw her down and might've been a little rough." Looking right at her as he said it with a grin, her hero. Listen to him. He said, "I hope I didn't hurt you."

There was nothing she could say to him, *nothing*, in front of these people. He was finished with her anyway, looking at McKenna now.

"You want to put TAC on me, huh?"

"I'm gonna insist on it, Big."

"I guess if you have to."

Lou Falco came in saying, "Five .22 casings, out by the pump house. The guy fired from less than fifty meters and broke a window, if that tells you anything. You can check the casings for latents, but I doubt you'll get any prints. They were in the mud where it's damp there. The guy walked all over them."

"We have a place to start," McKenna said, getting up as the sheriff rose from the table. "How do you want to handle security here?"

"Four outside and two in the house," Falco said.

"That's what I need," Gibbs said, "some boarders. Lou, how much can I charge you?"

Every one of them, Kathy noticed, smiled or laughed out loud in deference to this asshole who happened to be a judge. Even Gary, though he didn't give it much. She saw the detective who had gone to call the Belle Glade station coming out on the porch.

He said, "Sheriff, Dale Crowe Senior's in the hospital. He was at a dance in Clewiston the other night, got in a fight and some guy broke his jaw." The detective telling it with a grin. "No one's seen Dale Junior yet."

Sheriff Gene Givens started to walk away. He stopped and said, "I seem to recall old Dale has an artificial leg."

"Got bit by a gator," McKenna said. "Gangrene set in and they had to take it off at the knee."

Sheriff Gene Givens said, "I guess my question is, how's a one-legged man do the Texas Two-Step?" He seemed about to leave again.

Kathy watched him as the boys on the porch all had another good laugh. Gene Givens turned and looked back at the hole in the screen, stared at it for several moments before telling everyone present, "The connection with the alligator is what's gonna solve this case."

It made an impression on Kathy, the man not saying much, but then making that point. She believed it herself, a feeling she had.

They were all leaving the porch now, going outside or

into the house, all except Gary Hammond. As soon as he was standing by himself he came over to her.

"Something I was wondering about. What were you doing outside?"

"Looking at flowers."

"In the dark?"

"You think it was my idea?"

He said, "Well, it must've been pretty frightening, getting shot at."

Kathy nodded, looking up at him from the lawn chair. "It was, but I don't think he was shooting at us."

"That's what the judge said. Why didn't you back him up?"

"No one asked me."

"You were in front of the window, the light was on . . ."

"No, we weren't even that close to it. How could he see us? He's way back in the trees."

"Why shoot at the house?"

"Why put an alligator in the yard? You heard Givens, he thinks there's a connection. I'll tell you one thing, no, two," Kathy said. "Gibbs didn't throw me down, he froze. And I didn't come to see him about Dale. He called, said he wanted to talk about his wife. She's supposed to be in Orlando, but I don't believe it."

"Why would he want to talk to you about his wife?"

"He uses it as a way . . . What he wants is to go to bed with me. It's the only reason."

Gary said, "Oh," giving that one some thought. "You mean he says things like his wife doesn't understand him? They don't get along?"

"Yeah, only there's more to it. She thinks she's a little black girl who died a long time ago." Gary was giving her a funny look. "Or the little girl speaks through Leanne and it drives the judge crazy."

"I heard her," Gary said, "the little girl. I heard her voice. We were standing in the yard . . ."

"Come on, you did? What'd she say?"

Gary hesitated but kept looking at her. "We could have a lot to talk about."

Kathy said, "I think so," with the feeling, now this one was using the judge's wife as an excuse. She hoped so.

He said, "You want to have a drink somewhere?"

She said, "You mind if I ask, are you married?"

He looked surprised. "No, I'm not."

"You have kids?"

"I've never been married."

She thought of asking why not, but said, "Okay, where?"

15

Something about when he was in the judge's house bothered Elvin, sipping bourbon at the Polo Lounge as he retraced each step of the way in and out. The hell was it? Taking a big sip as he remembered, *Jesus*, the pizza box, and started coughing.

Now something else was bothering him. A little girl with curly blond hair and big seashell earrings next to him at the bar saying, "What's wrong, sugar?" and patting him on the back. Elvin recovered, took another sip and it went down okay. But now the curly-haired girl was saying, "I haven't seen you before. You with TAC, working undercover? I love your getup." Elvin looked at her with the pizza box on his mind and told her to hit the road. She said, "Well, pardon me all to hell," and slid off the stool.

Two more Jim Beams and the pizza box was nothing to worry about. Only a matter of seeing how others would look at it, cops going in the kitchen, what would they see? An empty pizza box sitting on the counter was all. If the shooter was outside he couldn't have put it there. By now one of the cops had most likely thrown it in the trash. That out of the way, Elvin wished the cops luck in getting the son of a bitch who'd done the shooting.

Under its other name this place had been popular with cops and Elvin, looking around, believed still was. Cops and guys throwing darts at three boards out in the front part of the room where you came in. The cops were the ones in the suits and ties, dinks from the Sheriff's Office that wasn't too far from here. It made Elvin think of his brother Roland's suits he'd stored in a trunk with mothballs. Maybe he ought to get them out. There were girls liked you looking spiffy and ones that went for the mean and dirty style of dress. Like the little curly-haired blonde or she wouldn't have come over when he started coughing before.

Elvin had a view of the whole place from where he sat at the back end of the oblong bar, stools on all four sides, a barmaid in the middle, a friendly woman who poured a good drink. It was kind of dark in here. He could see the curly-haired girl though, no trouble, down at the other end with her girlfriend. Elvin waited for her to look this way. When she did, he touched the brim of his hat. That was all it took. Here she came.

"I had something on my mind there before was giving me a hard time."

"Your job," the girl said, working her butt up onto the stool. "I understand, sugar, and know what you mean. You married?"

"I was, you might say, the same as married for ten years. Actually to different ones, but I'm free as a bird now."

"You work undercover, huh?"

Elvin gave her his dirty grin. "I'll work under your covers anytime you say."

"Hey, whoa. You might start a little slower if you don't mind. Since I don't even know your name."

"Yeah, but I'm hot to go. I haven't had none in so long I'm like a young virgin."

"You are *weird.* You just got done telling me you were like married. What *is* your problem?"

"I been away."

She said, "Uh-oh. You mean you were in jail?"

"Jail, shit, the big time. Honey I was up at Starke." He got her by the arm before she could swivel off the stool and hunched in close, his hat brim touching her curly head, his eyes on her great big ones, saying, "How'd you like a convict hasn't done it face-to-face in ten years? Huh, does it sound good to you?" He let go of her arm before she screamed or had a fit and that girl was *gone,* back to tell the other one her experience. Copfucker's all she was. That kind, they only went for the mean and dirty look if they knew it was fake.

Maybe her girlfriend was different. Elvin tipped his hat down on his eyes and kept staring, waiting for her to look over, this one kind of red-haired, a mess of it piled on her head. Just then he heard loud voices from out where the guys were throwing darts, some yelling like one of them must've hit the bull's-eye.

Elvin sat up to look, that part of the room lit brighter than in here by the bar. He saw the dart throwers and the heads of people sitting at a few tables out there. He saw a dark-haired girl that looked like . . . Jesus, it didn't look like her, it *was.* It was the little probation officer sitting with a guy wearing a suit, another one of them, except he didn't look like a cop, he looked like a dink state attorney.

The two of them at one end of a round table talking, look-ing at each other, not paying any attention to the dart throwers still hollering. Ms. Touchy sat back now and seemed to be laughing at something the dink said. Out having fun after getting shot at. It was the first time Elvin had seen her laugh. He had an urge to go over there and say to her, Well, hey, how you doing? You had a close one there, didn't you? See her face. Not say another word, walk away . . . And spend the night in jail, deputies ask-ing what was he doing there, delivering pizza? How come the best things you thought of to say, you couldn't?

Shit, he'd better not even be seen here. Use that side door before she spotted him.

She said to Gary, "I'm going to tell you what I think. You don't have to agree with me, but if you look down your nose I'm leaving. Okay?"

"What's that mean, look down my nose?"

"Cop that typical attitude, I'm only a probation of-ficer. What do I know?"

"Is this some kind of test?"

"In a way, yeah."

"Have I said anything to give you the impression—"

"Just listen, okay?"

They had been talking about the judge's wife, Kathy learning things that seemed to back up what she believed and she was anxious to tell him. The guys throwing darts were a distraction at first and she would glance over, but not now.

"I don't think anyone's trying to kill the judge."

"Even if he deserves it?"

"Look, he wants his wife to leave him and she did. He said to you, 'An alligator walked in and my wife walked out.' Right? He didn't send her to Orlando to stay with friends, she walked out."

"She still could've gone to Orlando."

"Where she went is beside the point. She sees an alligator and that's it, she takes off. Because when she was a mermaid, which the judge never mentioned to me, she was frightened by an alligator and almost drowned. Now the former mermaid is communicating with a former slave girl named Wanda Grace. The judge wants her to leave because she's driving him nuts, talking in this little-girl voice, or, so he can be free to fool around, or both. You see what I'm getting at?"

"All I know is she walked out on him."

"Because of the alligator."

"Okay."

"And you believe someone brought it. You're convinced."

"For the judge."

"How do you know it wasn't for his wife?"

"There's no reason to think it was."

"That you know of. Ask Leanne what she thinks."

"Nobody shot at Leanne."

"Nobody shot at anybody. Some guy broke a window, with a .22. Is that what you use you want to kill somebody? Lou Falco said the same thing about the alligator. There are better ways to do it." Kathy sipped her beer, letting him think about it.

"There's no apparent connection, though, between the alligator and the shooter."

"Your boss believes there is."

"Yeah, and if he's wrong who's gonna call him on it? You know what you're saying? Or what I think you are . . ."

Kathy said, "Yeah, the judge had the alligator delivered knowing it would scare the shit out of Leanne. And it did, it worked."

"What about the shooter? What's he got to do with it?"

"I don't know. Ask him."

She watched Gary raise his beer and then pause.

"There's no way I could question Gibbs about it. A *judge* pulling a stunt like that? I can't see it."

Kathy could, but didn't say anything.

"He reminds me of a guy in the movies," Gary said. "You know Harry Dean Stanton?"

It caught her by surprise—just as the dart throwers started to make noise, yelling and cheering at something one of them had done. Gary glanced over. Kathy didn't, she sat back in her chair and then couldn't help but laugh, because it was true and she wondered why she hadn't realized it before.

"You're right, he looks just like him."

Gary said, "You know who I mean?"

"Harry Dean Stanton. How many are there?"

"You like him?"

"I love him. I think he's great."

"Gibbs has the same kind of, sort of a farmer look."

"Exactly. The hair, everything."

"I don't think you look like Kathy Baker though."

Zinging her again. Kathy started to smile, but then wasn't sure. "You mean the one in the movies."

"Kathy Baker. How many are there?" Giving it back to her. "You see *Clean and Sober* with her and Michael Keaton, they both play junkies?"

Kathy was nodding—this cop in the blue suit coming off even better than expected. "Yeah, I loved it, because I *know* those people, I have them in my caseload." She moved her glass aside and leaned on the table looking at Gary, trusting him, a cop she could talk to. She said, "I'm going to tell you something else . . ."

And described the face or whatever it was in the kitchen window. Now he did sound a little more like a cop saying yeah, she might've seen someone. It's possible there were two of them. Then ruled that out. If there were, he would have waited to finish the job. Kathy said what job? To break the window? He backed off saying well, if she wasn't that certain to begin with, and since there's no way to confirm whether she actually did see anyone or not . . . "I can't say it was someone's face," Kathy said, "but that's the way I think of it. I know it was there, because then it wasn't." That made sense to him, or seemed to. He nodded thinking about it before ordering a couple more beers.

Kathy said, "There was a guy down at the far end of the bar . . ."

Gary looked over.

"I didn't get a good look at him. He's gone now."

"What about him?"

Kathy hesitated. "I better not tell you anything unless I'm sure."

Elvin located her Volkswagen, then moved the pickup to where he could sit and watch it without straining himself. The Polo Lounge was in a semi-mall of stores, all closed now except the bar.

What he was thinking, it might be good to learn where Ms. Touchy lived. If she visited the judge, walked around in the dark with him, maybe the judge visited her too. He'd no doubt have cops with him now wherever he went, guys in suits, and it would be harder to get to him. If he was to slip off to visit Ms. Touchy that might be the place to be waiting. Or work some way of using Ms. Touchy as bait. Like get her to call the judge, ask him over . . .

There was the curly-haired blond girl and her friend coming out, talking away—no doubt about her experience still—going to their cars now. He felt like honking the horn at her. Get Ms. Curlyhead over here and throw her in the back. Here he was again getting an urge and having to let it pass. In prison you couldn't do whatever you wanted. Out in the civilian world, though, he'd always felt you could.

Watching the curly-haired girl he missed seeing Ms. Touchy come out. She was almost to her car, walking along with the guy in the suit, before Elvin noticed her. Now they were standing by her VW talking. Didn't finish talking inside they had to talk some more out here. Elvin said, "Come on, God damn it, let's go." Gets shot at and stops at the bar with her boyfriend, the guy touching her arm. Elvin thinking, Kiss her good night or I will. Now she was touching *his* arm, still talking. Elvin waited for them to hug and kiss, but it didn't happen. Ms. Touchy went and got in her car, the dink waiting there now so Elvin had to wait, not wanting to start the pickup and have the guy look over. Now her rear lights came on red and the guy stepped aside and waved and, shit, stood there watching her drive off. She was heading out the lot onto Military Trail before the dink finally turned and walked off and Elvin was able to get after her.

He had her now and would keep her taillights in sight all the way home.

16

One time when Inez Campau's dog Buddy was running loose and neighbors complained it was biting their children, Inez was told to bring the dog to the shelter. She brought her sister's dog instead, a white-ish pit bull that was from the same litter and looked almost identical to Buddy. The sister, Mavis, was married to Dale Crowe Senior. When Mavis found out her dog had been put down in place of Buddy, she called the Belle Glade sheriff's station. That not only took care of Buddy it got Inez charged with stealing her dog and fined fifty dollars.

So Inez couldn't believe it when Mavis came to ask a favor. If Dale Junior could stay with her and Dicky awhile. Deputies were looking for him, wanting to charge him with trying to kill Judge Gibbs.

Inez kept her mouth shut and listened.

Mavis said it tore her up they'd think Dale Junior would do something like that. He was already supposed to go to prison, but now was thinking of going to California instead and maybe after while they'd forget about him.

Inez sighed, a wheeze of sympathy coming out of her sturdy two-hundred-pound frame in housedress and dirty apron.

Mavis said that having Dale Senior home didn't help none. Oh, but he could tear up the house when he got mad, 'specially when his stump bothered him, as it was doing now. Mavis said the only way to protect herself and all their dishes was to hide his artificial leg on him. His face would get red as fire when he tried to yell and carry on but wasn't able to, his jaw wired from when he'd had it broken in Clewiston.

Inez kept her own mouth shut, having no sympathy for Dale Senior and knowing it wasn't Dale Junior had tried to shoot the judge.

What she finally said was "Where's your boy at now?"

"In Pahokee, at his sister Clarissa's. They been checking on her two days now. Clarissa expects they'll be back any time with a search warrant. So I got to thinking, they won't ever look at your house, knowing me and you don't get along."

They never had. Not since years ago Dicky had hung out with Dale Senior, drinking on the ditch bank by day, going out in the lake by night in a Gillis boat to pick up bales of marijuana dropped to them from airplanes. Dicky had done jail time and Inez had blamed Mavis 'cause she couldn't blame Dale Senior to his face. He'd get drunk and bust her dentures.

The next question, "When's your boy have to go to prison?"

"Not till Monday."

"I'll keep him the weekend's all. I won't hide a fugitive."

"He'll be gone by then," Mavis told her, "either to

MAXIMUM BOB →

prison or California. But you have to go get him. That darn Elvin's using his truck."

Inez watched her stringbean sister cross through the hedge grown wild to Dale Senior's pickup in the street. Couldn't walk the few blocks from their place. Always tired from having a mean one-legged man in the house. Inez closed the door, walked through the musty front room dark with its shades drawn to the smell of fish in the kitchen, bluegill crackling in the iron skillet, burning up. She'd told Dicky to keep an eye on it while she went to the door. He was at the kitchen table, still hiding behind the newspaper he'd been reading all morning.

SHOTS FIRED AT JUDGE'S HOME

The first time he read it Dicky said well, they didn't know who done it, that was good. She told him if they did he'd be in the county jail having catfish for dinner, wouldn't he?

This noon it looked like they'd have blackened blue-gill. Add cayenne pepper and Tabasco and serve it Cajun style.

Dicky didn't say a word about it till the story appeared in the paper, on the front page of the *Post* with Judge Gibbs's picture, the same one they used with the alligator story Inez cut out and stuck inside the Bible. When Dicky got home the night before last, drunk and slurring his words, he told her someone was visiting the judge when he got there, so he wasn't able to see him and make a deal. Yesterday, Dicky had stayed around the house all day hung over, sickly. This morning when the paper arrived and he looked at it, the first thing he said was, "Uh-oh."

So Inez took the paper from him, read the story and

said, "Did you think if you shot him you wouldn't have to pay the fine?"

Dicky said what happened, Gibbs had a girl there with him. So he pulled back to wait till the judge was alone.

"You were drinking," Inez said.

He'd stopped for a couple on the way, yeah. Think about what he was going to say to Gibbs. Get the words straight in his head.

She had told him exactly what he was to say. *I'd like to borrow five hundred dollars, Judge,* looking him in the eye. And if the judge pretended not to get it, tell him, *Or else it could be learned you ordered a gator delivered.* That was the part Dicky had trouble with.

"You stopped for a couple and picked up a fifth."

He said a pint was all.

"You got drunk sitting in the woods feeling sorry for yourself," Inez said, "went and got your rifle and took some shots at the judge, thinking it would solve your problem."

Dicky said the judge was out in the yard with a flashlight, flashing it around, and at first he thought the judge was looking for him. But what he was doing, he was showing this girl his flowers.

"In the dark?"

Dicky said he never shot at the judge, he shot at a window where a light was on inside. He believed the kitchen.

Inez asked him why.

Dicky said to show him.

"Show him what, Dicky?"

That it wasn't fair the way he didn't keep his word.

"How's he suppose to know," Inez said, "that's what shooting at his kitchen meant?"

It was to show what could happen you back out of a deal.

"Oh."

"Don't you understand? I had to do *some*thing."

Inez said, "You poor soul, you still owe the court five hundred dollars and now you got more problems'n before."

Dicky said he didn't see how he could be in any deeper shit'n he was already in. Inez stuck his engineer's cap on his head and told him to go on up to Pahokee and get Dale Junior, their weekend houseguest. It gave her time to think, see if there was a way to get clear of this mess.

What bothered her most was the newspaper bringing up the alligator again, mentioning it in the same story with shots being fired, investigators looking to find a connection. Also their mention of security measures being taken to protect the judge. It would make it hard now to talk to him directly about a deal.

What Inez did like was the mention they already had suspects. The paper didn't give names, but if deputies were looking for Dale Junior then he had to be one. And if he was going to be staying here the weekend . . . What if Dale Junior could be traded for getting Dicky's fine taken off the books? Was that possible?

It wouldn't hurt to phone the judge and ask.

By the time Dicky walked in with Dale Junior, the boy showing his family trait, that sullen, mean expression, Inez was dishing up. She said, "You're just in time, sweetie." Wasn't that the truth? "I have your dinner all ready."

* * *

Gary found Kathy Baker with four other young ladies around a conference table at the Omar Road office, one of them handing out case folders. Gary said, "Is this where you apply for a job?"

They all perked up, looking him over. Kathy said, "He can take Roger's place." The guy, she had told him on the phone, who'd quit all of a sudden and they had to come in today to divvy up his cases.

He asked if he should wait in the lobby. She said, "You can sit over there if you want," and then zipped through an introduction. "Michelle, Karen, Paige, Terri, this is Gary. He looks like he sells insurance, but he's really a cop." Sassy with a grin in front of her co-workers. They said, "Hi, Gary," giving him different kinds of flirty looks, these nice young girls in shorts and jeans who dealt with criminal offenders. He knew that eight out of ten probation officers in Palm Beach County were women; what surprised him, not one of them here could be over thirty.

Michelle seemed to be in charge, the one passing out case folders before she sat down. Blond hair tied back, perfect posture, back arched in a way that accentuated her compact little can. Kathy had a nice one too. Both girls were right up there. If Michelle was an eight, Kathy, with those smart brown eyes, was an eight and a half.

Gary took a seat out of the way. It was strange, to hear these young girls talking about bad guys.

"Oh, God, I used to have this one. He'd call every day, ask if I needed a car radio, a new TV . . ."

"He was lonely."

"He was a jerk, but I liked him."

"We've got a bunch under Community Control," Michelle said. "Twenty house arrest and six on the anklet. One's a rich doctor with three cars he can't drive."

"What'd he do?"

"Drugs. Two years probation."

"They'll go to AA just to get out of the house."

"Listen, they'll even go to church. I had one."

"Nah, all they do is hang out. I go in there to check up on some guy, they think I'm a druggie. 'Yo, babe. Sit here with me.'"

"I know. They come up and give you hugs. Hugging's big. All that feely touchy stuff."

"Here's another one I had. Real skanky-looking guy, who wants him? He had a dirty urine twice in a row so I violated him."

"The last guy I violated, he drove here to report in a stolen car. Took it from this tire shop where he works? His boss called to tell me. The guy's sitting there nodding, all rocked out, while I go get a warrant signed. Then have to drive out to the Sheriff's Office to get it put in the system. I come back, call West Palm PD and West Palm goes, 'Is it in the system?' I go, 'Yeah, and the guy's right here, sleeping on my desk.'"

"I know guys who'd rather do time than Community Control, sit at home all night."

"Well, you can understand that. A year and a day of DOC time you do, what, ninety days maybe? A year on Community Control you do the whole bit, no time off."

"I catch this guy leaving his house after curfew? He goes, 'Oh, my phone ain't working. I was jes' going someplace to call you.' Like a bar."

"Or, you want a problem, they're under house arrest and get evicted for not paying their rent."

Michelle said, "We've got a doctor, a lawyer . . . We've got a woman and it's not drugs."

"No thanks, they're too fucking devious."

"Fraud, bank and credit card. She lives in Palm Beach."

"The guy with the two dirty urines? He told the judge I was hounding him. I wanted to say, 'Don't flatter yourself.' "

Kathy said, looking at him, "Gary wanted to bust me one time in Riviera Beach. He thought I was a rockhead."

In the car, the unmarked Dodge, he said to Kathy, "You look more like a Rockette. You know it?"

"One of the first times I made a house call in a black ghetto at night," Kathy said, "I walked up to the door—it was open and I heard a voice inside say, 'It's the Man.' I weigh a hundred and five, but that's who I am, the Man."

"I can't imagine any of you dealing with offenders, all you nice girls," Gary said. "What did they say about the other night, your being at the judge's?"

"I didn't tell them."

That surprised him. "Why not?"

"My name won't be in the paper, so why mention it?" She said, "Have you ever shot anyone?"

He turned his head to look at her. "No."

Wearing his sharp navy-blue suit again, or maybe a different one, white shirt and striped rep tie. All dressed up and she was in her jeans. "You ever have trouble making a collar, putting the cuffs on?"

He looked at her again. "Why?"

"I just wondered."

"They usually cooperate."

"Hold their hands out? Here, please."

"Behind the back."

"Gibbs said house arrest, wearing the anklet, is like being married." She waited for Gary to comment, but he didn't say a word, busy driving.

Last night she told him about her fourteen months with Keith—pardon me—Dr. Baker. Some of it. Gary said he went with a girl three years, they set a date to get married and a month before the wedding she changed her mind and went back to Chicago. He said the funny thing was, he felt relief. So then he wondered, what if he had married her? "You know what I mean? How can you be sure?" This was out in the parking lot. Kathy said, "Don't ask me." She could tell it was something he thought about. He said, "Would you get married again?" She said, "Of course. It's what you do when you're grown up. But that's the tricky part." He said, "What is?" She said, "Knowing when you're grown up. You're not doing it to play house and get laid whenever you want."

She could talk to him now and feel at ease, say whatever she wanted. The breakthrough was Gary liking Harry Dean Stanton and the other Kathy Baker, those two among all the people in movies. She believed it saved them months of finding out about each other. That one thing.

She thought about it now and said, "Who does Elvin look like, in the movies?"

That's where they were going now, to see Elvin. Gary had called the office and asked her to come along and they'd have dinner after.

He said, "I haven't seen Elvin in ten years," smiling a little as he looked at her. "I'll let you know."

She could tell by the look he felt something too, catching him looking different times last night. The trouble right now, she couldn't think of a movie actor Elvin resembled even a little. Though if Gary mentioned one after seeing Elvin again it might be worth saying yeah, that's the one I was thinking of. It would be okay to cheat. Or she might actually see the movie actor in Elvin.

She said, "I hope Dale's home."

"He wasn't this morning," Gary said. "Two of my guys stopped by to check. Elvin slammed the door in their face."

"He still could've been there, inside."

"You're right. There could be a .22 rifle in there, too."

"So get a warrant."

"I'd rather not barge in. At this point do anything to get Elvin upset. You know, hard to manage." Gary was quiet for several moments, passing cars in the freeway traffic. "I was thinking you might do it if I can't."

"Do what, go in their house?"

"You're allowed to, aren't you? Look for drugs, anything a guy on probation isn't supposed to have?"

"You're *using* me," Kathy said. "I go in and look around you'll take me to dinner, uh? Is that the deal?"

"I just thought of it this minute, honest."

"You tried for a warrant and the judge turned you down."

"That part's true, I happened to get a judge, he's either a civil rights nut or doesn't care if Gibbs gets shot. I haven't figured out which."

"I love that line, you can't imagine us dealing with offenders," Kathy said. "But it's okay if we're helping out a cop."

"My timing wasn't too good," Gary said, and paused, his eyes on the road. "It's not a bad idea though, is it? If Dale's there you get a chance to talk to him?"

"If he isn't I can still look for the gun."

"It's up to you. If you don't want to do it, I understand."

"You'll still take me to dinner?"

"Wherever you want."

The thing was, she liked the idea of doing a search. Doing no more than her job, really, but now it was police work and that added some excitement.

She said, "Okay, but what if Elvin won't let me in?"

"He has to."

"You mean he's supposed to."

He was sitting on the front steps with a longneck, cowboy hat down on his eyes in the late sun, bare arms across his knees in a sweatshirt with the sleeves cut off. His hat, eye-level to Kathy, showed sweat stains and crimps she hadn't noticed before. Here was the ex-con model repeat-offender. And here was Gary Hammond in his navy-blue suit giving Elvin a friendly hello. "How you doing?" Introducing himself, showing the shield pinned to his belt. "I wonder if we could go inside, have a talk."

"I like it here," Elvin said. "I get to watch your buddies in the Thunderbird up the street there. They got everybody around here ready to flush their product down the toilet."

Kathy stepped closer. "Elvin, where's Dale?"

"I ain't seen him."

"His truck's here."

"He's letting me use it."

"You're working?"

"I told you I was, didn't I?"

"Doing what?"

"This guy over in Ocean Ridge hired me to keep an eye out, see nobody messes with him. He's a rich doctor."

"What's his name?"

"I call him Dr. Tommy, and that's all I'm gonna tell you."

Gary got into it saying, "Were you there the night before last, Elvin, at the doctor's?"

"Let's see, what was that, Thursday? I might've been."

"We can check if you don't remember."

"No, you can't. It's against the rules to tell my employer about me if I might get fired."

Kathy said, "Where'd you hear that?"

"From a guy I know was on probation one time. Hey, but I wasn't over there anyway. No, I remember now, I was in Lake Worth getting a blowjob. In the front seat of that pickup there. You want to check, her name was . . . Shit, I forgot her name. Cute little Hi-spanic piece a ass. Like her," Elvin said, looking at Kathy.

She said, "I want you in for a urine test Monday."

"Is this for disease or dope? I don't do any dope. Never have."

"If I tell you to come in for a test, you come in. It doesn't matter what it's for."

"I'll piss for you right here," Elvin said, "in this beer bottle. You can take it with you." He opened his legs and let one hand slide down the inside of his thigh.

"You're out of line," Gary said.

Elvin looked at him. "Is that your opinion?"

"Why don't you behave yourself?"

"Why don't you get fucked?"

Kathy stepped in, raising a tennis shoe to the first step. "I'd like you to move out of the way, Elvin. I'm going in the house."

"Dale ain't in there, I told you."

"Are you gonna move?"

Elvin said, "I don't see why I should," looking at her with those stupid eyes under the hat brim, thinking this was funny. "What I'm wondering is why you brought this dink along says he's a police officer. Shit, I thought he was your sister."

"I'm going in the house," Kathy said. She started up the steps past him. Elvin put his hand out, touched her stomach and she grabbed a finger, the middle one, not the one she wanted, tried to bend it and he grinned at her holding it stiff. "Move," Kathy said, "or I'll violate you."

Elvin said, "That's the best offer I've had all day."

She saw his expression change, his face raise with a dumb look and his hat was gone, snatched from his head. She saw Gary close to her throw the hat aside and grab a handful of Elvin's hair, Elvin thrashing around now, pushing her out of the way, reaching for Gary's arm, but Gary's fist was in his hair tight and Elvin howled as she saw Gary dragging him off the steps, tripping him, throwing him down in the weeds along the front walk; Gary kneeling on him now, a knee planted on Elvin's chest as he brushed his suit coat open to grip the Beretta holstered on his hip. She heard Gary say, "If I pull it, I shoot it. You understand? It's up to you." Not angry or excited, more like he was reciting it from a manual. Kathy didn't move till he looked over and said, "Go on in. We'll wait here."

It didn't take long to look around, empty beer bottles and pizza cartons—*Pizza from Pisa* and a drawing of the Leaning Tower—palmetto bugs, dirty dishes, clothes all over the place, some she thought might be Dale's, but no rifle. In the kitchen she found a spoon with the handle sharpened to a point and a piece of wood taped to the other end.

Now they were standing in the yard talking, Elvin with his hat on again, their expressions mild but not telling much. Gary doing most of the talking. Elvin would shrug.

Kathy watched them from the front steps.

Elvin walked away now, through the weeds to Dale's pickup and got in. Gary raised his hand—she believed to the Thunderbird parked down the street—as Elvin drove off. Gary turned to the house and Kathy held up the sharpened spoon.

"No rifle. How about a shank?"

17

"It was on the kitchen table," Kathy said, watching Gary gnawing on a barbecued rib, his little fingers pointing out, the guy so neat. "But I don't know if a shank is considered a weapon outside." She watched Gary shake his head now, meaning he didn't know either. "Elvin couldn't have brought it with him, so I guess he made it, showing Dale how to do prison. What do you think?"

This time Gary nodded, sitting across from her in the booth with his suit coat off, cotton dress shirt soft and snowy white, an ad for Tide. Except he would never drip barbecue sauce on it to show how the detergent would get it out. He had asked where she wanted to go. She said she didn't care, as long as it wasn't dressy. He said how about Chuck's Bar-B-Que Pit, his favorite place.

It was okay. They served pitchers of beer.

"Dale acts tough," Kathy said, but he goes to FSP, he finds out he's just another punk. I'm thinking maybe Elvin talked to him. You know, advised him, showed him how to make a shank . . . Dale says holy shit, man, he'd rather be a fugitive than try to hack DOC time. Or Elvin might've told him, you're out, stay out. And he took off."

Gary nodded, Mr. Agreeable today, picking up his napkin. "Who do you think he looks like in the movies?"

"Elvin or Dale?"

"Elvin."

Kathy hesitated, then took a chance and said, "I don't think he looks like anybody."

"I don't either," Gary said. "Maybe some bit player. Elvin overacts, trying to be the bad guy."

"But he *is*. What did you talk about when I was in the house?"

"I asked him if Dale had taken off, where he might be. Elvin said he didn't know."

"You believe him?"

"It doesn't matter one way or the other. I can't make him tell me if he doesn't want to."

"He told you to get fucked—I thought you were going to hit him."

"That was for your benefit. He wouldn't have said it if it was just him and me."

"You weren't mad?"

"I might've been on the edge."

"Why didn't you pull your gun?"

"I didn't have to."

"I mean instead of grabbing him by the hair."

"Why? I wasn't going to shoot him."

"But you took a chance, he's a big guy."

"You had him distracted." Gary smiled saying it. "They teach you that finger hold at the Academy? Somebody your size, you ever have to get physical, I think you'd do better with a gun."

"You sound like my brothers."

"At least show it. That's why Elvin and I got along, after. I had a gun and he didn't. What can he do? Guy fresh out of prison, does he want to risk going back? He isn't that dumb."

"Yes, he is," Kathy said. "He doesn't think. You heard him say he's working for a doctor in Ocean Ridge? It has to be the same one Michelle was talking about, in the office."

"Michelle," Gary said. "She the one stands real straight? Has the nice posture?"

"You mean the cute ass. She's our Community Control officer," Kathy said, "getting back to the doctor, Tomás Vasco in Ocean Ridge. It has to be Elvin's Dr. Tommy."

Gary was paying attention now. "That's a familiar name, Vasco. What'd he do?"

"They had him on some kind of dope charge. He drew, I think, county time plus probation, Community Control on an anklet and had his license revoked, or suspended."

She watched Gary gnaw a rib clean, wipe his mouth with a napkin, but miss a dab of barbecue sauce on his chin.

"There was a guy named Vasco arraigned on a homicide, or he was called as a key witness, about a year, year and a half ago. I'll look it up. He's wearing an anklet, huh?"

"Two years," Kathy said, staring at the barbecue sauce on his chin. "I think he still has one to go."

"If Elvin's working for him . . . You allow that, offenders getting together?"

"Not if we think they're up to something. You hear him say I can't check on him if he might get fired? He doesn't know what he's talking about. That's a special condition you have to get a judge to okay. Elvin's the kind of guy thinks he knows everything and can beat the system. They're always pretty dumb, those guys."

Gary said, "It sounds like Dr. Tommy isn't too bright either. Hires a convicted felon? If he knows who Elvin is."

"Elvin would tell him, don't worry," Kathy said.

"Then the doctor would be risking a violation."

"That's right. So either he doesn't care, or, for some reason, he thinks it's worth it."

She watched Gary giving it some thought, the dab of barbecue sauce still on his chin.

He said, "Maybe we should have a talk with Dr. Tommy. What do you think?"

She liked the way he was including her and said, "With or without a search warrant?"

That got a smile.

She touched a finger to her chin.

He raised the napkin and wiped his.

She said, "So I add the doctor to my caseload?"

It seemed to Elvin every time he came here Dr. Tommy acted different, showing more of himself or a different side to him. Showing everything today, Dr. Tommy coming out of his swimming pool bare naked. Looking up at the cocktail hour sky and slicking his hair back with both hands.

Some kind of black thing, like a little box, was taped to his ankle.

Just then the sound of Latin booger music came on loud and for a second Elvin thought the black thing on his ankle was a transistor radio. But no, the music was coming from the house.

Elvin, still back a ways on the lawn, watched Dr. Tommy stretch his arms out to the sides and begin to move in time to the music, doing a booger dance Elvin believed was called the mumbo. Now here was Hector coming from the patio in a little jockstrap type of bathing suit that showed the cheeks of his butt, the dink popping them side to side to the music and carrying what became a silky white robe, holding it open now as Dr. Tommy gave him a sexy look over his shoulder—Jesus Christ— and slipped into the robe.

Now there was a picture.

The two of them doing the mumbo back to the house, grinning and touching each other, the doc slapping Hector's bare butt with the sash ends of his robe and Hector saying stop that or something in Spanish, acting more like a girl than ever.

Elvin could identify behavior under certain drugs even though he didn't believe in them. Why go to all the trouble to buy that shit, have to deal with niggers mostly, when you could get all the beer and whiskey you wanted driving no more than two blocks in any direction? On the way here Elvin had stopped at a cocktail bar in Boynton Beach. He left Dale's pickup outside for the guys in the Thunderbird to watch—the ones who'd followed him from home—slipped out the back way and rode a taxicab over here, having made plans for the future.

He found the two boogers in the kitchen:

Dr. Tommy on a stool, sitting at a high butcher table in the middle of the room, still moving his shoulders to the music as he rolled a joint. Hector was mumboing around a blender, pouring different things into it from bottles on the counter.

"I see I'm just in time," Elvin said. "You girls having a little drinky?"

Dr. Tommy looked up but didn't stop moving, too much into what he was doing or doped up to act surprised. He had the joint rolled and was wetting it in and out of his mouth. Hector had the blender going, holding his hand on it. Dr. Tommy said something in Spanish and Hector laughed, nodding his head, his hair in a greased ponytail today. Now Hector was talking in Spanish.

"You two're cute," Elvin said, "but impolite." He saw Dr. Tommy smoking the joint now, sucking in on it. "What was it you said to him?"

"You come in, I said, 'Ah, it's the great shooter of windows.'" Dr. Tommy spoke in that strained voice of a weed smoker, holding his breath.

"That's pretty funny," Elvin said. "You think it was me the other night shot at the judge?"

No answer. Hector came over with creamy yellowish drinks in big wineglasses. He served Dr. Tommy first and toked off the joint before shoving a glass across the table toward Elvin, saying something in Spanish in that strained voice. Dr. Tommy seemed to get a kick out of it. Elvin heard his name in whatever was said. He stood at one side of the table, between the two boogers at opposite ends.

"He said something about me, huh?"

"Hector says if you ever want someone's kitchen shot, you're the one to hire."

"Shit, he's funnier'n you are. It wasn't me, Doc. We better get that straight."

Hector was talking again in a girlish way, moving his shoulders, Dr. Tommy grinning at him. Couple of dinks. Elvin picked up the glass and took a sip. He said, "Jesus," and wiped his hand across his mouth. "What is this thing?"

"Banana daiquiri," Dr. Tommy said. "You don't like it?"

Hector was talking in Spanish again and laughing at whatever he said, this queer that put bananas in a drink, saying his name. Elvin thought of stepping over to smack him, but then had an idea he liked better and threw his banana drink in Hector's face.

"Talk English in front of me. Hear?"

It stopped him moving his shoulders, all that creamy shit dripping from his face onto his hairless body. Elvin turned to Dr. Tommy. "You too. Talk English from now on." He heard Hector's stool scrape on the brick floor and looked to see him running out of the kitchen like a girl.

Dr. Tommy didn't seem to mind. He drew on his weed and held the smoke in a long time before letting it out. He said, "Okay, it wasn't you."

"Listen," Elvin said, "it not only wasn't me, I almost got hit standing in the man's house. You hear what I'm saying?" The doc's eyes didn't look too clear. "I was in there waiting on Gibbs to come in from the yard."

"You were in his home?"

"I *told* you how I'd walk right up to him, didn't I? Well, now he's got police around him and I have to think of something else."

Man, it was a job holding this guy's attention. Now he was climbing off his stool, his robe coming open to show a bare leg, and Elvin said, "What's that thing on your ankle, looks like a little radio?"

"It's how they keep track of me." Dr. Tommy was at the counter now putting more rum in his drink. "You never saw an anklet? You wear it, you can't go no more than a hundred and fifty feet from your telephone. There's a receiver in this thing and a box hooked to the telephone line, like you have with your cable TV."

Elvin didn't have cable TV or know what he was talking about, but said, "Yeah?"

"A computer calls my number every now and then and if I'm not in the house or close by, the computer doesn't get a signal back and it lets them know."

Elvin had heard of that. "You're on pro*bat*ion? Shit, so am I."

"Is that right?" Dr. Tommy was coming back to his stool. "I don't think you told me that."

"It don't make any difference. They can't check on me coming here." He watched Dr. Tommy sip his drink, not saying anything. "Why don't you take the goddamn thing off and set it by the phone?"

"You'd have to break it." Dr. Tommy stuck his leg straight out. "You can, all it has is the strap holding it on. But there's some kind of sensor in there, tells them if it isn't on your leg."

"You mean you can't ever leave the house?"

"Only to go to Alcoholics Anonymous, twice a week."

Shit, this was working out perfect. "Then you don't need your car, do you?" Elvin told him why he couldn't use Dale's pickup with cops watching it. Then Dr. Tommy had to think about it, his mind fuzzed with weed, before he said, "You have my gun, now you want a car? There's a difference. A gun doesn't have a license plate on it."

Elvin noticed Hector was back, standing at the counter now with one of those Cuban shirts on over his jockstrap, and his hands held together over his crotch. The booger music had finished playing. That was good to hear.

"I need a car for getting around in," Elvin said, "as I track the judge, figure where I'm gonna hit him. Then when I'm set up I either swipe a car or use my brother's truck. He don't drive no more with one leg. He does, but ain't suppose to. They took his license on account of he keeps running into things."

Elvin got that booger stare before Dr. Tommy said, "You look different today."

"I'm letting my beard grow."

"Wants to look like a rogue," the doctor said to Hector.

In English, so it was okay. "I'm thinking I may use dynamite. I know how. I shoot it sometimes I go fishing and I don't have all day. My brother always has some."

He had to wait then while Dr. Tommy relit his weed, took another drink and stared, trying to appear casual. He said after a minute, "Okay, you can have a Cadillac or a Lincoln. Hector likes the Jaguar to go to the store."

His dead brother Roland had owned a Cadillac. It was Elvin's choice without having to think about it. He said, "I might stay here too, since I know you have room."

"Now you want to move in?"

"I'll see, but I think I better while I'm working this out. Your probation officer comes by I'll hide in the closet."

He watched Dr. Tommy shrug inside his silky robe and give Hector a nod, the doc easy to deal with on his weed trip. So Elvin said, "I'll need a couple hundred for expenses. So I won't have to stick up a liquor store, your car sitting out front."

The doc gave another shrug looking at Hector. Then had to say, "Give it to him," when Hector didn't move, still holding his hands by his crotch.

Something funny going on here. Elvin squinted at him. Dr. Tommy said some words in Spanish, his voice quiet, soothing, different than before. Hector slipped his hand under the Cuban shirt and drew a little bluesteel automatic from his jockstrap. Elvin said to him, "You little booger, you weren't gonna shoot me with that, were you?"

"Hector worries about me," Dr. Tommy said. "It's all right. He won't shoot you unless I tell him. He's a very good boy. Aren't you, Hector?" Hector turned his head to look away. Like a girl. Like he wasn't ever going to speak to the doctor again.

These guys were creepy. Elvin took his expense money and the Cadillac and went back to West Palm to get laid.

"I was going to kill him," Hector said in Spanish. "Shoot him at least several times and make up a story for the police."

Dr. Tommy listened to this thinking, Not again, please. He said to Hector, "Don't worry about it."

"He has your car, your gun—don't worry about it?"

"What gun?" Dr. Tommy said. "I don't own any guns. Listen, he could be lucky and do it. You know why? Because he's a fool. He doesn't see what could stop him."

"But this was something you thought about, when, a year ago. Now you're thinking about it again?"

"I wasn't, until I saw that in the paper, the judge and the alligator. See, I'm beginning to entertain the possibility again and this one walks in, a convict, tells me yes, of course, he'll be happy to do it."

"Like Saint Anthony answering your prayer," Hector said, in a better mood now. "But what if he's arrested?"

"If he is, or the time comes I can't bear the sight of him, I report my car stolen."

Hector came over with the blender and began filling their glasses. "I wanted so much to shoot him."

"I know you did. Listen, it could still happen."

"But if he does kill the judge, will you pay him?"

Dr. Tommy picked up his glass. "Are you serious?"

They were having coffee now and wondering what to do this evening. No more talk about work. Go to a movie, a bar, listen to a band. Gary asked if she liked to dance. They could go to the Banana Boat. Kathy said she'd have to go home and change. She said the only trouble with the Banana Boat, sometimes she ran into probationers and they always wanted to buy her drinks. Or they'd bother her till she'd finally have to leave. Gary said, "Oh?" stirring his coffee. "You go there alone much?"

She said, "If you want to know do I go there to get picked up, ask me. Don't be afraid." He used milk and sugar and stirred his coffee forever.

"Do you?"

"No, I don't. I go with friends. You want to drive by Dr. Tommy's house, see what it looks like?"

"Tomorrow. I'd like to check on him first."

She thought of Elvin hanging out at a million-dollar home on the ocean. It was hard to imagine. She could see him in Dale's house, no problem, among the longnecks and pizza cartons. Pizza from Pisa, with the drawing of the Leaning Tower. The same kind she saw in the judge's kitchen, after . . .

"We could go to my place," Gary said. "Talk, listen to music. I'm down in Boynton, right off Hypoluxo."

Kathy raised her eyebrows as if to say, oh, that's an

idea. Talk and listen to music. Uh-huh. She said, "Well, okay," not wanting to sound too anxious. "Drop me at the office to get my car, I'll follow you."

"Or I can drive you back later."

She didn't like that idea. "I only live about five miles from you, in Delray. You want to drive all the way up here, and then we both have to drive all the way back?"

He was stirring his coffee again. "I don't see a problem. It's not that far."

"I'd have to leave my car on the street all night."

They were looking at each other across the table as she realized what she said.

"I mean, you know, it might be late."

He wasn't stirring now. He said, "We can get your car whenever you want."

18

Elvin said to his big brother, Dale Senior, "How do I look?"

It didn't matter Dale Senior couldn't answer him, metal pins sticking out of his sunken cheeks, wires holding his jaws shut tight like he was gritting his teeth, which he did most of his life anyway.

Elvin had looked at his reflection in the bedroom mirror and had to grin at himself, man, in that bright blue suit from Taiwan China and a bright yellow shirt with the collar spread open, duds that had once belonged to Roland and Elvin had stored in the attic of Dale Senior's house before going off to prison.

Dale Senior was most likely trying to tell him with his beady eyes he looked like blue shit tied in a bow, this old man big brother sitting at his kitchen table one-legged. Elvin stooped to make sure. No, that's all was under there, just the one leg and a stump.

"Buddy, where's your plastic wooden leg at?" No answer. "I hear you got in some trouble over to Clewiston."

This man had worn nothing but bib overalls or state clothes all his life. Had been up to Starke on a Corrections bus, but never over to Palm Beach, forty miles away. Had thought their brother Roland was leaving this world when all he did was move down to Monroe County. Dale Senior had a jelly-glass jar of Rebel Yell bourbon he was sucking in through a straw, glaring, the booze putting words in his head he was dying to say but couldn't. All it did was bulge his veins where he was going bald in front.

It reminded Elvin he had to get a haircut. He'd shaved off the week's worth of beard before putting the suit on. It was driving the Cadillac last night had changed his mind about looking rough and ready. The Cadillac and the go-go whore he picked up at the bar after she was done and took to Dale's house. He said to Dale Senior, "Bud, I was with a girl last night had her puss shaved near clean. Told me so she wouldn't look like a female gorilla up there in her G-string. I thought of ones me and you use to take out on the lake? Man, there were some of those old girls had bushes on 'em—I'd say I ain't going in there without a gun and a flashlight. Remember? This one last night was like a little girl down there 'cept she was grown."

One of Dale Senior's big ugly hands, all spotted and gnarled up with arthritis, was scratching at the oilcloth cover on the table, putting nicks in it, like a hound pawing on the end of a chain. Cut him loose and look out.

"This here's a go-go rock whore I'm talking about. Does it to buy crack and get high. That's the new thing, crack. They can get scrappy on you."

Insulting too, this one, calling Dale Junior's house a rat hole. This whore appraiser named Earlene, hand on her hip saying, "Drive a Cadillac and live like a nigger." He gave her a look at the shank he'd made for Dale, sticking it up under her nose. Oh, is that right? You calling me a nigger? It changed her tune quick, eyes about to pop out of her head. He told her he had already killed a man, was about to get him another one and to watch the newspaper if she thought he was blowing smoke at her.

But she was right in a way, what she said. What was he doing in this dump if he drove a Cadillac Fleetwood only three years old and looked brand-new? Or why dress as he did and look like he stole the car?

It was the reason he came here this bright Sunday morning and pulled Roland's trunk from the attic where it had laid ten years untouched—not counting his getting the hat and boots out of it. Animals had scratched at the trunk, but none had got in to mess up the clothes. Three suits, a bunch of shirts and ties and undies. All he had to do to complete his changeover, besides get a haircut, was move in with Dr. Tommy and that little puss Hector.

He said to Dale Senior, "You know where Ocean Ridge is at? You go on over to Palm Beach and turn south." Elvin would catch himself talking loud, as if the man couldn't hear as good with his jaw wired, and have to lower his voice. "I'm moving into a house over there, big one, right on the ocean. How's that sound to you?" Dale Senior could at least nod his head. Shit, it was like talking to the wall.

He turned as Mavis came in the back door and walked right past him, looking concerned and heading straight for Dale Senior.

"I'm home," Mavis told him, in case he didn't see her standing there. "I come right back like I said. Can I dish you up a nice bowl of soup? It's split pea with bacon in it, your favorite."

Elvin watched Dale Senior swipe the jelly glass,

empty now, clear off the table with that big ugly hand of his.

"I think he wants another toddy," Elvin said to Mavis, and looked over at the cast-iron pot of soup on the stove, bubbles popping in it. He said, "I bet, thirty years with the old sweetheart, you've thought of adding roach powder with the bacon. Look at him. He's afraid I'm giving you ideas." He said to Dale Senior, "You better be careful what you suck into your mouth there, Bud."

Mavis stopped to get the glass from the floor and came up sniffing, her nose in the air.

"What's that smell?"

"If you mean me," Elvin said, "it's my suit of clothes, from being in mothballs. I think it'll air though."

Mavis was getting the bourbon off the sink counter.

"Where's his leg at?"

She said, "Shhh," putting her hand up by her mouth. "Don't mention it." Now she was pouring Dale Senior another three inches of whiskey and setting fresh straws in the glass, telling him, "Honey? You know I brought some soup over to Inez's for Dale Junior? He's still there, doing just fine."

Elvin said, "That's where Dale's at?"

Mavis gave him a scared look, the kind, when you're caught saying something maybe you shouldn't have. Then seemed to decide it was all right and told him, "Since yesterday. They been looking all over for him, deputies have."

"That ain't a problem," Elvin said. "What is, he's going to prison tomorrow. Man, I know if I was I wouldn't be staying over at Inez and Dicky's, Jesus. I'd be in every bar in West Palm. No, I wouldn't either, I'd find that little girl I was with last night."

"I don't know as he's decided he's going or not," Mavis said.

Elvin had to grin at the woman thinking you had a choice. Just then Dale Senior began making growling sounds in his throat and blinking his drunk eyes, his way of trying to speak.

"Too bad he never learned to write," Elvin said, watching his big brother, this old man of fifty-six struggling with himself, spit coming from between his sealed lips. Elvin raised his hand. "Buddy? Let's see you wave bye-bye. Like this, move your fingers." All he got were those beady eyes staring at him and veins turning blue. Elvin said to Mavis, "I think I'll stop over and see Dale. Show him my new car."

They were in Michelle's office eleven o'clock Sunday morning, her desk piled with case folders left over from the meeting yesterday. She said to Kathy, "How would you like to open one of these and see it's a guy you used to go with?" Michelle picked up a folder. "This one." And dropped it. "At the time I thought he was a sweet guy. He threw his girlfriend's TV set out the window. His ex-girlfriend, her apartment's on the fifth floor."

"The sweet guy discovered crack," Kathy said.

"He has to pay almost five thousand in restitution."

"That must've been some TV set."

"It hit a car."

"You're not taking him, are you?"

"Hardly. If you want him, he's yours."

"I wouldn't mind that doctor in Ocean Ridge."

"Dr. Vasco, another sweetie," Michelle said, looking for his case folder. "Why do you want him?"

"Something different."

"But you don't do Community Control."

"I could. I've been here long enough."

"And you must love it," Michelle said, looking up. "I got here at eight this morning and there's your car in front. I thought you were up in your office." Michelle acting, her expression going from innocent to puzzled. "No, wait a minute. Gary picked you up here yesterday . . ."

"You want to know if I left my car and spent the night with him."

"Listen, I wouldn't blame you, he's a neat guy, very clean-cut, polite . . . I love his hair. He doesn't come on like most cops, does he? He seems . . . you know, gentle."

Michelle was waiting now to have this verified.

"He's nice," Kathy said, "he's smart, likes to read. Majored in sociology at U of M. Spent eight years with Palm Beach PD, likes to work homicide . . . What else do you want to know? His folks live in Boca, he goes there for dinner every other Sunday. He has a younger sister, she's there sometimes. His dad's retired."

Michelle said, "Really?"

Kathy said, "I know how Community Control works and you need help, right? You could let me have Dr. Vasco on a temporary basis, thirty days?"

"Yeah, I suppose, if you really want him." Michelle had the case folder open and was glancing through it. "He's on twenty-four-hour house arrest. Allowed two AA meetings a week. Has a houseman, Hector, who does the shopping. The doctor goes in swimming with his anklet on. It's supposed to be waterproof but they had to replace three the first year. He bitches constantly about his phone bill, even though he's loaded. You know an anklet adds about a hundred and twenty bucks a month." Michelle closed the file. Handing it across the desk she said, "I like that dress. Is it new?"

"This?" Kathy pinched the front of her beige cotton knit that was like a long T-shirt with a belt. "It isn't new and I didn't have it on last night, but we did go to his apartment."

That seemed to make Michelle happy. "Was it nice?"

"The apartment? It was neat, nothing lying around. He rents movies, listens to music. He likes Neil Young, The Band, Bob Dylan . . ."

"No new stuff?"

"Dire Straits."

"They're not new."

Kathy said, "He has ten years of *National Geographic* magazines," looking Michelle in the eye, "he keeps in chronological order in a bookcase. He has about four hundred books, all kinds, in alphabetical order by authors."

Michelle took a moment. "He does?"

"He's reading one about Siberia he says is a honey."

"Siberia," Michelle said.

"The gulags, slave-labor camps. Twenty-five million people were sent there during Stalin's time, anybody he didn't like. Russian soldiers captured during the war, they came home they were sent to Siberia. They shouldn't have let themselves get captured. A man was overheard saying to an American his boots were better than Soviet boots. He got ten years. In one camp they shot thirty people a day to keep the rest of them in line."

"That's what you talked about, Siberia?"

"They call the convicts over there *zeks*. No, we talked about different things. Gary opened a bottle of wine."

"Yeah?"

"I didn't spend the night."

"You didn't?"

"It got late, he took me home."

"Yeah?"

"Picked me up this morning and dropped me off, that's all. We're going to meet later."

"Nothing happened last night?"

"You mean did we go to bed? No. What do you want? We just met. You go to bed with every guy you meet and happen to like?"

Michelle paused. "No, not every guy."

"Just the ones throw TV sets out the window."

"Why're you upset?"

"I'm not. You want to know what happened, I told you. Nothing."

Now Michelle seemed to be appraising her, eyes narrowed. "Are you saying he didn't try anything or you didn't let him?"

"It wasn't like that."

"Like what? You're alone in his apartment . . ."

"That doesn't mean he has to jump me, does it?"

"No wonder you're upset. What's wrong with him?"

"Nothing. He's a nice guy. He wants me to go with him next Sunday, meet his folks."

"Well, I guess if you hang in there long enough . . . I really like his hair. He'll never get bald."

"And he's clean-cut, he's polite," Kathy said, "and you think he's a little weird, don't you?"

"I wouldn't say weird."

"What he does with his *National Geographic*s."

"Well, that. No, but I think he *is* different. You know, maybe he's shy. I mean with women."

"He might be."

"Self-conscious, afraid of being turned down. When they're like that you have to let them know it's okay. Bring them out, so to speak."

"Like unzip their fly?"

"That would work. You know the old saying," Michelle said, "once you have their balls in your hand, their minds are far from Siberia."

Inez came around from the side of the house where she was hanging wash and yelled at Dale to get back inside, what was wrong with him? Elvin waved at her and brushed through the opening in the hedge that hid the street and his black Cadillac sedan. He was only going to show it to Dale, how it told you all kinds of stuff on the dash panel when you pressed buttons; but when Inez started yelling he said, "Shit, get in the car."

Dale was in the front seat before Elvin was even around to the other side. He yelled at Inez, "We going for a ride. Be back directly."

Driving off he saw Inez in his rearview mirror standing out in the street, the size of her, like a man wearing a housedress. All you could say about Inez Campau, there was a big ugly woman. He said to Dale, "You don't want to stay there no more, do you?"

"She's making me leave by tomorrow anyways," Dale said, "once I'm a fugitive."

"You run, you know what they'll do."

"I don't care, I'm not going to prison."

"They'll add on five to the five you already got."

"If they catch me."

Sounding like the boy had made up his mind.

Elvin said, "Prison ain't that bad, you get the hang of

it . . . find yourself some buddies, a little housekeeper to take care of your wants . . ."

Dale wasn't talking.

They drove out of this back-end part of Belle Glade where people like the Crowes and Campaus lived in old frame houses, their pickups and boat trailers in the yard alongside rusted washing machines, car parts, skiffs past use. Old boys sitting on porches drinking beer waved at the Cadillac driving past.

Now it crept down the main drag of storefronts, Elvin always amazed at the sight of cane cutters, hundreds of black faces on the street buying Walkman radios and little TVs to take back to Jamaica, their season almost done. Elvin said, "I ain't gonna say nothing but, Jesus Christ, how come we bring all these people here when our own niggers could be doing the work? I know it's a filthy dirty job and you can get hurt swinging them machetes, but they could at least try it, shit. Don't let me get off on that, the invasion of the boogers. You think they're gonna be happy staying only six months? Pretty soon they'll be living here, as the Cuban and different other kinds are, taking our jobs."

"Excuse me," Dale said, "but when did you ever work?"

Elvin didn't like Dale's snippy tone of voice, but let it go, the boy scared and angry at the same time.

"I took folks for airboat rides," Elvin said. "I even took rich boogers for airboat rides and it like to killed me. I had a mind to dump 'em in the swamp. I got a deal on right now with a rich booger. He's paying I mean top dollar for me to do a special kind of job. If it was only for pay, shit, I wouldn't do it. But it turns out it's for me and you mostly. You know the guy, Dr. Tommy, the one in Ocean Ridge. You want to guess what the job is?"

The boy didn't answer. Not interested or too busy feeling sorry for himself.

"I understand where you're at," Elvin said, "facing up to a system known for not being fair."

Dale said, "Shit, all I did was hit a cop. Why're they any different?"

Elvin said, "I know, I've done it and paid. I've learned if you're ever angry enough to hit somebody, don't do it. Cool down and get yourself a pistol. There's a cop pulled my hair I was dying to hit. Unh-unh, I'm waiting till the right time." Elvin hunched close to the steering wheel, turning his head as he gazed up through the windshield. "Look it how they live."

They were passing migrant housing now, two-story concrete barracks, wash hanging to dry on the upstairs rails.

"Day off, they drink rum and chew sugarcane. You go inside there, everyone of 'em's playing a radio. I never saw people liked radios so much."

Dale said, "When'd you ever go in there?"

Looking for an argument in his frame of mind.

"I worked one time for a guy ran the *bolita*. You know, the numbers? I'd have to go in those places they lived, be the only white person in there, boogers looking at me like they wanted to cut my balls off with a cane knife. Ugly people but, man, did they love to play the *bolita*. They'd love this car too, wouldn't they? They'd keep house in it."

Out on the highway the sky to the south was full of black smoke where they were burning off the last of the fields. Trucks whipped past hauling cane stalks to the sugar house for processing. They drove their Ford tractors fast, dumped the loads off the trailers and headed back for more. It was a job Dale used to have and Elvin thought he would brag on it now, but he didn't. That's how mean his disposition was.

"Oh my, what to do," Elvin said. "All right, I'm gonna make you a proposition."

Dale didn't even ask what it was. Didn't say one word till they'd driven the forty miles back to civilization, took the freeway down to Boynton Beach and turned into the parking lot of the cocktail bar on S.E. 15th.

Dale said, "That's my truck." Not snippy at all now, more surprised than anything.

Elvin checked, didn't see any surveillance, before saying, "Why yes it is." The pickup still sitting where he'd left it yesterday. "And the keys are in it."

They sat in a booth with their drinks, Jim Beam and 7-Up, dark in here this Sunday afternoon, Elvin relaxed with something he was anxious to tell, but irritated the drinks were served in skimpy glasses. He'd wave to the waitress for two more. She'd bring them and he'd quit talking and tell her to take it from the change on the table. The waitress would poke through the pile there, car keys, bills and silver, Dale's cigarettes and matches, and pick out what she needed.

Elvin spoke of prison for a while, about sports and movies, making it sound not too bad. Though advised Dale to get laid tonight; be his last shot at some front-door lovin'. Dale wouldn't talk about it. So Elvin said, "All right, you made up your mind." On their third drink by this time. "Go on get in your truck and take off. By tomorrow they'll have detainers on you clear across the country. But if that's what you want to do . . ."

On their fourth round Elvin was telling him about the deal with Dr. Tommy. Top wages to shoot the judge and he'd give Dale, let's see, two thousand to drive for him. How did that sound? "Take off in your old beatup truck or drive a Fleetwood Cadillac while we set up the judge."

It got Dale to fidget around some in the booth.

"I'm thinking we'll move in with Dr. Tommy," Elvin said. "Have a party out there tonight, huh? Get some girls. I'll tell you one I'm thinking of having sometime, that little probation lady. I've had Cuban puss and it ain't too bad. We could have us some tonight, you want. Or this go-go whore I had over to your house last night."

"You want to kill the judge?"

The boy finally waking up.

"I call it paying back. How about you?"

"They already think it was me tried."

"Listen, that dink, whoever it was, he's an amateur. You're working with a pro here. I've *done* it."

"And you went to prison."

"Hey, that's something else entirely. We set this one up right, it'll work slick. You take off after with some cash on you."

Dale was quiet, looking at his drink.

"Come on, what do you say?"

"I'm thinking."

"While you're doing that," Elvin said, "I'm gonna go shake the dew off my lily."

He got up and walked to the men's room, all the way in back. Elvin was gone maybe five minutes. He washed his hands after, for no reason, then had to hold them under one of those goddamn machines you pushed the button and it blew hot air as you were supposed to briskly, it said, rub your hands together. That's what took the time. Then after that drying his hands on his shirttail and having to stick his goddamn shirttail in his pants again. When he got back to the table Dale was gone.

The waitress said, "He didn't leave but a minute ago."

Elvin ran outside hoping to catch him driving off. Beat some sense into the boy if he had to. He stopped short in the parking lot, around on the side of the building. Dale's pickup was still there, nosed against the cinder-block wall.

It was the space where he'd parked the Cadillac that was empty.

They must have seen him drive up in the taxicab. Hector opened the door and Dr. Tommy was standing in the hall waiting for him.

Elvin said, "You know what happened?"

Dr. Tommy said, "Tell me."

Elvin said, "Somebody stole your car."

19

They stopped a hundred feet or so from the entrance to Dr. Tommy's, on the opposite side of Ocean Boulevard. It was dark inside the unmarked Dodge, going on ten. Through a wall of trees and sea grape they could see lights on in the house. Gary said, "I guess you know what working surveillance is like," as she was thinking this could be the time to bring him out, if he was willing to be brought. But no grabbing. With the right words, tone of voice.

"I do it a lot," Kathy said, "keeping track of my cases. Okay, where were you? The drugstore, had to get some medicine. Why didn't you come in today? I was sick. The same thing over and over."

"You're bored."

She wanted him to touch her and they'd kiss. She was dying to kiss him. She said, "No, this is different."

The idea was to see if Elvin was around. He wasn't home in Delray Beach and he wasn't using Dale's pickup. Yesterday he'd left it in Boynton. This morning TAC pulled off its surveillance and gave the job to Boynton PD. Well, requested they keep an eye on the truck. Elvin could be here, at Dr. Tommy's. But if he was, Gary said, it didn't make sense.

He had looked up Dr. Vasco. Key witness in a homicide. Almost implicated. Fingered his houseman, Sonny, who was convicted and drew twenty-five to life at FSP.

"Where Elvin was," Kathy said.

Gary said he'd thought of that, wondering how Elvin had found Dr. Tommy. So he called the prison and what do you know. Elvin and Sonny were sweethearts. Elvin would cut anyone who even looked at Sonny with lust.

"With lust? A corrections officer said that?"

"I think it was 'looked at Sonny's ass.' "

"That's more like it."

"Sonny tells Elvin about Dr. Tommy, who fingered him and, for all we know, might have been implicated."

"As an accessory?"

"Sonny claims he killed the girl trying to protect the doctor. They got in a fight, the doctor accusing her of blackmailing him with some home movies, and Sonny hit her over the head with an iron poker. The doctor says no, it was Sonny who wanted to blackmail him, but not with home movies, something else, writing phony prescriptions. They had him on that anyway. He said on the stand the girl told him what Sonny planned to do and that's why Sonny killed her."

"What were the home movies?"

"Porno stuff, the doctor and different girls. Sonny's lawyer wanted them admitted as evidence, but the judge ruled against it. They had Sonny cold, picked him up driving the girl's car, her body and the murder weapon in the trunk. The funny thing is, the tapes are still in our evidence room. Never returned because the doctor said they weren't his. Sonny must've taken them without his knowledge."

"Did you look at them?"

"There must be at least a dozen tapes."

"What are they like?"

"The usual, mostly kinky sex. I only saw a couple."

She said, "What's kinky to some people isn't to everybody."

"These were kinky."

"I'll have to take your word."

"Well, like in some of them the doctor had more than one girl in bed with him."

"I thought you only saw a couple of tapes."

"I might've looked at three or four, to get an idea."

"Yeah? You learn anything?"

"I meant get an idea what they were about."

"They turn you on?"

"You're not serious."

"Yes or no."

"Is this another test?"

"Come on, I won't tell anybody."

He said, "Well, they weren't bad for home movies."

Was he smiling a little? She wasn't sure.

"Even the kinky ones?"

"I mean the camera work."

She said, "You're not shy, are you?"

"I never thought I was."

"But you're steady, always composed?"

"I'm not sure what you mean."

"You don't like to take chances. You're cautious."

"I suppose, up to a point."

"Really? You let go sometimes?"

"If I know what's gonna happen."

"You're safe," Kathy said, moving close enough to take his face in her hands. She kissed him on the mouth, lingered and said, "Relax, okay?" She kissed him again, staying on it longer this time before she said, "I've had enough surveillance for one night. How about you?"

Elvin brought the go-go whore in the front way, opening the door with a key on the ring that had the keys to the Lincoln, the car he was driving since Dale stole the Cadillac this afternoon.

Elvin'd had to argue Dr. Tommy out of reporting it. "You want police coming here while we're working our deal? My nephew won't hurt your car. By the time they pick him up the job'll be done." Then had to argue the doc into letting him use the Lincoln, a big gray one. "You want me to ride in taxicabs while I set up the judge?" Dr. Tommy had seemed nervous at the way things were going, not as cocky, but stoned and half drunk was easy to handle. He might not like it, but what could he do?

Booger music was coming out of hidden speakers and the go-go whore was moving to it on the terrazzo floor, looking around bug-eyed like she'd died and gone to whore heaven. "Mumbo on down the hall," Elvin said. He followed her cute butt sliding side to side in a little skirt that barely covered it, no backs to her high heels clicking on the marble. She wasn't too bad looking for a crackhead junkie. Had her G-string on under the skirt to give Dr. Tommy a show.

There he was in his den, lamps shining on the gold wallpaper that looked like stucco: the doc crapped out in a fat sofa full of pillows, swallowed up in there, his drink on the round gold-metal table: the doc a drunk prisoner among all this glitter shit, eyes closed. . . . Elvin said to the go-go whore looking over the den, hand on her hip the same way she'd checked out Dale's house, "See that rug? It's the hide off a skinned zebra. Feel the wallpaper."

Elvin noticed Dr. Tommy had his eyes open now but didn't seem about to move, bent low in the sofa with his legs sticking out, barefoot and glassy-eyed. "Sunday night," Elvin said, "how come you aren't watching TV?"

The doc blinked his eyes and then rubbed them. He was looking at the go-go whore now.

"Doc, this here is Earlene. She's gonna do her go-go number for you and then I'm on take her upstairs. You want, you can have a turn after. Hey, Earlene?"

She came over from feeling the wall, hips sliding, eyes sparkling with crack.

Elvin grinned at her. "Honey, show the doc your little G-string."

It was good to see a guy in his underwear again, a nice guy this time, not anything like Keith. Keith, taking his clothes off, would be looking at himself in the mirror on the door to the closet. The mirror still there, full-length. Gary, taking his clothes off, looked at her taking hers off. She pulled the dress over her head and he was motionless, looking. Even when they were in bed Keith, the catalogue model, would watch himself in the mirror, very serious. Gary came over to the bed in his shorts, pushed them down and said, "I'm on the wrong side." She said, "There is no wrong side." There was to him. He crawled over her as she squirmed her way to the middle of the double bed and now he was on the left side. "Is that better?" She could see him in faint light, the bed close to the window. He seemed happy. He said, "From driving a car . . ." She didn't ask what he meant and he didn't say more than that because it was getting good now, doing all the things with a man she had not done in a long time, getting to the best part, letting go and letting him hear small private sounds come out of her until, finally . . . silence.

It was nice.

It wasn't the kind where you get totally carried away, lost in it or quite like falling off the edge of the world. It wasn't sweaty.

It was . . . nice.

He said, "When you made out in a car the guy's on the left, because usually he drove."

"You like to do it in a car?"

"I mean when you're younger."

"Or on surveillance," Kathy said, getting out of bed. She stepped into white panties.

"Is that it for tonight?"

It gave her hope. "Don't move. I'll be right back."

She went to the kitchen, turned on the light and got two cans of beer from the refrigerator. As soon as Gary mentioned being in a car, that business about the left side, she was in the unmarked Dodge again seeing the dark street, the doctor's house—it reminded her of a British colonial building in the Bahamas. If Elvin was there it would be for one reason. If the doctor put the stuff on Sonny at his trial and Elvin was Sonny's boyfriend and the biggest thing in Elvin's life was paying back . . . Something didn't make sense.

In the bedroom again with the cans of beer, she placed Gary's on the nightstand and turned on the lamp. He seemed happy to see her navel looking him in the eye.

"You think Elvin wants to kill the doctor?"

"That was my first thought," Gary said, finally looking up, reaching for the can of beer.

"Then what's he waiting for? He's been on the street ten days. He told me the only reason he shot the wrong guy and went to prison, he waited too long. What's he waiting for this time?"

Gary sipped his beer. "Maybe that's his problem. He puts things off."

"Would he tell us he even *knows* the doctor if he's going to kill him?"

"You said he's pretty dumb."

"Elvin's into something, with the doctor."

"Like what?"

The beer can was cold in her hand, but it was something to hold on to standing topless in her panties; that wasn't planned. "You talk to Elvin, you get the feeling he's dying to tell you something, but he can't. You see it on his face. How did he introduce himself to the doctor? Did he walk in off the street looking for work? That isn't Elvin. I think he came with a story, something about Sonny, or he wouldn't have got in. Well, the doctor has a story too, doesn't he? He wasn't convicted of killing that girl, Sonny was. You know he could convince Elvin . . ." Kathy stopped. "Who presided at Sonny's trial?"

Gary was smiling a little. "Guess?"

"You've thought of this, haven't you?"

"I might've. Keep going."

"I had a feeling it was Gibbs. How about Dr. Tommy's trial?"

"Gibbs. You feel that one too?"

"I was hoping. And Gibbs put Elvin away. What do you think?"

"About what? Elvin's always been a suspect."

"I mean Elvin *and* Dr. Tommy, both in on it."

"But you said no one's out to get the judge."

"I've changed my mind."

"The shots were fired at his house, you said. Not at him."

"I still think so, but I see these two guys . . . You don't like the doctor in it?"

"I might. I haven't talked to him yet."

"He could have the same pay-back motive as Elvin. Gibbs took his license, put him on house arrest. He can't *move* because of this judge and he's a problem case, always bitching. He's already been implicated in a homicide . . ."

"As a suspect, never indicted."

"He's an offender, Gary. They're dirty once, they can get dirty again."

"You sound like a twenty-year cop."

She gave that a moment. "I do, don't I?"

"Learn procedures, you'd make a star investigator."

"But start out in uniform."

"I like the one you have on," Gary said.

Kathy hooked a thumb in her panties, getting back in the mood. "Yeah, but where would I keep my gun?"

The gold walls shimmered and the zebra moved, ready to rise from the floor. The zebra could be explained: Earlene the go-go whore doing the salsa on its skin in her G-string, topless. Sorry, Dr. Tommy said, no rock and roll. The only rock had cost Earlene twenty-five dollars. He paid her for it anxious to do crack, his first time. Elvin drank Scotch whiskey complaining there was no bourbon, while Dr. Tommy and Earlene smoked chips from the rock. When he couldn't find a pipe she made something like a bong by cutting a hole in a beer can: an amazing, resourceful girl, too thin, arms like sticks and small breasts, never smiled, hated Elvin, slowly killing herself . . . But when he asked her, "What do you think it's like?" Doing crack. She said, "Being born. Coming into the light of day." That wasn't bad. He told her he thought it was like doing the best coke and the best weed at the same time, because while you space out everything becomes much clearer too, yes, bright, and you want to, not so much fly, as hover above the ground. She wasn't listening. Elvin was telling her to take off her G-string. She wasn't listening to him either. Elvin telling her then, "Show the doc your haircut." What? She had long limp hair. Dr. Tommy said wait, he had to go to the bathroom.

Each time he left the room he would stop by the kitchen where Hector, fluttering, afraid to come out, would have another observation to make. This time:

"What if the nephew is arrested?"

"I'm sure he will be."

"In the Cadillac you haven't reported stolen."

Hmmm. "I say I loaned it to him? Listen, you may have to go out and get some more." The trouble with crack, you were no sooner up, you were coming in for a landing, hitting the ground.

Hector said, "The man is taking over your house."

Also, it left an unpleasant taste.

"You hear me? He's taking over your *house*."

"Hector?"

He looked away, pouting. "What?"

When he did this you had to win him back.

"The man wears an electric-blue polyester suit made in China that smells of mothballs."

Dr. Tommy returned to the den to hear Elvin saying

20

Monday afternoon in his chambers Gibbs said, "I get my picture in the Sunday paper and what amounts to the story of my life. . . . You see it?"

Kathy, in the low sofa, nodded at his head and shoulders behind the desk, the judge out of his robes.

"So this morning my courtroom's packed, all these people come to see the judge some screwball wants to assassinate. I have standing room only and what happens?"

"I was there," Kathy said.

It didn't stop him.

"A defendant starts using vile, obscene, and abusive language. Tells me to kiss his ass. Calls me a racist motherfucker in front of all those people. Now I've been called a racist before and I don't know why, 'cause I got nothing against the colored. One time I was written up in the *Judicial Conduct Reporter* for what they considered a racist remark. I was trying a man who had shot and killed his wife when he found out she was having an affair with a colored guy. I happened to say as I was charging the jury, they had to decide if a willful act of murder was committed, but also take into consideration the infidelity involved and be willing to call a spade a spade."

"You actually said that?"

"Just kidding, I wasn't serious. Now, on account of what happened this morning, they want to put me in a dinky little courtroom. TAC does, so they'll have tighter control. Here's this defendant mouthing off, using obscenities—he's already serving five life terms for rape, kidnapping, and robbery. He knows I'm gonna give him three more plus fifty years for good measure. What's he got to lose. He starts yelling—bad as he is he's got friends in the courtroom, so they get into it. 'Right on.' You heard 'em. 'Fight the power.' All that kind of talk they use. What am I gonna do, clear the courtroom?"

"You could have called a recess."

"Like hell. I warned the defendant, 'One more outburst of any kind, I'll order the bailiff to gag your mouth shut and chain you to your seat.' Well, he found out I meant it, as did everyone in the courtroom. I give my word, I stand by it. But it'll be in the paper tomorrow somewhat different, wait and see. 'Maximum Bob strikes again. Lowers the boom.' Having fun with me. Maximum Bob, that's what *Newsweek* named me the time I was on their cover."

Kathy watched him shake his head, tired, maybe the strain getting to him, but the next moment wide awake.

"You happen to notice last year, when that federal court judge sent Jim Bakker away? . . . The TV preacher."

"Jim and Tammy Faye?"

"That's the one. A judge in North Carolina, Robert something or other, gave Jim Bakker forty-five years plus a half-million-dollar fine. So they start referring to him as Maximum Bob. The press, they take my nickname and use it. Hell, I'd have given the preacher more'n forty-five years, and not in any minimum-security country club. They drove him there in a Chevy Impala. He'll do ten working in the cafeteria and be right back in business. A man is sentenced it should be hard time, or what's the good of it."

"Hard time," Kathy said, "makes the boy the man. Is that how it goes?"

The judge grinned at her. "You got it."

"Dale Crowe's facing ten years now."

"It's his choice," Gibbs said, "he signed the guidelines waiver. You don't report when you're suppose to . . . Honey, I don't send offenders away, they do it themselves."

"I think Dale got some bad advice."

"Well, why didn't you set him straight?"

"I couldn't find him."

"You know law enforcement will. They'll pick him up on a fugitive warrant, no problem. His lawyer then'll piss and moan, 'If they can find him, how come Ms. Probation Officer can't? Did she try?' It'll be your fault this boy has to do ten years. Can you handle that?"

"I didn't sentence him" Kathy said.

The phone on the desk rang, once. Gibbs ignored it.

She saw his solemn Harry Dean Stanton face change, start to grin. Saw his bare arms, pale and bony, raise as he leaned back in the chair and locked his hands behind his head. She was pretty sure he dyed his hair, slick and shiny in the light. He said, "I love young girl probation officers. They most always surprise me. Here you are looking sweet and innocent, but underneath it you're a tough little thing, aren't you? No, you didn't sentence him, but you did bring him into my court. I didn't go out in the street and drag him in." The judge's gaze moved.

Kathy looked over to see one of his bodyguards from TAC in the doorway: a young hot-dog cop named Wesley, blond hair down on his forehead. In the JA's office earlier, Kathy waiting to come in here, Wesley said to her, "You must be the judge's friend I've heard about." His coat open and hands on his hips so she'd see his .357 mag. He told her he usually worked undercover, but got stuck with this baby-sitting job. Wesley's tone was different now.

"Judge, can I interrupt?"

Gibbs said, "If you feel you have to."

"There's a guy on the phone wants to talk to you."

"He give his name?"

"No sir, but this one's different than usual."

Gibbs came forward to rest his bare arms on the desk, looking at Kathy. "I've had a dozen or more calls already. They say, 'I hope he gets you, you son of a bitch,' for whatever I did to their boy or their husband. . . . One said, 'If he don't do it, I will.' Full of talk. I thought I'd met all the flakes in my courtroom. Saturday they found a snake in my mailbox."

The TAC cop, Wesley, said, "Judge?"

Gibbs ignored him. "Every call that comes in is recorded out in my JA's office. Course they never say who it is, but we had Southern Bell put a trap on the line. It tells what number they're calling from, so then they look up to see where the phone's located. Now TAC's rounding up all these smartass anonymous callers." Gibbs looked toward the doorway. "What's this one, another threat?"

"He says it's about Dale Crowe."

"There's a warrant out on him. Tell the guy to call the Sheriff's Office."

"He says it's something you'll want to know about."

Kathy looked from one to the other. Now at Gibbs picking up the phone. He winked at her as he pressed the "speaker" button and said, "This is Bob Gibbs. What can I do for you?"

A voice came over the speaker saying, "Is this the judge?" With that country accent you heard in the Glades.

"I just told you it was, didn't I?"

"I like to make sure's all."

"Say what you want or I'm gonna hang up."

There was a pause before the voice came on again. "If you want Dale Crowe Junior, I can tell you how to find him."

"All right, how?"

"I know who he's with and the kind of car they're driving."

"Tell me," Gibbs said, "and we'll both know."

There was another pause on the line.

"Remember that gator was in your yard?"

Now it was the judge who paused.

Kathy watched him frown, looking up at the wall above her, maybe wondering what the voice was getting at, or deciding what to say next. Then surprised her. All he said was "What about it?" But in a different tone, his voice lower, serious.

The voice said, "You don't know what I mean? Or who this is?"

The judge's eyes raised to the wall again to stare with a look of concern that wasn't like him. He said, "I'm afraid I don't."

Lying—Kathy was sure of it. Because if he didn't

know who it was he'd snarl at the voice to quit wasting his time.

The voice said, "Come on, Judge." Then paused a moment and said, "Wait a minute, okay?"

Kathy watched Gibbs's hand creep across the desk toward the phone. She said, "Is this being recorded?" and the hand stopped. Gibbs looked at her, stared a moment and nodded. Now his fingers, close to the phone, began to drum on the desk, without making a sound. She had the feeling he wanted to press the "speaker" button again, turn it off, but now it was too late.

The voice came on saying, "Judge? I won't mention that business about the gator if we can make a deal here. Otherwise, what I'm gonna do . . ."

"Is that right?" Gibbs said. "Well, since I don't know what you're talking about and I don't think you do either, I'm gonna hang up this phone."

Wesley was motioning now, shaking his head, but Gibbs wasn't looking at him. He said, "Judge, don't." A second too late.

Gibbs hung up.

"Who's he think he's talking to? I don't make deals. That's between the state attorney and the guy's lawyer, they want to work out a plea deal. He called the wrong party."

Wesley said, "Judge, you have any idea who it was?"

"Some flake. Could've been anybody."

"He seemed to think you knew him."

" 'Cause he was in my court one time I'm suppose to remember him?"

"Well, if he's still where he called from," Wesley said, "he's ours."

Gibbs began to nod with a thoughtful expression,

looking at Kathy again. She saw the worry in his eyes before he looked away, looked around, anxious. Wesley turned to go and Gibbs said, "Wait a minute . . . I'm wondering if it might be this guy from Belle Glade I sentenced the other day. If I can recall his name . . ."

He was putting on an act and it made Kathy think of Harry Dean Stanton again. The judge had lied and now was trying to cover his ass before he got caught. She watched him hit the desk with the edge of his fist and look up at Wesley, still in the doorway.

"Dicky Campau. I bet anything that's who it was. I had Dicky up for shooting a gator, used a rifle he keeps in his truck. Listen, you call out to the Glades tell 'em to be careful, hear? Approach with caution."

Kathy watched the judge lean back in his chair and look over, his old self again and proud of it. He said, "I'd like you to ride out to the house with me. One of the deputies can drive you back after."

Dicky and Inez were in the kitchen, Dicky getting a drink of water at the sink. He wished it was to chase a good belt of Seagram's, but knew if he started drinking Inez would get on him and it would take the pleasure from it. She was snapping beans at the kitchen table where she had snapped at him all the time he was on the phone. That was what got him confused. Trying to talk and listen to her at the same time. When he told her the judge had hung up, Inez said, "I don't wonder. You sounded like you were asking him a favor. I said tell the son of a bitch here's the deal, whether you like it or not. *He's* the one wanted the gator. We didn't even get her hide out of it."

Inez had been after him ever since the alligator was

in the paper, like it was his fault. She'd been the one said the alligator was dead.

"You told me don't say too much."

"I told you don't say your name. Let him figure it out."

"I'm pretty sure he did."

"Then how come he hung up on you? If you had said what I told you instead of thinking up your own words . . ."

Dicky, looking out the kitchen window with the glass of water in his hand, said, "Inez?"

"What?"

"They's deputies in the yard with shotguns."

"Well, you're the talker," Inez said. "Ask what they want."

The first time Elvin woke up that morning he went out to the hall and banged on doors till Hector came out of one in his robe and an ugly disposition. Elvin got a couple of painkillers off him and went back to bed. No sooner was he lying there he smelled the go-go whore, her perfume, jumped up and went out to bang on Hector's door again, wanting to know where Earlene was. Hector said, "I drove her home. You don't remember?" Elvin said oh, yeah. Got back in bed again and let the painkillers put him under.

The next time he woke up, dying of thirst, dust blowing around in his head, it was past noon. He left the guest room this time in his undershorts and cowboy boots, a cold beer in mind, and ran into Hector standing in the hall, Hector with big eyes and a finger pressed to his mouth.

"The hell's wrong with you?"

"A policeman is here."

"So? I ain't done nothing."

Elvin made a move for the stairway and Hector took hold of his arm. "He ask to know are you here."

Elvin pulled his arm free. "Where's he at?" Hector gestured with his head and Elvin moved to the French doors that opened on the sun deck.

There they were by the swimming pool. Dr. Tommy, bare naked except for his anklet, hands on his hips, talking to the cop in the dark-blue suit. Elvin *knew* it was going to be him. The one pulled his hair, Ms. Touchy's boyfriend.

Elvin hurried back to the guest room, his head fuzzed but feeling purpose, an urge to get it done and not let anything stop him. He saw his suit of clothes and Earlene's G-string hanging over the back of a chair. Saw the empty Scotch bottle on the bureau, what had hung him over the way Beam never did, squeezed his skull. Was he still tanked? Some. Enough not to give a shit. What he didn't see anyplace was his gun, the Ruger Speed-Six. He noticed Hector in the doorway watching and asked him, "Have you seen my piece?"

"What?"

"My goddamn three-fifty-seven."

"It isn't your gun."

Elvin, looking through the bedcovers now, catching whiffs of the rock whore's perfume, straightened up quick.

"You take it?"

"It isn't *yours*."

Now he was ducking out of the room. Elvin tore after him, caught the dink in a headlock right by the stairway and almost threw him down it, he wanted to so bad.

"You gonna tell me where it's at?"

What was the guy doing, crying?

Man, this was a creepy place. The doctor out there bare naked talking to a cop and this dink whimpering like a girl, begging not to be hurt.

"Where'd he go?"

Dr. Tommy looked up to see Elvin at the top of the stairs to the sun deck: Elvin in his cowboy hat and underwear holding a revolver, bare legs, boots planted in a stance to keep him erect. The man still drunk.

"His beeper went off and he left."

"He was asking about me, was he?"

"He wanted to know do you work here." Dr. Tommy saw Hector appear on the deck, somewhat behind the assassin in his underwear. "I told him you come by now and then, work in the yard. What were you going to do, shoot him?"

"I wouldn't mind."

He wouldn't mind. Dr. Tommy scratched his stomach looking up at the deck. Elvin wouldn't mind shooting the policeman. He wouldn't mind shooting the judge. Hector wouldn't mind shooting Elvin, or pushing him down those stairs. . . . What is it, Dr. Tommy thought, you wouldn't mind? More than anything.

Right now?

Well, a twenty-five-dollar rock and a decent bong, not a beer can, to start with.

21

They drove out to his house in what Gibbs called "the Dodge Motorcade," a green-and-white leading and two unmarked cars following the one they were in, Wesley the TAC cop driving, Gibbs talkative.

He said to Kathy, "I miss my pickup. You know what's a kick? Drive over to Palm Beach for a function and have one of their cops stop me. Wait for him to swagger up to the window and then let him have it. I've been to places, these big condo layouts, drive up to the gate going to a cocktail party, the security guard says, 'No trucks after five P.M.' I look at him. 'Boy, you happen to know who you're addressing?' "

He said, "I'm getting too much attention of the wrong kind. What I need is a good capital felony, an open-and-shut first-degree murder. Send the defendant up to sit in Old Sparky and get my image restored." Kathy saw Wesley's eyes in the rearview mirror and Gibbs said, "Boy, watch the road. Never mind what's going on back here. You TAC guys are on the ball, but I can't say you're fun to live with." Two inside the house at all times, he told Kathy, another four placed around the property. The TAC guys in the cars following them would relieve the crew that was here all day. They turned into the gravel drive, Gibbs saying, "They're quiet as mice, but you know they're around. We'll sit and relax, have a drink, talk of something pleasant for a change. Then I'll show you my garden."

"I've seen it," Kathy said.

He told Ms. Spunky, well, you haven't seen *everything*.

She was not as appreciative as Stephanie, now selling real estate, damn it, in Orlando. Steph would love the motorcade, all the attention. He might've misread this one. She didn't just talk to be talking like most girls he knew. Barely spoke till they were in the garage, going in the house, then looks at the pile of trash waiting to be picked up and asks if they delivered pizzas way out here. He told her he wouldn't know. Cops ate pizza, he didn't.

Now they were settled on the porch with drinks and the first thing she said, looking at the patched screen:

"I was surprised, the guy on the phone mentioning the alligator."

He should never have put that call on the speaker.

"It surprised me too. Least I won't get any calls here, the number's unlisted. I'll have to play the tapes for you sometime, the ones called hoping to see me killed. You imagine the kind of person would do that?"

"He seemed to think you'd know who he was."

"Well, last week I fined a poacher five hundred bucks. I mentioned him, Dicky Campau? Shot a gator in the Palm Beach Canal."

"But he was talking about the one in your yard."

Bob Gibbs saw he had to take another tack. He hated to act dumb, give this girl the wrong impression. "Well, the only thing I can think of . . . he's the same one brought the gator. Put it in the yard beforehand, mad as hell, *knowing* he was gonna get a heavy fine. What do you think?" He saw her start to tell him and moved on saying, "The guy's wife was in court at the sentencing. Now there's a woman *looks* like an alligator, homeliest female I ever saw." Hoping to slide off the subject.

No, Ms. Spunky stayed with it saying, "Didn't he want to make some kind of deal?"

Why was she asking these questions? A girl. Cops, you told them how you saw it and they got the picture, fast, they knew how the system worked. He wasn't worried about Dicky Campau. Maybe he was for a minute there on the phone till he realized, hell, whatever story Dicky told would be an offender's word against his. So pick him up, let him say whatever he wanted.

Now he couldn't remember what it was she'd asked him.

It didn't matter. She had another question. "You think he's the one shot at us?"

Gibbs almost said, Who, Dicky? before he realized it wasn't a bad question. Why couldn't it be Dicky? Kept a rifle in his pickup. He'd even mentioned it to the TAC cop. When he did, though, he wasn't thinking of Dicky as the shooter. He saw Ms. Spunky waiting to know what he thought.

"Honey, are you reading my mind or what? I thought of Dicky Campau as we lay there on the ground, before the shots had even faded out. How's your drink?"

"It's fine. But you didn't mention him to the sheriff and his guys."

"I wanted to think about it awhile first."

"Did you mention him to anyone before he called?"

"Let's see now. All last week I had a full schedule, plus these TAC guys in my hair . . . You could use some ice."

She said, "How would he know where Dale was?"

Gibbs had their glasses now, leaving the porch. "I'll be right back."

In the kitchen he dialed his buddy McKenna's home number.

"Bill, I think they're picking up Dicky Campau on one of the anonymous calls."

"They already have," the colonel said.

"They should look for his rifle."

"They have it too. It's in the lab."

"Let me know, all right?"

"Soon as I hear."

He doused their glasses with bourbon and took a good sip of his, beginning to believe he might have to strangle this girl if he couldn't get her drunk. Maybe this wasn't a good time to be thinking of romance. Gibbs opened the back door and stepped into the garage. Wesley and another TAC guy were out in the driveway talking. Gibbs said, "Wes?" and watched him look this way.

"Sir?"

"Ms. Baker's ready to go home."

Wesley had the radio tuned to a top-forty station before they were out of the drive. He asked Kathy if she wanted something else. She said no, that's fine. But then reached over and turned down the volume.

They were on Southern Boulevard before he said, "So you're a friend of the judge's, huh?"

She shrugged, her mind on something else.

"You want my opinion, he's too old for you."

"He is," Kathy said. "You ever stay at his house?"

"You mean, on security detail? Every night."

"What do you have to eat?"

"What do we *eat*?"

"What kind of meals do you have? You cook or send out?"

"We cook on his grill."

"You know any evidence techs?"

With each question he'd glance at her.

"I know every one of them."

"Would they bring pizza on a job?"

"Pizza?"

"Last Thursday night, at the judge's house."

"When the guy shot at him?"

"Yeah, would they bring a pizza?"

"You kidding? With the sheriff there?"

They didn't say anything for several minutes. Wesley turned the volume up a notch. Coming to Military Trail he asked if she'd like to stop for a beer. Kathy told him she had to pick up her car at the courthouse and get home. They drove along. Wesley turned the volume down again.

"I usually work undercover."

"When you're not baby-sitting?"

"Yeah." He liked her remembering that and grinned. "I make buys, set up the bust. Since I've been with TAC we've busted seventeen dope houses I was in on. One time I run around to the backyard and here's this dude coming out with a MAC-ten in his hand. I'm cocked, I got the tension off the trigger. I go, 'Put it down, man, or you're fuckin' dead.' I mean it was close."

"Have you ever shot anyone?"

"Not yet."

She drove home on that one. "Not yet." Dark now, almost seven. Traffic on the freeway erratic, slow drivers in the fast lane. Have you ever shot anyone? Gary said no; her brothers, even Tony, said no and she had the feeling they hoped they'd never have to. But there were cops who believed it would happen or who looked for the chance. *Not yet.* Maybe the next time he was cocked, tension off the trigger . . . She parked in the lot in front of her apartment building, got out, locked the VW. A door slammed in the dark.

Gary walked up without saying a word and kissed her. He tried to step back, but she had hold of his tie and wouldn't let go until they'd kissed again, putting some meaning into it. Now they could play around.

She said, "I think my affair with the judge is over. I ask too many questions. How was your day?"

He said, "I heard about Dicky Campau and I learned Dr. Tommy has a dark-brown penis. It's almost black."

She said, "We always have something to talk about, don't we? Let's go upstairs and have a beer."

He said, "How about coming with me first. I want you to meet somebody. It won't take long, she has to be at work by nine."

"What is she, a hooker?"

He smiled. "Part-time. There's your cop instinct again. Earlene dances topless at a joint on Lake Worth Road and turns tricks on the side."

"To buy crack and beam up," Kathy said. "Outside of

that, and having a name like Earlene, what's her problem? No, wait. Her pimp beats her up and she's pregnant."

"I'm sorry I mentioned your instinct. You want me to tell you, or you'd rather keep guessing?"

"She owes her dealer and *he* beat her up." Talkative because she was glad to see him.

"It's nothing like that. This girl, Earlene, told a friend of hers about a guy she was with and the friend, who did sell drugs at one time, happens to be a confidential informant of mine. He tells me about it, says she's afraid of this guy and doesn't know what to do. I'm interested, so my informant gets back to her. Will she talk to me? Well, she's a little nervous about it and he has to convince her it's okay."

"This is a very devoted snitch you have."

"He cooperates with us, like any good citizen."

"Or you'll put him away."

Gary said, "We all have choices to make, don't we? But he does want to help his friend. He's worried about her."

"So you got to talk to her?"

"Just a little while ago. What's bothering her, a john she was with told her he's going to kill somebody. He said he's already killed one guy. Now he's going to do it again, and if she doesn't believe him, watch for it in the paper."

"Elvin," Kathy said.

"Maybe. He took her to a house in Delray."

"It's Elvin. Can she identify him?"

Gary smiled at her in the dark.

"That's where you come in."

Kathy waited in the backseat, the Dodge double-parked in front of a rundown apartment house in Lake

Worth. Gary brought her out to the car: a girl in her early twenties, long hair, pale skinny arms in a tank top, a small shoulder bag in her hand, holding on to it. Don't leave home without your stash, or at least something. Gary opened the door for her and she hesitated, seeing Kathy in back. Gary said, "Earlene, this is Kathy Baker, the probation officer I mentioned. The guy we're talking about might be one of her cases." He got her in and closed the door.

Kathy said, "How are you, Earlene?"

No answer. Earlene tossed her head, getting her hair out of her eyes, watching Gary circle the car. He acted different. As soon as they were moving he said, "We're off," like they were going for a ride in the country. Then, on the way, gave his views of the weather, the traffic, ethnic restaurants along Federal Highway: Gary making small talk—it was funny—to the part-time prostitute smoking cigarettes, nodding to some beat in her head, not saying a word. Earlene had told Gary she remembered the street in Delray but didn't know the address. Maybe if she saw the house. Kathy asked what night it was he brought her there. Earlene said Saturday. Kathy asked if the guy wore a cowboy hat and Earlene said, hey, yeah, that's right. Gary turned into the street of old frame houses and trees. Pulling up in front of Dale's he said, "Is this the one?"

Earlene wasn't sure. She said, "I can tell by the inside, but I'm not going in if he's there. No way."

Gary looked at Kathy in the backseat. "You mind?"

"You can see no one's home."

"For Earlene?"

For Earlene—for Gary. Save him the trouble of getting a warrant.

"If the door's locked, do I break in?"

"My guys checked yesterday. You can push it open."

That's what Kathy did, walked in and turned on the lamp without a shade, then the lights in the kitchen and the bedroom. Gary brought Earlene in. She said, "This's the house. Man, all the beer bottles and shit." She crossed to the bedroom but didn't go in. "This's where he practically raped me."

Gary said, "Practically?"

"He was so rough, and he smelled. I go, 'How can you live in a rat hole like this and drive a Cadillac?' and he got pissed."

Gary glanced at Kathy.

"He was driving a Cadillac? You didn't mention that."

"Yeah, a black one."

Earlene walked over to the kitchen, Kathy watching the way she moved in her short skirt and backless heels in a kind of confident slouch, a low-speed sway to her hips. She kept her hand on the small beaded purse hanging from her shoulder. Earlene was looking in the kitchen now.

"Jesus—see that thing? He stuck it up my nose."

The shank made from a spoon, lying on the kitchen table. Gary edged past her and picked it up. "I thought he didn't threaten you."

"It was when I said the place looked like a rat hole? He goes, 'You calling me a nigger?' I forgot that part. See, it was right then he told me he had killed a guy and was gonna do it again."

Gary prompted her saying, "And if you didn't believe him . . ."

"Yeah, I'd see it in the paper."

"But even if there was a story about a homicide," Gary said, "how were you supposed to know he did it?"

"He said it would be a big headline on the front page, with a picture. Not some nigger got killed."

"You went in the bedroom then?"

"Yeah, and the bed smelled worse'n he did."

"He mention it again, after? About killing someone?"

"Not a word." Earlene turned from the kitchen. "Or last night either."

She moved in a kind of slow motion that seemed natural to her, heels scuffing the floor. Gary came out of the kitchen shaking his head at Kathy. One surprise after another.

"Earlene? You were here again last night?"

We went to a guy's house, over on the beach."

Gary looked at Kathy again.

"What's his name?"

"I don't know, some guy."

"Where was it, Palm Beach, Lantana, Ocean Ridge?"

"I don't know, one of those. He made me get down on the floor. In the car, going over there."

"He was driving the Cadillac?"

Earlene frowned. "It might've been a different car. This other guy drove me home. He didn't make me get on the floor, but I was so bummed out it didn't matter. I'm getting out of the car this little greaseball goes, 'Don't ever come back again.' I go, 'Hey, I came with a guy has a key to the house, if you don't fucking mind, okay?' This's a guy that *works* there talking to me like that."

"Would you know the house if you saw it again?"

"I didn't *see* the house, where it's at. You understand? Hey, can we go? Jesus."

Getting antsy. Beamed up on the way here and now

coming down. Kathy went over to her. "You have something, don't you, take the edge off?"

Earlene said, "You gotta be kidding," her eyes going to Gary watching them.

"No, it's okay," Kathy said, moving Earlene to the sofa and easing her into it. She sat down next to her saying, "You have something in that purse, don't you, help you relax? It's okay, really. He doesn't care."

Earlene opened her purse, glancing at Gary again. She brought out a pack of cigarettes and a book of matches. Kathy took the matches. Earlene worked a thin, tightly rolled joint from the cigarette pack and Kathy gave her a light. Earlene sat back in the sofa to take long, slow drags, Kathy sniffing that familiar aroma, wondering if Gary ever smoked grass. She and Dr. Baker would do it on weekends when he was still in school, using forceps for a roach clip, Keith the only person she knew who could smoke and never crack a smile.

She said to Earlene, "The guy who owns the house, what was he like?"

"He was nice."

"You go to bed with him?"

"He wasn't in the mood. He said next time."

"You're going back there?"

"Maybe. I don't know."

"The guy in the cowboy hat, he and the guy who owns the house must be pretty good friends."

"They didn't act it especially."

"Didn't you say the one who took you had a key to the house?"

"He opened the front door with it," Earlene said. "Oh, and he got all dressed up for me. Had on the ugliest suit I've ever seen in my life."

"Pretty bad, uh?"

"It was this real bright blue. You had to see it."

"You go to bed with him last night?"

"Yeah, and you know what? The son of a bitch never paid me. The first time in my life I didn't ask for it up front, that's what happens. I go, 'Hey, come on, man, I don't give freebies.' He says it was for fun, like I get laid on my day off. I'm still sore. He tells me, when he picked me up? Bring my G-string, they're gonna pay me to dance. Only all they have is a bunch of South American cha-cha shit. The nice one gave me a hundred bucks. But you know what? I left my G-string there. My best one, black with silver sequins on it."

"I'll see if I can get it," Kathy said. She gave Earlene's arm a pat, got up from the sofa and motioned to Gary. They went into the kitchen. She said, "Is Elvin living there now?"

"It sounds like it."

"She isn't upset that he's going to kill someone. It's because he didn't *pay* her."

Gary was nodding. "I got that."

"You want to know something else?" Kathy stepped to the table and picked up an empty "Pizza from Pisa" carton. "There's one just like this at the judge's house, and he never eats pizza."

She was thinking that getting one on the way here was a mistake. Or they should have gone to bed as soon as they walked in the apartment and microwaved it later instead of opening cans of beer, sitting down with the pizza and arguing about a flat square cardboard box that had held another pizza at one time and was in the judge's garage, Elvin Crowe's fingerprints all over it.

Gary said, "If you're lucky."

He was eating his pizza with a fork.

She said, "Okay, maybe not all over it. Maybe you get only one or two good latents. How many do you need?" She said, "If you have trouble seeing yourself walking in the Sheriff's Office with a pizza box, let me do it."

Bad. Much too confident, even brash. When he didn't smile she wanted to take it back and was afraid now his tone would be condescending, putting her in her place. It wasn't, it was polite. So she had to be polite and listen. He was methodical, maybe a little cool, telling her this is what you have and this is what you don't.

"Assuming we're able to lift prints that match Elvin's, we'll know he had the box in his hand at one time or another. But that doesn't necessarily place him at the judge's house last Thursday night. Let's say we have evidence to show the box was there in the kitchen. We know the judge doesn't eat pizza and the evidence techs didn't bring it. That still doesn't mean Elvin did. Even if you could somehow place him at the house," Mr. Methodical went on, "there's no way you can prove criminal intent. What did he do? Did he break in, take anything? Not that we know of."

"He was there," Kathy said. "I saw him."

"You maintain you saw *some*thing, or someone."

"Yeah, that's what I do, I maintain."

"Isn't that what you told me?"

"Gary, we know he wants to kill the judge."

"Or someone. And we have that on hearsay from a not too reliable witness who claims he owes her money for engaging in unlawful sexual congress."

"You make it sound political."

"I'll run Dr. Tommy through Motor Vehicles. If he

owns a Cadillac, it'll be put on the list to watch for. And we'll locate Elvin and keep an eye on him. What else do you want?"

"Get hold of the pizza box," Kathy said. "It connects him to the judge and you might need it."

She watched him shrug, take a sip of beer and pick up his fork. She didn't want to argue, feel that knot in her stomach. "There's another piece," Kathy said. "Would you like it?"

He was chewing and shook his head.

"Would you like to go to bed?"

He swallowed and said, "Get political?"

She felt better already. "Engage in a little congress."

It was nice. Maybe even nicer than the first time. They were getting to know each other. His beeper went off in the silence. He said, "Work work work," slipped his shorts on and went out to the phone in the living room.

Light from the window lay across the sheet pulled over her. She listened for the sound of his voice, but heard nothing. He was quiet. She liked that. She wondered if he thought she was too emotional. He worked criminal investigations and was methodical. He'd better be. There was nothing wrong with eating pizza with a fork or arranging magazines in chronological order. He had a new album by one of the Dire Straits guys, *The Notting Hillbillies,* she should've mentioned to Michelle, who liked his hair but didn't know him at all. He had a nice body too. She saw it in the living room light, coming to the bed now in his white shorts.

"Dicky Campau signed a statement. He did the shooting."

She said, "Now what?"

"That's it, the case is closed."

22

Kathy's friend Marialena Reyes, the assistant state attorney, said, "His bond was set at fifty thousand, so Dicky will be in at least another six to eight weeks, till the arraignment."

"His lawyer accepted that?"

"He didn't want to. But I told him before the hearing, try to live with whatever the judge comes up with and we'll talk about it after. That's what took me so long."

It was Tuesday morning. They were in the snack bar on the first floor of the Palm Beach County courthouse, standing at a counter against the wall with their coffee, Marialena telling Kathy about Dicky Campau's probable cause hearing.

"The lawyer looks at all this stuff Dicky told the sheriff's people and sees it as unusual and mitigating circumstances, enough to get Dicky released on his own recognizance. And he has a point, there's considerably more to this than meets the eye. But I've already been prepped, in fact told what to do." Marialena took a sip of coffee. "I'm referring not to the shooting, but the business with the alligator."

Kathy said, "Gary filled me in on some of it. That's not in Dicky's statement, is it?"

"No, of course not. Just the shooting."

"But he claims Gibbs ordered him to bring the alligator to his house. Isn't that it?"

"His story is he was given a choice. Bring the alligator or do time on a poaching charge hanging over him. Dicky says if the alligator had been dead—he thought it was—none of this would have happened. He says he doesn't know why Gibbs wanted a dead alligator, but was in no position to refuse. Our office talked to Gibbs this morning, he flatly denies having anything to do with it. So we have to assume Dicky's lying." Marialena shrugged inside the wide shoulders of her brown linen suit. "Why would Gibbs want an alligator delivered to his house? It doesn't make sense."

It wasn't asked as a question, so Kathy didn't tell her. She said, "But the alligator business will come up at the arraignment, won't it?"

"That's what I spoke to Dicky's lawyer about," Marialena said. "I told him we don't see any merit in getting Judge Gibbs involved, since Dicky's story won't hold up anyway. If he'll plead to shooting into a dwelling, a second-degree fifteen-year felony, we'll offer six months county time and probation. But if Dicky insists on talking about alligators, then we'll offer him the whole fifteen years."

"What'd the lawyer say?"

"Nothing, but he'll take it. He doesn't have a choice. I came out of the hearing, I thought Dicky's wife was going to take a swing at me. You ever see her, Inez Campau?"

Kathy shook her head. "I don't think so."

"We're accepting as mitigating circumstances Dicky was drunk," Marialena said. "TAC did find an empty pint bottle with his prints and there wasn't anyone in the house he could have been shooting at, so . . . By the end of the year Dicky could be one of your cases. No, that's right, he lives in Belle Glade. Thank God for small favors, uh? You won't have to meet his wife."

"He did say he was shooting at the house?"

"At the kitchen window. His explanation, because he was mad at the judge. And, of course, drunk."

"He didn't see anyone."

"If you were both outside, how could he?"

"I mean, I wonder if he thought he was shooting at someone, in the window."

"He ever admits that, we're talking about attempted murder," Marialena said. "Let's keep it simple."

Kathy said, "Oh shit," and Marialena looked around.

Bob Gibbs was already in the snack bar, the judge in shirtsleeves, grinning, raising his hand to people, Kathy thought like he was giving them his blessing. He came over to where they stood at the counter against the wall, saying, "Well, they've called off the dogs, I'm a free man again. Marialena, honey, would you excuse us? I have something to say to this little girl."

Marialena stooped to get her briefcase. "I was leaving anyway, Judge."

"I have to go too," Kathy said. "I have appointments at the office." She picked up her purse from the counter and Gibbs put his hand on her arm.

"Offenders are used to waiting," Gibbs said. "They spend their life waiting for trial, waiting to get out of jail . . . Listen, I'm free of those TAC boys, there's nobody shooting at me, so I'm safe to be with. I'm thinking, why don't you and I go out and have some din-din this evening?"

"No more protection around you?" Kathy said.

"Don't need it."

"You know that man wasn't shooting at you."

"He claims he wasn't and I'll accept that. I'm just glad to get those strangers out of my house."

"But what if there is someone who wants to kill you?"

"Listen, I got another one of those phone calls this morning. Some cuckoo, he'll get picked up and thrown in jail for it. But now they'll read in the paper the shooter was apprehended and it'll be over. The nuts'll have to think of something else to do."

"Maybe," Kathy said, "but I don't think so." She tucked her purse under her arm. "They shouldn't have pulled the protection off you. Not yet."

"You're concerned about my welfare?"

"I don't want to see you get shot."

"Honey, that's the nicest thing anybody's ever said to me. Let's have dinner this evening. Come on."

"I'm sorry, I really can't."

"You have a date?"

"I just won't do it."

"If you're afraid of us being seen, come out to the house. I'm all by myself now, my wife gone, run out on me."

"I thought she was visiting friends."

"Yeah, but now it doesn't look like she's coming back."

"She afraid," Kathy said, "another alligator might show up?"

Gibbs stared back at her with a mild expression that

was almost a smile, a gleam, mischief in his eyes. This old-man judge acting like a little kid with a secret.

"You don't think I'd have a live ten-foot gator brought to my home, do you?"

"I heard it was supposed to be dead."

"You believe that story?"

Kathy said, "Yeah, I guess I do," nodding.

Now he did grin at her. "See, that's why I like you. You aren't afraid to speak right up to my face. I saw it that time in my court I called you Ms. Bacar?"

"You always called me that."

"You know the time I mean. You said, 'It's Baker, Your Honor. It's *always* been Baker.' I got a kick out of the way you stood up to me. You know what I thought? Why I wanted to talk to you after? I thought, well, I'll be damned, this girl and I think the same way."

"Excuse me," Kathy said, "but you gave Dale Crowe five years and I tried to argue that was excessive."

"You're being picky now. What I'm talking about, you and I aren't afraid to say what we believe. Hell, we could have more fun disagreeing with one another than most people have getting along. Listen, I can show you some sights, take you to society functions over in Palm Beach'll knock your eyes out. Argue all the way over there and back."

"We can talk about anything?"

"Pick a subject."

"If you made Dicky Campau bring that alligator . . ."

"Who says? Listen, you want to know the honest truth? I told him bring me a little bitty one sometime. For fun, not to hurt anybody. I'd forgot all about it. Then one morning there it was. Yeah, it scared Leanne and she left. Of her own free will."

There was that gleam in his eyes again.

"Why don't you let him off?"

"Who, Dicky? It's out of my hands. Listen, if he appeared in my court for sentencing I'd give him at least five years. You can't fire a gun at somebody's house and get away with it. But since it was *my* house I'd have to recuse myself anyway, step aside. So they'll cut a deal, offer him six months and he'd be dumber than he looks if he doesn't take it."

Kathy said, "And no one'll ever know . . ."

"It's no one else's business. I can tell you 'cause we think alike and I know I can trust you with a personal matter," Gibbs said, leaning on the counter close to her, confiding. She could smell his aftershave, look into his sad brown eyes and see a movie actor playing the judge, reciting his lines in the courthouse snack bar. He said, "You know I could be influential in your behalf. Couple of years from now see you named head of the Probation Department. How's that sound to you? Big step up, lot more money."

"Run a probation office," Kathy said, "what I've always wanted to do."

Gibbs, still with the sad look, said, "It's a shame, you've got devilment in you going to waste. Well, I'm not gonna get down on my knees and beg, I'm feeling too frisky for that. You don't want to have fun, there's plenty others'll jump at the chance."

Elvin sat in Dr. Tommy's gray Lincoln across the street from the Probation Office, a queer-looking pink building, two stories, but hardly any windows in it. Maybe so the poor assholes getting questioned in there would pay attention and not be looking outside, thinking of better places to be; though what you saw around here was all industrial, places to work and the sound of the freeway close by. Elvin had been in Ms. Touchy's office on the second floor when he first reported. Sat cooped up in that dark-paneled shoebox while she filled out a postsentence form on him. Prison time. Extent of Victim's Loss or Injury. Socioeconomic Status. What? Vocational Skills. Alcohol Usage. Hobbies. Shit. He was thinking of going up there again to give her his new address, except now he forgot what it was. Six something, three other numbers, North Ocean Boulevard. He'd have to make it up. Tell Ms. Touchy he was working full-time over there on security and when she came to check on him bring her swimsuit. Or don't wear one if she didn't want to. Go in bareass like Dr. Tommy. Not a stitch on but his anklet, like some creature they had tagged in the wild to keep track of. The doc was turning into a crack dog since the other night with Earlene. When he was high the doc acted nervous and liked to go into his dance. Earlene said there was no such thing as the mumbo, it was the cha-cha. Take her word for it. The doc hardly ever spoke. Hector either. What Hector did was sneak around watching him wherever he went, making it hard to find where the doc kept his cash. Upstairs somewhere. Hector would go up there and come down with a hundred-dollar bill for crack cocaine or to go to the liquor store. About the only time Hector spoke was to ask him, You shoot the judge yet? Elvin believed he might end up shooting Hector. They had picked up none other than little Dicky Campau for shooting at the judge's house. It was in the paper today and Elvin had phoned Inez to ask her the hell was Dicky up to? Ready to tell her Dicky had almost shot *him,* for Christ sake. But nobody was home. What it didn't say in the paper was whether the judge was still being protected or not. Walk in the court building you had to go through metal detectors. So the judge's house was still the place to do it. Get hold of another pizza box once the bodyguards cleared out. Elvin had not noticed any tails on him driving the Lincoln— even though that hair-pulling sissy cop was at Dr. Tommy's yesterday and must've known he was there. It might be since they had Dicky in custody they weren't looking for anybody else.

What'd be funny, press charges against Dicky for trying to shoot him and see Inez's face. Here was still another instance, something you'd like to do but couldn't.

Or ask Ms. Touchy would she like to have noon dinner with him and get turned down. He had always believed Hi-spanic girls would bust their ass to go out with a white man. If Ms. Touchy went with that hair puller she wasn't any different. The thing to do was take the cop out of the picture.

Elvin got out of the car and crossed Omar Road to the building, trying to decide what color it was. Sorta pink, but not exactly. There were two colored boys in the lobby who looked like convicts and two young white guys, addicts of one kind or another. Elvin gave the woman at the reception window his name and Ms. Touchy's and sat down to wait. Now the two white boys were looking him over, boots to cowboy hat, one of them making remarks to the other, grinning like a monkey. Elvin said, "You boys behave now, hear? I'll have to take you outside." The colored boys watched with sleepy looks. Up at Starke they'd tell you same old same old, in that peculiar way they spoke.

A guy in a dark suit of clothes came in the lobby.

Elvin glanced over and then looked again, the guy standing at the reception window now. Jesus Christ, if it wasn't the sissy blue-suit cop, Ms. Touchy's boyfriend. He didn't have to wait there but a minute. Somebody opened the door next to the reception window and was talking to him as he walked in. Elvin watched, thinking, Hey shit, I was here first.

Kathy was waiting for him outside her office. The first thing she said: "Did you see Elvin? He's in the lobby."

Gary walked up to her in the narrow hallway. "There were some guys—I didn't notice." He followed her into the office. "He's here to see you?"

"He was. Should I have him come up?"

"If he's still there."

Kathy said, "I doubt it," turning to her desk. "I should've had the receptionist tell you." She was anxious now. He was too, but in a different way watching her pick up the phone and punch numbers, wanting to touch her, run his hands over familiar places, the feel of her ribs, her stomach sucked in, slim legs around him, seeing her tan lines in the dark and knowing where they were beneath the white skirt she was wearing. "This is Kathy. Is Elvin Crowe still there?" He liked the way her hair was short in back and showed her slender neck. She turned now, looking this way, waiting. He liked the way she moved. He liked her eyes, the way she looked at him and seemed to know things. She said, "Thank you," and hung up, shaking her head. "He left."

Gary smiled; he couldn't help it. "You look good enough to eat."

She gave him that bland, knowing look. "With a fork?"

He said, "With my fingers," and watched her raise her eyebrows and move in a kind of lazy shrug. Another one to remember, store away, along with hooking her thumb in those narrow white panties and cocking a hip. He wanted to take her home, right now, but had to see a man about a Cadillac. He told her that Dr. Vasco, it turns out, owns a Cadillac and Dicky Campau says Dale Crowe was last seen in a Cadillac, driving around with Elvin.

"I'm gonna stop by Dr. Tommy's later on this afternoon, if you'd like to come."

"To get you inside? Sure, why not." She was nodding, thinking of something else now, he could tell. "You wouldn't want to take a quick run out to the judge's house first, would you?"

Gary said, "For what?" without thinking, and said, "Not to look for the pizza box. Don't tell me that, all right?"

"It's evidence," Kathy said.

"Of what? You want to go through it again? Elvin hasn't done anything."

"Not yet."

"Or is planning any kind of criminal act we have evidence of, outside of what a rockhead thinks she remembers him saying."

"But you'd like to talk to him."

"About Dale. Dale's now a fugitive and the Cadillac's a lead."

She said, "All right, I'll go by myself." Matter-of-fact about it, telling him if he didn't want to go, fine. He liked that about her. She was direct, didn't put on any kind of an act to get what she wanted. Telling him now, "I'll pick up the pizza box and I'll put it on your desk, as a favor.

Then it's up to you. You can take it to the lab or throw it away. But if you do, you'll be destroying evidence."

"You're sure of that."

She said, "Reasonably," starting to turn away, and looked at him again. "If you want, you could come along for the ride. I'll drive."

He had to smile at her, wanting to go and said, "I would, really, but I can't. I have to get a haircut."

"You've been saying that for the past week."

"I was leaving to come here, that same captain stopped me."

"The one with the body shirt."

"Yeah, he goes, 'I don't want to see you again, Sergeant, without a haircut. Have I made myself clear?'"

"And you told him," Kathy said, raising her hand to touch his hair, "your goal in life is to live up to his expectations."

"I just told him I'd get it cut."

She said, "That's too bad," moving her fingers through his hair on one side and then smoothing it. "Have it thinned a little here and in back, but not too much, okay? I love your hair."

23

All Elvin had to do was spot the blue-suit cop coming out of the building alone, he changed his mind like that about seeing Ms. Touchy. She'd be around the next five years to fool with. The blue-suit hair puller was here and now and chances didn't come along every day.

Elvin had been sitting in the car with his hat off rubbing the red line it made in his forehead: thinking the two would come out together, it being noontime, and go eat someplace: thinking he'd most likely pick himself up a burger and fries, couple of beers, and come back here to wait on her to get dropped off.

But, Jesus, seeing the hair puller all by himself walking to his car, no idea he was being watched, got Elvin excited with the urge to get it done. Right now. No more thinking about it. The best time always when they least expected. Slip up on him in broad daylight driving along the street maybe. That could work. He had the Ruger Speed-Six in the glove compartment. Or wherever the dink was going, like someplace to have his dinner. Walk in, do it and walk out. Do it so fast nobody in there would see a thing. All this in his mind at once was making him more anxious. There, he was backing his car out now, the gray Dodge, from in front of the building. His name, he'd said that time at Dale's showing his badge, was Gary something. Gary the hair puller.

Man, but strange things happened in life.

Thinking of this squirt grabbing him by the hair.

Thinking, as he followed the Dodge over to Dixie Highway and turned south, he had planned to get a haircut yesterday, but was too hung over to make it.

And where does the Dodge pull up to the curb and park? In front of a place called "Betty's Hair Studio," the name written big across the window.

Wouldn't you know, Elvin thought, looking for a place to park, a hair puller would go to a beauty parlor?

The garage door was closed. That was the first thing Kathy noticed driving up to the house. It gave her a sinking feeling. She got out of her car telling herself it wasn't locked, that all she'd have to do was grab the handle and lift up. She tried. Grabbed it with both hands and tried. Kicked the aluminum door and tried again. It was locked. Shit. Gary would ask her, well where is it? Gary with his new haircut. She caught a glimpse of him as a skinhead and got rid of that one. Saw him with the sides shaved Marine style and crew-cut on top saying to the crew-cut captain in the body shirt he was trying to live up to his expectations. With a straight face. He was actually a cool guy. He acted natural, didn't pose or try to impress anyone. She should have cut his hair last night, in his undershorts. Kathy stepped away from the garage to look at the front of the house, the door, sunlight on the windows. No one home, the place shut tight. She turned, wondering what to do, looking at the dense growth across the drive now, young palms and a lot of fern, and saw the car parked in tree shade.

A Ford Escort, dark blue, nosed into the cover of an old laurel oak.

The judge drove a pickup truck but could have a car too, whether he used it or not; it seemed reasonable. Unless it belonged to someone else, visiting.

Kathy walked to the front door and rang the bell, waited, tried it again. She could hear it ring inside.

The car could belong to a TAC guy still hanging around somewhere. They drove all different kinds of cars, whatever they appropriated. If a TAC guy was here she would have to tell him what she was looking for . . . Oh, a pizza box. Have to go into all that, explain her theory. Or make up a story. She lost an earring. In the garbage? Maybe swept up and thrown in the trash. And thought, You think too much. You know it?

But, if a TAC guy was still around and happened to be out in the yard, he wouldn't have heard the doorbell. She walked back past the attached garage to the north end of the house, looking out at scrub growth and a line of Australian pines in the distance. The canal curved off in that direction toward the lake.

Kathy stopped.

She heard voices. Or thought she did.

Another few steps would take her around the corner to the screened porch and the backyard, the judge's gardens, his orchids hanging in trees. She stood listening before moving again, from coarse grass to the edge of the brick patio in sunlight, looking at the screened porch now, dim inside. Kathy stood motionless.

In the silence a woman's voice, coming from the porch, said, "I told them, I refuse to only work dry. Stand around being a hostess or have to do that awful bird show."

Another voice, much higher, a child's, said, "Wasn' the reason atall."

"It was too."

"You lef' account of your thighs lookin' how they do. Be with those young girls and everybody see how chubby you is now? No, *ma'am.*"

"I am not chubby."

"You is too."

"I am not."

There was a silence.

The woman's voice said, "Is someone there?"

Kathy moved toward the screen door. "I'm sorry to bother you."

"No, please, come in out of the sun."

Kathy said, "Thank you," opening the door and stepping inside.

The woman was alone on the porch.

Pretty in a kind of old-fashioned way, a pleasant smile. Blond hair to her shoulders with a small blue velvet bow to one side. She did appear chubby in her flowery print dress. Nice legs though in a dark shade of hose and white sensible shoes. She stood waiting for Kathy.

"I thought I heard you talking to someone."

"Oh, Wanda. Yes, she left."

"You're Mrs. Gibbs," Kathy said.

"Leanne, please. And I bet I know why you're here."

* * *

They had porch furniture out here where you waited to get your hair done, a table of magazines, a counter full of hair products, and a white lattice fence separating this part of Betty's Hair Studio from where they did the work.

Elvin stepped over to the fence and peeked through the crisscrossed slats. He saw four beauty parlor chairs in there, two on each side, mirrors on the walls behind them, everything the same turquoise color floor to ceiling and nobody in there. He no sooner straightened up he heard a woman talking.

Now when he looked through the fence again he saw the cop, Gary, coming out from the back with a turquoise cloth over him like a cape, his hair wet to his head and this woman leading him, a tiny woman with rouge on her cheeks. She had on a smock that same turquoise color and appeared to be Hi-spanic. She was. Elvin could hear her talking again as she got Gary in the beauty parlor chair and spun him to face the mirror.

Seeing him sitting there, the cloth draped over him, made Elvin think of a book Sonny had read to him up at Starke. Not the whole book, part of it. It was a western where this guy is getting his hair cut, the good guy, and the guy who's supposed to be the bad guy comes in, he's in a hurry, and tells the good guy to get out of the chair. The barber's done with the guy, has slicked down his wavy hair, but now the fucker won't move, acts like a girl and won't get out of the goddamn chair. The guy in a hurry, Frank, has a rifle under his arm. The pissy good guy— Elvin couldn't think of his name—you *know* doesn't have his six-shooter on him, but Frank isn't too sure. He doesn't want to get shot by a gun hidden under that barber cloth.

Elvin stepped back from the latticework and squared his Ox Bow straw over his eyes thinking about that barbershop in the book. A real barbershop, not a beauty parlor. He touched his right-hand suit coat pocket where the Ruger Speed-Six rested heavy. Then unbuttoned the coat.

What happened in the book was Frank got so pissed off at the good guy he stepped up to yank him out of the chair and the guy hit Frank with this mirror he was holding the barber had given him to look at his haircut. Wouldn't fight him like a man, hit him across the head with a mirror.

With the cop, if you got too close and weren't minding, he'd pull your hair. There was no doubt in Elvin's mind this cop had his gun on him. Except it was around on his hip and would be wedged down in there between him and the beauty parlor chair. Watch his right shoulder. If he lifted it he'd be going for the gun.

Elvin readjusted his hat, put it lower on his eyes. Now he brought the revolver out of the pocket and slipped it into the waist of his pants, a bit to the left side, and closed the suit coat over it. There. Ready?

He took another peek through the latticework. The beauty parlor woman was snipping away at the cop's wet hair now.

Ready.

Elvin walked in. He saw the woman pause, holding her comb and scissors in the air. He saw the cop raise his head and saw his eyes in the mirror. Elvin said, "You do men in this place or just women and sissies?"

"I felt you in my energy field," Leanne said to Kathy, "so I knew you were there. But it's so bright out I didn't see your aura good till you came inside."

Kathy said, "You can see it?"

"Oh, my yes, it's a soft blue. You're acquainted with the judge—you should see his aura."

"I think I have, almost."

"You'd know if you did. Here, let's sit down." Leanne pulled a chair out from the metal table. "You came for a psychic reading, didn't you? Not knowing I've moved. Well, I haven't *act*ually moved. I've left here but haven't as yet relocated. There'll be a notice in *The Third Eye* and some of the other papers when I do. I have to be going pretty soon, but sit down, please. I only stopped by to get something I forgot."

Kathy took a chair next to her saying, "When you left here, you went up to Weeki Wachee?"

"I did," Leanne said, "with the idea of picking up where I left off. But then after I thought about it a while I decided no, I have another life now."

Kathy watched Leanne's eyelids begin to flutter.

The other voice, the child's, came out of her saying, "What you have is thighs shake when you walks."

"They do not."

The child's voice said, "Try and zip up a mermaid tail, see how far you gets."

"You hush up."

Leanne closed her mouth, tight, Kathy watching. Now she closed her eyes for a moment, opened them and said, "Wanda's been picking on me ever since I left Big."

"You mind if I ask," Kathy said, "how you do that?" Not sure what to call it.

"Communicate with my spirit guide? Oh, there's different ways." Leanne leaned toward Kathy, confiding now. "You can resonate by grounding yourself to the earth. See, that allows you to vibrate at a higher level, so you become a conduit for the other being. But now

Wanda," Leanne said, sitting back again, "she sneaks in on my energy level just about whenever she wants. I love her dearly, but she's getting to be a pest. See, she's upset 'cause I left."

Kathy said, "She wants you to stay here?" and saw the woman's eyelids flutter.

"She ain' finish her woik," the child's voice said.

Leanne's eyes blinked. She said, "Now you stop that. When I want to hear from you I'll get in touch." Looking at Kathy again Leanne said, "Wanda gave me a time in the car, driving up to Weeki. Kept grabbing the steering wheel to turn us around. I don't know why we didn't have an accident."

"There's so much I'd like to ask you," Kathy said, hunching over the table now. "You don't mind?"

"It's what I'm here on earth for," Leanne said. "To answer those who ask." Her eyes for an instant began to glaze and she straightened, hitting the table hard with the edge of her fist. "No! Now you stay put, darn it."

Kathy waited a moment. "Are you all right?"

"I'm fine."

"I won't ask you anything personal."

"I've spoken to thousands of people," Leanne said. "My life is literally an open book."

"Well, something I've always wondered about—when you're performing underwater, how do you stay down? I mean keep from rising up."

"Controlling your depth, a lot of it is in the breathing, something you have to learn. You don't just put on a tail and you're a mermaid." Leanne cocked her head, her eyes shining with an inner wisdom. "When people from out of town ask how do you get to Weeki? A mermaid will always answer, 'Practice.'"

"That's good," Kathy said. "Do you mind talking about the alligator?"

"Which one? The one here or at Weeki?"

"Both, I guess. The one at Weeki first."

"You want the whole story? My out-of-body experience and what happened in the hospital after?"

"Everything," Kathy said.

"Well, it began just after one in the afternoon of a gorgeous day." Leanne's gaze moved to the backyard. "I remember rising from the underwater chamber behind the screen of air bubbles we use as a curtain and seeing the surface of the spring, above me, shimmering in bright sunlight . . ."

As soon as Gary was in the chair she turned him around and he saw their faces close together in the mirror: Gary's pale next to her bright glow of makeup, the woman coming on to him, running her hands over his shoulders as she studied his reflection. She was in her fifties, not bad looking, full of energy. Sang to him in Spanish shampooing his hair in the back room.

"I just want a trim."

"Don't worry, I take good care of you. Like last time."

"I don't think you've cut my hair."

"I haven't? Good-looking guy like you? I'm surprise. You sure you don't have me before?"

"I'd remember you."

She liked that. Getting her comb and scissors from the counter she gave him a wink.

"Are you Betty?"

"Of course. Who else? Maybe it was Helen you had. Helen quit. No, it must be it was Isabel. You like how she fix your hair?"

"Yeah, that's why I came back."

"It was Isabel. She isn't come in yet, has trouble with her car. But listen, I can take care of you good, don't worry. Put your head down." She began working on him, humming, hitting her scissors against the comb in rhythm.

Gary raised his eyes to the mirror, saw his head sticking out of the turquoise cover, Betty lifting his wet hair and snipping with a flourish, moving her shoulders as she hummed. He thought of Kathy touching his hair and then saw her in bed in early morning light, her eyes coming open and for a moment or so not aware of him. Both times when they were together and she woke up, felt him close and there he was, she said, "What're you doing?" A murmur, sleep still in her voice. He said, "I'm looking at you." His head raised from the pillow. He was so close to her she said the first time, yesterday morning, "You must need glasses." This morning she looked at him and didn't say anything, waiting, and he said, "I love to look at you." She said, "We're moving right along, aren't we?" with that quiet expression in her eyes, knowing things. She raised her hand to his face, touched his mouth with the tips of her fingers . . .

He saw the cowboy hat in the mirror.

Elvin saying, "You do men in this place or just women and sissies?" And Betty turning, saying to him, "We do everybody. Have a seat, mister. You next."

Gary almost said his name, but now the hat was gone from the mirror. He waited and finally heard Elvin say, "Is that you, Officer?" And Betty say, "Oh, you know each other?" She swiveled the chair around and now Gary was facing him, Elvin saying, "I thought you were some woman getting a marcel," as he eased into the chair across from Gary's, filling it with his bright blue suit.

Gary said, "You getting a haircut?"

Elvin smoothed the front of his suit coat. "Yeah, and I'm in a hurry too."

Betty said, "Isabel will be here soon. You wait, okay?"

"I never had nobody name Isabel cut my hair," Elvin said, "or been in a beauty parlor."

Then why did he come? Gary thought, Betty saying, "We do hair designs. This is no beauty parlor, no. But I can make you beautiful if you want, mister. Fix you up."

"I wouldn't mind being beautiful," Elvin said, "if I don't have to wait."

"Isabel, she be here soon."

"But I don't want Isabel. I want you."

"Sure, in a few minutes. It won't be long."

"I mean I want you right now," Elvin said.

"The reason I came back," Leanne said, "I left my rare and beautiful window crystal buried in the backyard." She looked out that way. "See the two petticoat palms? They look like women, don't they, in fancy dress. The crystal is buried between them."

"In the ground?"

"To revitalize its energy. The earth, you know, has wonderful restorative powers. What a window crystal does," Leanne said, "used for meditation, it allows you to look into your soul and see the real you. Not the one you see in the mirror, the one you're pretending to be."

Kathy said, "Oh."

"It's like using a crystal ball to see things about yourself aurawise, you might say."

"You can see into the future with it?"

"Some. Or you can use it to locate missing persons or help others see themselves. If I aimed a window crystal at you and then looked into it with my third eye, I'd get a pretty good idea of your inner self. Wanda was always after me to use it on Big."

"Why didn't you?"

"I couldn't get him to even touch the crystal. Wanda says 'cause he's afraid of it, but that's no reason I shouldn't keep working on him."

"Is that why she didn't want to leave?"

"Partly. She likes it here, it reminds her of her home in Clinch County, Georgia. But mostly she thinks I should be able to save Big, change the way he is. Wanda says he's gonna have an awful time on the other side if he doesn't learn to open his heart. But try and get him to think about dying."

"You might have better luck with him now," Kathy said, "after what happened. You know he was shot at?"

"When I saw it in the paper," Leanne said, "I wondered if it had changed him any. Would you say?"

Kathy thought about it and nodded. "He seems less sure of himself."

"Aware of his mortality in this life?"

"I don't know if I'd go that far," Kathy said. "But I think you could get to him now, do him a world of good." Kathy hesitated, then went straight ahead saying, "I mean if you could find it in your heart to stay here and be his wife again." She took a breath and said, "Big needs you."

Leanne was looking at her in a strange cockeyed sort of way, unfocused, like she was stoned. Maybe using her third eye, Kathy wasn't sure.

"You were sent here," Leanne said.

"Actually I came to look for something in the trash."

It brought Leanne back. She said, "The trash was picked up this morning," and seemed concerned. "Hauled away. Is this something valuable you lost? Maybe I can help you find it."

Kathy eased back in the chair, quiet for a moment. She said, "Thanks anyway," not wanting to get into it with Leanne. "It's not that important." And saw the woman giving her that strange look again, as if in some kind of trance.

Leanne said, "You were sent here. Did you want me to contact someone for you? A deceased relative?"

Kathy shook her head. "I don't think so."

"You brought a message," Leanne said, "instructing me to stay and help Big. I feel I should give you one in return. I believe I'm sup*pose* to. Wait now. Wanda's telling me about someone . . . Who? . . . She doesn't know. It's someone who passed over recently."

Kathy said, "I don't know of anyone."

Leanne said, "Shhh," glaring at her. Then stared cock-eyed again or stoned and raised her hand. "Wait, this person hasn't passed over." She said, "What?" And said, "Oh, my Lord. He's passing over right now, as I speak."

Kathy saw her eyes squeeze closed and heard her little-girl voice say, "They's two of 'em, Leanne."

This was good, the woman trying to take it as a joke, but not too sure now, getting nervous, saying, "I can't leave this man sitting here, can I?"

"Why can't you?"

"He's here first, with an appointment. He's a good customer."

The cop was staring at him not saying a word, no doubt wondering what in the hell was going on. Was he being played with or what? Meantime the woman was working on him again, scissors clicking away, trying to get it done quick.

"I know who he is," Elvin said. "I still want you to come over here and cut my hair. I want it cut real short too, so nobody can pull on it."

The woman said, "If you can be patient for jus' a few minutes," in her Hi-spanic way of talking, and the cop's left hand came out from under the cloth.

He raised it to her saying, "There's no hurry. Take your time."

Almost just like in that book. It made Elvin think of it again: Sonny reading, getting to the part where Frank starts to put his rifle on the guy to move him out of the chair and the guy tells him if he raises it another inch he'll kill him. With what? Elvin knew he was bluffing. Why didn't Frank? Sonny read some more, but Elvin had lost interest in Frank, knowing he'd be dead before the end of the book, so why read it. Instead of talking, letting himself get faked out, why didn't he use the goddamn rifle? That was the difference between a book and real life. In a book, the one who was supposed to be the bad guy always got killed in the end.

Elvin pushed out of the chair and moved behind it to a washbasin and counter, glancing at himself in the mirror. He picked up a hair dryer that looked like a Buck Rogers gun and thought of smashing the mirror with it. He could see them watching. First ask the woman if she's ready to cut his hair. She starts to argue, smash the mirror and then say, Now are you? And the cop would be out of that chair so fast . . . Best not to touch anything. Keep it simple. He moved toward the opening in the lattice fence saying over his shoulder, "Seeing you're so busy, I'll come back later. Have Isabel cut it."

"Is okay with me," the woman said, "you go someplace else."

Let her think whatever she wanted.

Elvin walked through the room with the porch furniture to the front door, opened it and let it slam closed. There were all those things you wanted to do and couldn't, and finally there was something you could if you had the nerve, if you quit thinking about it and *did it.* He moved back to the lattice fence not making a sound, the Speed-Six revolver in his hand now, peeked through the slats and—Jesus, the cop was pulling the cloth over his head, shoving it at the woman, about to push out of the chair—and Elvin had to step quick to the opening. He shot Gary as he was standing up and it punched him back in the chair. He shot him again sitting in it, starting to slide out. He shot the woman as she was screaming. It knocked her off her feet and shut her up. The hair puller, Gary, was on the floor getting to his hands and knees, straightening up now—Jesus, with his gun in his hand—and Elvin shot him again and then one more time before he got out of there, that sound ringing in his head.

24

Tuesday afternoon Hector said to Dr. Tommy, "You believe there's another dermatologist in the world who sunbathes?"

Dr. Tommy, lying naked on the patio in a chaise, said he was no longer a dermatologist, so it was okay.

He was no longer anything, on a crack cocaine binge, his new thing, and looked at himself in mirrors making faces, as if talking to himself. He was always a little crazy, but they had fun. Now, since doing crack with the go-go whore, he was crazy in a different way. In two days he had become a rockhead. It was all he wanted, saying, "Where have I been?" *Where?* Right here doing cocaine, the best weed, Quaaludes. At least then he was aware and made sense when he spoke. Now he called the creature, Elvin, "the assassin in underwear," knew that much, but didn't care Elvin was taking over his home.

Hector would say, "You *know* he can get us in trouble. You *know* he isn't going to kill the judge. It doesn't matter to you now if he does or not. Why don't you make him leave?"

The doctor would seem to be considering a way to do it and then say, "We need a source we can rely on. We buy it from the go-go whore, she adds her profit on top. I don't blame her, but it isn't the most economical way to buy it. Unless you bring her here, give her what she paid and share it with her. No, wait. If I do that I would be getting less, wouldn't I? That would be okay, though, I like to watch her. Do you know she's killing herself? She doesn't know it yet, but she is. Ask her."

"What, if she knows she's killing herself or if she wants to come here?"

"That's an idea. She stays here, it would save you going back and forth. We let her use a car to make the buy."

It was all he thought about.

"Maybe she can cook," Hector said, "and clean the house."

"Maybe. Ask her that too."

See? Now he was seriously crazy.

"I'm trying to get rid of the assassin," Hector said, "and you want to bring his girlfriend here to live with us."

"She hates him," Dr. Tommy said.

Again missing the point. Though it got Hector to realize that, given a choice, he would prefer to have the go-go whore in the house than the creature, the animal that wore a suit. And if there was a way to get rid of him the doctor wouldn't care.

He would like to shoot Elvin, feeling this since almost the first time he saw him, and had been thinking of ways to dispose of his enormous body. Drop it in a canal or the Intracoastal. Take it to a woods. Steal a car and put it in the trunk. If he knew how to steal a car.

The doorbell chimed.

Hector put on his silk robe and left Dr. Tommy baking on the patio. By the time he reached the front door the high-low ding-dong chimes had sounded at least ten times. He peeked through the spy hole before opening the door, saw a young woman with short dark hair waved to extend out on each side. Cute hair, a little-girl face. The beige jacket and white skirt were *okay*, nothing special.

She said, "Dr. Vasco?"

Hector shook his head. "He's not in."

"That's too bad," Kathy said, flipping open her ID case to show her picture, her name, and those official words, *Department of Corrections.* "I'm his new Community Control officer."

"Oh, you know something? I thought he went to AA, but he's sleeping," Hector said. "Please, come in." She moved past him and he said, "I like your hair. It's much more chic than in the picture."

His voice so delicate, didn't go with his coarse features, a little guy with a big nose and a ponytail in a robe that touched the floor. Kathy said, "Thanks, Hector," turning to face him and saw his eyes light up.

He said, "You know my name," pleased but still surprised.

"I know all about you," Kathy said.

"Now, I don't believe *that.* You may have a complete dossier on the doctor, but *me*? No, you couldn't."

Close to him Kathy said, "Will you tell me things I don't know?" Playing with him.

He liked it. He said, "I might."

"Would you wake up the doctor for me?"

He said, "You can, if you want. He's on the patio."

Following him along the hall she asked if a Sergeant Hammond was here earlier. Hector stopped.

"He was here yesterday."

"You've been home all day?"

"Yes, so I would have seen him."

"Is Elvin around?"

This time he hesitated. "I'm sorry, who?"

"I thought we were getting along," Kathy said. "You like my hair, I like yours. Why spoil it?"

He smiled at her and said, "All right, I haven't seen him."

"Is he staying here?"

"I wouldn't say he's *stay*ing, no."

"What would you say?"

"He's here two nights, that's all."

"You know where he went?"

"No, but if I did . . ."

Kathy waited.

Maybe too long, giving Hector a chance to change whatever he was going to say to: "Is he your business?"

"I'm his probation officer."

"He isn't any of *my* business, so I don't want to talk about him, okay?"

"I think you want to," Kathy said, "but the idea makes you nervous." She said, "Anything you tell me, Hector, would be in confidence. I'm not a cop."

He said, "No? Well, you sound like one," and motioned for her to follow: the rest of the way along the hall and through the gold-wallpapered den to glass doors open on the patio. "There he is," Hector said, stepping aside.

"In the flesh," Kathy said, looking at the man lying naked, the anklet on his right leg, tanned a deep brown all over and Gary was right, what he'd said last night, the guy's member was darker than any part of him. A cop's observation, something to keep in mind for possible identification though not conclusive; there could be others that dark, weird, almost black.

"You going to check his equipment," Hector said.

"You kidding? I wouldn't touch it with a stick."

"I'm talking about that thing on his ankle."

Sure he was, acting innocent.

"I wouldn't touch that either," Kathy said, turning from sunlight to the semi-dark room with its glittery walls. She sat down in the sofa, sinking into it. Hector remained in the doorway, in light. She had to turn her head to see him.

"You worried about the doctor?"

No answer.

"What's he on?"

Hector looked over now. "I'm not stupid."

"And I'm not a narc," Kathy said. "Come and sit down, talk to me. You have a convicted murderer living in your house, the doctor doesn't seem to care and you don't know what to do about it. Am I close?"

Hector came over, taking his time. "You think you know everything."

"No, I need you to tell me."

"Why? There's nothing you can do."

"How do you know that? Please, sit down with me. I can be your friend if you want."

"I don't think so."

"Will you tell me one thing? Why the doctor lets Elvin use his car and gives him a key to the front door."

Hector was staring at her now.

"Talk to me," Kathy said, "and I won't look for dope. I

imagine Earlene brought a few rocks Sunday night, but they're gone, uh? Listen, I won't look for guns either."

Hector kept staring at her. Now he glanced toward the patio. Now she watched him sink to his knees in front of her—a slow, fluid motion in the robe, a priest in vestments—and sit back on his heels. He said in his delicate manner, "You're making serious accusations."

"Of course I am," Kathy said. "I'm putting you on the spot. You know I can search the house if I want. Look for Earlene's G-string she left here? . . . What do you think of her?"

"Nothing. She's a whore."

"She turn the doctor on?"

"He doesn't need someone like that."

"Elvin brings her?"

"He did once."

"I told her I'd pick up her G-string."

"Well, that was presumptuous of you."

"Why do you say that?"

He had sounded offended; now he shook his head. "It doesn't matter."

This was a weird guy. Kathy watched him. She said, "You want me to tell you something I know?"

"You're going to anyway."

"Maybe I should whisper it," Kathy said, paused and said, "Elvin and Dr. Tommy are going to kill a judge."

It hooked him good. He said, "No. Oh, no," shaking his head, but too late to hide that look of panic in his eyes, there and gone.

Kathy eased toward him, laying her arms on her knees. "They change their mind?"

"It's crazy what you're saying."

"The police know it."

"You're making that up. There's nothing for them to know."

"You want to protect the doctor. Of course you would. But if I know it, you think the police don't? Come on."

"Believe me, please, he isn't doing anything."

"The doctor, but what about Elvin?"

"I don't speak for him."

"You want to tell me something without saying it," Kathy said. "That's hard to do."

"I don't want to tell you *any*thing. Look at him," Hector said, getting a plea in his voice, his eyes. "You said yourself he doesn't care about Elvin, what he does." His gaze moved, came back and he lowered his voice saying, "There was a story in the paper, somebody trying to kill the judge with an alligator. You think that was Dr. Tommy?"

Kathy hunched in closer. "I think it gave Dr. Tommy the idea." She saw Hector shaking his head again and said, "But the doctor was putting Elvin on. 'Look at this, someone's trying to kill that judge we both know intimately. Not a bad idea, uh?' Having some fun with Elvin. Was it like that?"

"Exactly," Hector said, going for it, "and Elvin thought he was serious. The doctor has even forgotten it. Ask him—he'll say, 'What judge?' "

"Stay high, you don't have to think," Kathy said. "He can absolve himself of responsibility." She shrugged. "It might work. But you have clear eyes, Hector, you know what Elvin's doing. You don't want to say anything because you're afraid of him. Listen, I am too. But I know a guy who isn't afraid. The detective that was here yesterday, Gary, a good guy. He's coming back. When he does, why not talk to him? What do you say?"

Nothing. Not a word.

"Tell him what you've told me."

"Or you will? Is that what you're saying?"

"Gary knows all this," Kathy said, "what we've talked about. But it doesn't do him any good unless you tell him, yes, it's true. Hector, you're the key witness. You don't want Elvin here, you can get him put away, sent back to prison."

Hector was frowning now. "But what's he done? Nothing yet. You going to wait for him to do it?"

There it was again, Gary's objection.

"He's conspired to commit murder," Kathy said. She saw Hector on the edge, wanting to believe her. All she had to do was push him over.

"Hector, I've told you things no cop ever would. I could even be accused of blowing their investigation by confiding in you, revealing what they know. But I don't care. You know why? Dr. Tommy's one of my cases and I don't want to see him get in trouble, have to go to prison. Hector? . . ."

He was looking past her. Scrambling to his feet now. Kathy straightened and turned enough to see Dr. Tommy coming in from the patio, still naked, scratching his groin.

He said to Hector, "You have my robe on."

Hector shook his head. "This is my robe."

"Are you sure?"

"You left your robe by the swimming pool."

Dr. Tommy said, "Oh." As he turned to go back he noticed Kathy in the sofa. He gave her a nod, said, "How are you today?" and kept going. Still scratching himself.

Kathy watched him walk out into the sunlight, the doctor's rear end somewhat lighter than the rest of him, the doctor holding a straight course but all the way gone, stoned out of his skull. She turned to Hector.

"What're you doing?"

He had his back to her and was bent over, taking something off inside his robe. He turned to her and extended a G-string hanging from one finger. Black with silver sequins.

Kathy said, "Thank you," and got out of there.

Bob Gibbs had skipped his after-work stop at the Helen Wilkes and come straight home to put on a clean sport shirt and be ready for an interview this evening. A little girl from somewhere like the *Port St. Lucie Shopping News* wanted to talk to him about judging people's character. She'd stopped in his chambers to set it up, a little wide-eyed cutie with country ways about her. He liked country girls, they learned early about nature and how animals did it. This one—he couldn't think of her name— was brand-new at her profession, not yet cynical or slick at telling lies. The kind would write down everything he said and laugh at his wit.

In the kitchen he poured himself a Jim Beam thinking about character and how to judge it. The best way, you look at their priors. He saw offenders standing before him in their state-blue outfits and began thinking about auras —strange—not his own, other people's, wondering what it would be like to see colors glowing off their bodies. It was something he had never given a thought to without Leanne bringing it up. He could tell the little girl from Port St. Lucie that's what he did, checked their auras. She'd say, Really? Tell her you can do it once you have the gift. If you're perceptive. First, of course, you have to be able to clear your mind of—what was the word, prejudicial or preconceived ideas? Something like that. You had to open your mind and heart, get rid of negative thoughts.

He was facing the window above the sink, looking out as he sipped his whiskey, so that the voice came from his left.

"Big?"

From the doorway to the dining area where Leanne stood smiling at him.

He said, "Jesus Christ."

And she bowed her head at the reverence in his tone. "You've changed, Big. I can see it. The messenger told me you had, but I was doubtful till now I see it with my own eyes."

He said, "Leanne?"

Not to question her identity. He wanted to know what she was doing here, but couldn't get the words out.

"The messenger, Big, confirmed what my entity has been telling me all along, that it was selfish of me to leave when I know I can be the source of your enlightenment. Big? . . . I'm home."

He said, "Oh, God."

Leanne answered, "Praise be."

Elvin wanted to see her. He wasn't sure why, other than he wanted to look at her knowing what he knew.

He stopped at a bar right after leaving the beauty parlor. The bartender, watching him throw down that first one, asked had he almost got run over or was some old girl's husband after him? Elvin still pumped up at the time, but okay now.

He'd waited in the car about an hour, then walked up to the entrance and checked her apartment number, 219. When a couple in casual retirement clothes came along and entered, he went in with them, the guy in his golf hat giving him a look and Elvin said, "I'm going to see my probation officer. Is that all right with you folks?" He walked upstairs to 219, knocked on the door to make sure, then sat down on the floor with his back against the wall. He had to tip his Ox Bow forward as the brim kept hitting.

An old woman in a housecoat came by carrying her trash down the hall. She looked worried glancing at him, but didn't speak till on her way back.

"Can I help you?"

Elvin had to take his hat off to look up at her.

"Do what?"

"Are you all right?"

"I'm fine and dandy."

He wondered what the woman would say if he told her he'd just shot two people. Watch her face. He couldn't help but grin thinking of it.

"I'm waiting on the girl lives here? She's my probation officer."

"Oh," the woman said, and got inside her apartment and shut the door. He could hear her throwing the bolts.

It wasn't hard to scare people. Knowing it about them could serve you, too. He knew Ms. Touchy was afraid of him. What might work, use it to get her in bed then, hell, she finds out she likes it. You gonna tell on me? No way, Daddy, gimme some more. He wondered if she might've heard anything by now about her boyfriend. If she was a person they'd inform. He'd stopped by her office after leaving the bar and was told she was on the street.

Elvin must've waited almost another hour before he heard the elevator door open and close and there she was, coming along the hall with a bag of groceries, one finger dangling a ring of keys. Elvin got to his feet and put his hat on, noticing she seemed calm.

"What're you doing here?"

He said, "Lemme help you," reaching for the groceries, but she pulled back.

"Elvin, what do you want?"

"Just to talk to you, that's all."

"We talk at the office. You were supposed to come in yesterday for a urine test."

"I forgot all about it."

"Tomorrow, or you're in trouble."

"I was in today, you weren't there."

"You came and left."

"I had some business to take care of. Can't I come in for just a minute?"

"Elvin, get out of here right now. Leave."

She didn't seem upset, like she'd heard anything yet.

"I'm working tomorrow," Elvin said, trying to keep it going. "You know my job I told you about?"

It stopped her. He could tell the way she was looking at him she wanted to say something.

Just then the phone started ringing inside her apartment.

Now as she turned to the door getting the key ready, he said, "Here," and took the grocery sack from her. She glanced at him getting the door open, not wasting any time. But now she seemed in doubt whether to take the groceries back or run answer the phone, leaving him out here holding them. He said, "Go on, I'll set 'em down inside," and she did, more anxious to get the phone than worried about him coming in.

Elvin walked over to a table in the dining-L with the groceries. Nice place, pictures on the walls . . . Ms.

Touchy stood at a desk in the living room, her back to him as she talked on the phone, saying "Yeah?" a couple of times, but mostly listening. Elvin set the groceries on the table and stood watching. He heard her say, "Lou, just tell me what happened." He heard her say, "Oh, Jesus," and then, "Where is he? Is he all right?" Elvin sure now they were talking about her boyfriend, the hair puller. He saw her turn then to look this way, directly at him, as she said, "He's dead, isn't he?" It gave Elvin a funny feeling the way she kept staring at him as she listened to what was said to her. She said something else he didn't catch and saw her hang up the phone.

Still looking at him.

He said, "You get some bad news?"

She didn't answer. Just kept looking, like she was in some kind of state.

He said, "Well," and moved to the door. It was as he reached it, about to go out, he heard her say:

"You followed him, didn't you?"

Elvin kept going. There was no talking to an upset, emotional woman.

25

She called her DEA brother, Ray, and he came up from Miami late Wednesday afternoon. She said, "You know what it's like? It's like getting kicked in the stomach."

Ray said, "I know."

She said, "I haven't seen him yet. They're doing a post today. Then he'll be at the funeral home. I don't know which one yet. He was shot four times, in the stomach and the chest, and they're doing a post to determine cause of death."

Ray nodded. There were silences because he didn't ask her questions, not at first. They had the same features, the same thick dark hair. Both wore jeans and T-shirts sipping beer Ray had brought.

"A girl who works there found them," Kathy said. "Isabel something. She called nine-eleven and Fire Rescue rushed them to Good Samaritan, on Flagler and Palm Beach Lakes Boulevard; it's not too far from the hair studio. They worked on Gary, but he was dead on arrival.

The woman, Betty, lasted a little while. I think she was shot in the back. She was never conscious long enough to tell what happened, give a description . . . I know who did it," Kathy said, "but it doesn't seem to help much. He was standing right by that table when I got the phone call. I was looking at him. I said to Lou Falco, 'He's dead, isn't he?' Lou said yes and I'm looking right at the guy who killed him. You know what I thought of doing? I wanted him to wait there while I went in the bedroom and got the .38 Tony gave me. Remember that gun? I still have it, I clean it every once in a while, keep it loaded. . . . The guy is standing right there by the table. Elvin Crowe. I said, 'You followed him, didn't you?' He walked out. Oh, but before that. I hung up the phone and he said, 'Did you get some bad news?' The guy who shot him."

Her brother raised his eyebrows at that one, but still didn't say anything.

"I called Lou back," Kathy said. "I told him about Elvin, everything I knew, where he's staying, the people he's been hanging out with . . . They couldn't find him, not till this morning. They picked him up for questioning and he was released this afternoon. Lou called just before you came. He said they have nothing to hold him on. I said, 'What about Earlene?' There's a girl involved I mentioned to him last night. Lou said they put Elvin in a lineup and she failed to pick him out. I know she was with him Saturday, she told me. Sunday she spent the night with him . . . But she saw the paper today, Gary's picture . . . They talked to the doctor, he owns the house where Elvin's staying, and his houseman. They both know it was Elvin, they *have* to. But if they were afraid of him before . . . now, you know they won't say anything."

Ray said, "You're getting ahead of yourself."

She said, "Gary was really a nice guy. And he was *good*. I mean at his job, I *saw* him, he was tough, he was careful . . . What I can't understand, how he let a guy like Elvin, this clown . . . You know what I mean?"

"I know," Ray said. "Listen, why don't you tell me the whole thing, from the beginning."

She said, "He's dead because of a fucking alligator, if you can believe that. An alligator he killed. Now it's killed him."

Elvin found Hector in the kitchen running the blender.

"Well, life goes on, don't it? You guys sure like to party. Act like nothing bad can ever happen to you. The doc's out there in the gold room with his music on, talking to a dead zebra else he's talking to hisself. Smokes rock and then weed, up and then down, I said to him, 'Why don't you make up your mind?' He goes, 'Huh?' Like, where am I? Stoned and smashed at the same time. What're we making there?" The booger didn't hear him, or pretended not to. "Shut that goddamn thing off."

He let it go another few seconds before flicking the switch. There were banana peels on the counter and the color of the mixer was pale yellowish. Hector was getting a couple of glasses ready. He had on clothes for a change, what looked almost like a regular shirt tucked into tight black silky pants. His high-heel Cuban boots brought his ponytail up even with Elvin's chin, Elvin leaning against the butcher table.

"Making more of that banana shit?"

Hector turned his head to the side. "You want one?"

"Not if I was on fire. What'd you tell the cops?"

"Nothing much."

He had to be drunk to sound this calm.

"They get tough with you?"

"Why would they do that?"

"Scare you. People get scared, they tell things before you even ask. What'd they want to know?"

"Last night it was all about you. Where are you? What do you do here? Today they had a warrant and searched the house. They took the doctor's hunting rifles."

"Aw, his flamingo shooter? That's too bad. They find where you hide the money?"

"They weren't looking for money. They asked about the Cadillac, what happened to it."

"Yeah, they knew it was gone, didn't they?"

Hector turned from the counter wiping his hands on a dish towel. Elvin watched the way he laid the towel over his shoulder then and picked up one of the drinks.

"I told them you took it."

Speaking right up. Elvin judged he'd drunk a load of that banana shit already.

"Well, what I told 'em when they asked, I said yeah, I had the car at one time, but my nephew Dale borrowed it. 'Cause he did. They're gonna find him anyway. I said he prob'ly went up to Disney World to see Mickey and Goofy. What'd you tell 'em about Earlene?"

Thinking it would catch the booger off guard. But all Hector said was, "Not much," and took a big sip of his drink, still calm.

"Wipe your mouth." He had foam all over it. "They ask if I knew her?" Elvin watched him pass the back of his hand across his mouth and then lick his hand, his tongue turning that yellowish color.

"I said she was here that one time with you."

"What'd you tell 'em about me, last night?"

"They wanted to know where you were. I said I didn't know."

"I expected they might come by. What they like to do, they think you're a suspect, is put you in jail overnight and not talk to you till the next day. So I was gonna stay at a mo-tel, come back here this morning and let 'em take me. Which they did as I drove up."

"I saw it," Hector said.

"But then last night I thought, why spend the money on a mo-tel? I'll go on over to Earlene's when she gets done working. I went, I had to throw this dink out just taking his clothes off. Earlene looks at me, she goes, 'I never said a word to nobody. Honest.' See, there she was telling me something I never asked, 'cause she was scared. I go, 'When was this you never said nothing to nobody?' I find out the hair-puller cop and Ms. Touchy was both talking to her the other night."

"I don't know who you mean," Hector said. "But did you beat her up, Earlene?"

Listen to him. "No, I didn't," Elvin said. "I don't hit girls or queers."

"Which do you like better?"

Elvin squinted at him. "You must've had a couple jars of that banana shit talking like you are. When I was in the joint I cut one or two of you, but I never hit any. So you're fairly safe, less I decide to shoot you in the head. You understand me?"

"Why are you so upset?"

"Why'm I upset? Listening to you? All I want to know is how the law found out about Earlene. You told 'em, didn't you?"

Hector shook his head, still calm. "They already knew."

"How could they?"

"I don't know, but they did. The woman knew it, your probation officer."

"She was here too?"

"In the afternoon, before the police came. She's also Dr. Tommy's officer."

"Since when?"

"How do I know. She said the cop was coming back who was here before? Then I look at the paper today, I see why he didn't make it. I thought they arrested you."

"For what?"

"Well, you did shoot him, didn't you?"

This booger kept talking right up, not acting a bit nervous. Elvin stared at him trying to figure it out.

"You think it was me, huh?"

"It was all you talked about the other day. The cop was here—remember how you took hold of me, almost threw me down the stairs?"

Elvin watched Hector roll his eyes, acting cute.

"You little booger, I would've you didn't give me my gun back. But you didn't mention that time to the law, did you?"

"I'm not crazy," Hector said.

"I figure you didn't, else I'd still be up on Gun Club Road with the deputies."

"I've told them nothing and I don't intend to," Hector said. He took a sip of his drink. "I have a feeling, without anyone telling on you, you'll be back in prison before you know it."

"I'll pull some stunt'll get me caught?"

"You'll do *some*thing."

"You think I'm reckless, huh? Well, the way I see it, taking chances is the hot sauce you put on life to make it tangy. Otherwise I'm no better off'n you are sitting, watching it go by."

"Did you make that up?"

"Buddy of mine said it and I like the ring of it."

"A prison buddy?"

"Up at Starke, yeah."

He watched Hector cock his head to one side, holding the glass at his mouth and peering over the rim. Acting cute again.

"You play at being the hellraiser," Hector said, "but there's more to it than that."

This was good, the booger trying to read him.

"You're saying I'm not the genuine article? Take a look at my sheet, it'll make your hair stand up."

Hector said, "Only my hair?" Raising his eyebrows like he was flirting. Then was serious again saying, "You're a bad boy, Elvin, but why? I think because you want to get caught."

Elvin had to grin. "I never heard of that one."

"So you can go back to prison," Hector said, "and be with your friend Sonny."

Elvin wasn't grinning now.

Ray Diaz watched his sister hang up the phone and come over to the sofa.

"That was Lou Falco. There'll be a service for Gary at St. Ann's this Saturday and another one—Lou said a military-style ceremony with police from all over Florida—at Queen of Peace Cemetery. Gun salutes, all that. I said to him, 'When's Elvin's funeral?' "

"I heard you," Ray said, watching her sit down again. She seemed worn out.

"TAC has surveillance on him. He's back at the doctor's house right now."

"If he did it they'll put it on him sooner or later," Ray said. "If he was in that hair place the chances are they'll find evidence of it, prints, *some*thing."

She said, "But if the evidence doesn't show he was there between twelve-thirty and one yesterday afternoon, it isn't evidence, is it?"

His sister thinking like a criminal investigator when he was trying to console her. Ray said, "Or someone saw him go in or come out," still trying. "Or they'll find the gun."

She said, "If it wasn't in the doctor's house or the car Elvin was driving it could be anywhere, in a canal, the ocean . . . Ray, even if he's brought up on something circumstantial, what's his motive? A payback? Because Gary threw him down one time and kneeled on him?" She said, "You know why I think he killed Gary? Because of me. Because he wants me."

Ray knew she ached; her eyes would fill talking about Gary, what a nice guy he was, sounding like she was in love with him. She was in the middle of this but could talk about it objectively, too, shut out her feelings, and it surprised him, his little sister.

"How do you mean he wants you?"

"In bed. How do you think? That's why he came here after. To tell me what he did without saying it."

"That he killed for you?"

"That he killed to get me, yes."

"I don't know—"

"He's primitive, Ray. He says, 'How many people you take care of ever killed anybody?' In my caseload. He says, 'I'm your star.' I could be seeing him every month for the next five years."

"He won't last that long, even come close."

"I know *I* won't," Kathy said. "I'm ready to quit any time."

"Join the DEA and see Latin America. I'm going to Panama Friday, but don't tell anybody." Ray picked up his beer from the table in front of the sofa and sat back again. "You're good at getting people to talk to you. Like with Hector. That was pretty neat."

"But I didn't convince him to tell the police."

"About what? That alligator business inspiring them? I don't see a connection between doing the judge and what happened to Gary."

"No, but Elvin loves to talk," Kathy said. "I'll bet he tells Hector and the doctor everything he does. He might even tell me if I ask him."

"Don't," Ray said.

"He'd hint around first."

"Please don't."

"If I wore a wire and TAC was close by?"

"And if he finds it on you," Ray said, "when he tears your clothes off?"

"It's just an idea. If I can talk to Hector, that might be enough."

"What will you do if Elvin's there?"

"I don't know, Ray. I'd have to wait and see."

Elvin said to Hector, "I never hit a queer but, man, I can start, you keep talking like that."

First the booger would do things with his eyes and mouth, acting cute, then look surprised and motion with his hands like a girl as he spoke.

"Why? You and Sonny were lovers, weren't you? Why can't you talk about it?"

"We weren't lovers, for Christ sake."

"You didn't make love to him?"

"Jesus Christ, will you quit talking like that? No, I never made *love* to him."

"What did you do then?"

"You don't know *nothing* what it's like in prison."

"So why don't you tell me about it? Ten years, you must have had other boys besides Sonny. Unless—did they allow conjugal visits?"

"I'm gonna pop you right in the fucking mouth."

"What did I say now, *conjugal*? That means your wife, if they let her visit."

"I don't have one or never did."

"I didn't think so."

Elvin said, "I want you to get something straight," watching Hector pour himself some more of the banana shit. "I like girls, women, all shapes and sizes. Even Hispanic puss is okay. You understand?"

The booger shrugged, like he was waving his shoulders. He said, "It's okay to go both ways."

Elvin shoved him, hitting his goddamn shoulder. "Quit talking like that."

"Owww, you don't have to hit me."

"I didn't hit you."

"I'm not going to tell anyone."

"Then shut up."

The booger shrugged his goddamn shoulders again and said, "Well, if that's how you feel," and stuck his big honker of a nose in the air.

Something Elvin hated, a guy acting like he was better than you. Elvin gave him another shove.

The booger said, "Stop it!"

So Elvin shoved him again, harder.

He said, "El-vin!"

In that girlish way he had, like he was going to cry. Elvin hated it worse than the snotty look. He said to him, "Sonny'd whine like that, you know what I'd do? Hold a pillow over his face so he couldn't breathe. He'd kick and squirm, I'd say to him, 'You gonna be good now? Are you? Show me.' He quit squirming I'd let him up."

"Then he was good?"

"Knew he better behave hisself."

"When you're holding the pillow over his face," Hector said, "did that excite you?"

The booger giving him that flirty look with his eyes as he said it and Elvin grabbed him around the neck, wrenched him down against his side in a headlock, the booger's face in his blue suit, and held him there.

"You gonna quit talking like that? Are you?"

He let up on him to hear an answer and the booger slumped to the floor at Elvin's feet, lying against them. Elvin gave him a kick with his cowboy boot as he stepped back. The booger didn't move. Elvin stooped over, noticing Hector's neck bent funny. He reached to touch it and felt around good. There wasn't any pulse.

Elvin said, "Shit," out loud.

He poured himself a short one from the blender and took a sip. It wasn't too bad this time. He took another sip and looked down at Hector thinking, Man, you're on a roll, aren't you?

26

It was dark by the time Dr. Tommy came sleepwalking out to the kitchen. Elvin was fixing himself bacon and eggs and asked was he hungry. No, he was looking for Hector.

Elvin said, "I haven't seen him."

Which was true. Not since he'd stuck him in the broom closet. Dr. Tommy said he needed Hector to get him something. He walked through the back hall saying he might have already gone, and opened the door to the garage. No, both cars were there, the Lincoln and the Jaguar, the one Hector would have used. The doc asked where he could be, sounding pissed and in bad shape, in some pain.

"Went for a walk on the beach," Elvin said, "looking for seashells. Don't worry about it, I'll go out after I eat, get what you need. I'm going out anyway." The idea, to look around good, see if one of their unmarked cars was parked on the road and would it follow him if he was to go anywhere.

Peering over the doc's shoulder into the garage, he said, "You don't have a boat, do you?" Thinking of something else he had to do. Dr. Tommy said he didn't care for boats. Not since coming here on one from Cuba in '59. What he had, Elvin noticed, was a rubber raft hanging on the wall, yellow with a blue bottom. It was small but would do the job he had in mind.

They went back in the kitchen and Elvin poured Dr. Tommy a banana drink, telling him, "Here, you work on this while I eat. Then you can give me the money for what you need." The doc wanted to go right then and get it, but Elvin made him wait while he had his bacon and eggs, mopping up the yolk on his plate with bread. The bread was stale and the bacon strips had green spots on them, these dinks not being serious eaters. Elvin was hungry so he didn't complain.

After, they went upstairs to Dr. Tommy's bedroom for the money, Elvin dying to see where he kept it. They went in a walk-in closet and the doc started poking through his shoes, what must've been thirty pair on shelves that sloped down, a wood strip holding them by their heels. Elvin had never seen so many shoes outside of in a store. The doc went along feeling inside them. He pulled out clear-plastic Baggies of coke, grass, different colored pills —there, he found a shoe with cash in it. He said Hector hid the money in different places; that's why he had to look for it.

Elvin wondered why the cops hadn't grabbed his dope. It must be 'cause they were looking for a gun held mag loads and that wouldn't fit in any of these pointy shoes. He said, "You keep all your money here?" The doc didn't answer, unfolding a wad of hundred-dollar bills. He handed one to Elvin, telling him to get what it would buy. Elvin kept after him, asking, "How much you keep in the house?"

The doc thought about two thousand. He called it "walking-around money," except he couldn't go anywhere.

"Well, where's the rest?" The doc told him it was in the bank and Elvin said, "A *bank*, don't you know banks get robbed?" kidding with him. Then was serious again. "Don't forget we still have a deal."

Man, where was he? His head all fuzzed. He looked up to ask, what deal? His eyes red and shiny.

Elvin said, "When things quiet down and I do the job, I'll drive you to the bank to get my money. No checks. This's a cash deal."

The doc wasn't following the conversation. He said he had a terrible taste in his mouth and to hurry up and get him his rock.

While they were still upstairs Elvin said, "I had to chuck that piece you give me. Where's your other one, up here?"

He'd dropped the Speed-Six in a Dumpster behind a liquor store when he went in to get a fifth of Beam. After leaving Ms. Touchy's. He had not wanted to part with that gun till he remembered there was another one in the house. Now he remembered that fifth was still in the car from yesterday.

The doc was telling how the police found his rifles and confiscated them. Elvin said, "I mean that gun Hector pulled out of his jockstrap. When was it? Saturday. I bet you still have that one." Dr. Tommy asked why he needed it, not wanting to give it to him. Elvin said, "Keep talking, see if I go get you your rock." A junkie was the easiest person in the world to handle.

Now they went into Hector's room where there were all kinds of different shaped pillows and a couple of stuffed animals—Jesus Christ—on the bed, a little white doggie and a furry green alligator. Dr. Tommy hefted the one, then the other, zipped open the gator and pulled out the bluesteel automatic Elvin recalled. A little seven-shot Walther .32 you wouldn't even know was in your pocket. Elvin had felt naked not having a gun. Now he was back in business, looking toward what he saw would be a long night.

The first thing, drive over to the club where Earlene worked and have her make a buy for him. She'd do it right on the premises, all the dealers and dope fiends they had in there; she'd be happy to in her scared state.

Look to see if he was being tailed, of course. They might even try to give him a hard time in that smarty way cops had of talking; but they weren't going to run him in on any two-bit dope charge.

The second thing, later on in the dead of night, load Hector onto the rubber raft, something heavy tied to him, paddle out in the ocean a ways and put him over the side. Come back and open that fifth of Beam. Hear Dr. Tommy moaning, Where's Hector at? Have you seen him? I don't know, Doc, maybe he went swimming.

God *damn*, he wished there was somebody he could tell all this to and watch their face.

She stared at the ceiling in the dark bedroom wondering if there was a way to turn off your mind.

Thinking that if she had cut Gary's hair Monday night he wouldn't have gone to Betty's.

Imagining the place, Elvin walking in, Gary in the

chair, Elvin knowing what he was going to do, speaking to Gary. She could hear his voice but not the words.

Then wondering if she would have shot Elvin standing by the table, the bag of groceries, if she'd had the chance. If he had waited while she came in here to get her revolver, walked back into the living room . . .

Then seeing it a different way, looking at him with the gun in her hand when Lou Falco said yes, he was dead. She might have shot Elvin in that moment. *Might have.* And thought, That's the best you can do. Maybe you would. The gun in your hand. But then realized she was thinking about it *now,* after the fact or as a fantasy, and thought, So you don't know what you would've done in that moment, the gun in your hand.

She imagined Betty's Hair Studio again and saw Gary dead with his gun in his hand. Never fired, the paper said. She remembered Gary saying to Elvin the other day, "If I pull it, I shoot it. You understand?" That was the trouble, he did understand. He would know enough to walk in and start talking and Gary would think, oh no, have to sit here and listen to this guy and his bullshit, trapped, and Elvin would have him off guard, the nice guy putting up with him. It could have happened that way. Gary pulling his gun too late.

You had to be ready for Elvin.

Armed. A gun on you he didn't know about.

A gun in your hand beneath the cloth they put over you to cut your hair, the moment you saw him come in.

She slipped out of bed in her T-shirt and got the .38 revolver from the top drawer of the dresser: a stubby S&W Chiefs Special with a two-inch barrel: the same model she had fired at the Academy during her training and again with Tony, when he gave this gun to her. He said she was a pretty good shot. A little more than a pound of metal fitting her hand. She brought the revolver back to bed with her and laid it on the night table.

She could see it in the wash of light from the window and began to think, You can't change any of that. What are you getting ready for? He doesn't want to kill you, he wants to play. He'll make you come to check on him, kid about his urine and one day open his pants with that stupid grin on his face and get on top of you. That's what it was about, what she saw in her mind and heard him saying, "Did you get some bad news?" He wanted to talk about it. Wanted *you* to tell *him* and then he'd put on his act and hint around, because if you don't know he did it . . .

You *have* to know. It's important to him. Gives you that stupid grin waiting to see what you're going to do about it.

She was looking at tomorrow now instead of yesterday and could feel her heart beating with the idea of walking up to him. Look him over. Give him a chance to put on his act. Ray said, "You're good at getting people to talk to you," and she had thought of wearing a wire. But that could come later, if TAC went for the idea. The thing to do now was give Elvin a chance to show off, give his opinion maybe tell something that wasn't in the paper. Talk to Hector first, if that was possible. Check out Dr. Tommy. Get a feel of what was going on in that house.

She was wider awake now, a few minutes past midnight, than when she came to bed. She set the alarm for 5:30 and thought about what she'd wear. Jeans, her navy blazer, a shoulder bag with the .38 in it. They could fire her, she was going to pack it from now on.

27

Wesley, the young TAC cop, sat low behind the wheel of the Thunderbird with a clear view of the doctor's property, the brick posts with lamps still lit where the drive circled in and came out. There wasn't much going on this early, a few cars now and then; people living in the big homes were still in bed, or else they'd gone north and their places were closed till next season. He heard a horn beep behind him, once, looked at the mirror and saw a VW close to his rear end. Wesley got up higher in the seat as he saw the girl—the judge's friend, Kathy—coming up on his side. His window was already down. He was glad to see her and got ready to ask what was she doing here, but she beat him to it saying hi.

"Just want to tell you I'm going to Dr. Vasco's. He's one of my cases."

"You know what time it is?"

He saw her look at her watch. "Twenty past six."

"I mean, don't you think it's kinda early?"

"It's how you check on Community Control cases,"

Kathy said. "Drop in when they least expect a visit. What's happening, anything?"

"Not much. The Lincoln went out last night. I tailed it to a go-go bar."

"That must have been Elvin."

"The one with the cowboy hat."

Hunched down by the window she nodded her head. "Alone or with Hector?"

"By himself."

She said, "I hope he isn't hung over this morning."

"He wasn't there a half hour. Came right back."

Now she said, "Oh, picking up a rock for the doctor."

"Well, shit, I better go in there with you," Wesley said.

"No, it's okay. Let's keep the doctor happy; I can violate him anytime. He's not the one you want."

Wesley knew she meant the one with the hat and said, "If it was the cowboy shot Hammond, we'll get him."

She said, "Did you know Gary?"

"I met him. I hear he was a good guy. I'll tell you something," Wesley said. "If that cowboy's the one, I'd sure like to get a crack at him. Have him come at me."

"Cocked?" Kathy said. "The tension off the trigger?"

"You recall my telling you about that, huh? At the crack house that time?"

"I remember," Kathy said. "But what if he shot you first? I mean Elvin."

"I wouldn't let it happen," Wesley said. "What you do, you watch their eyes."

She said, "Oh, I wondered," and walked away.

He watched her VW pull out past him, drive up the road and turn in at the doctor's place, disappearing into all the foliage there. She was a pretty good-looking girl but weird. Makes a house call before anybody's up. Goes out with that old-man judge . . .

* * *

No one answered the chimes. It was possible they weren't heard upstairs in the bedrooms. Kathy left her car by the front entrance and walked around to the ocean side of the house in clear morning sunlight. She could hear the surf breaking off beyond the pool, the sweep of lawn, the edge of the bluff lined with palm trees. Not the typical home of a crack cocaine addict. A rubber raft lay upside down on the patio. She gazed up the stairway at the deck, sun reflecting on the windows, walked past the stairs to a door with glass panes and put her hand on the knob as she looked in at the kitchen. The knob turned.

Inside, she was immediately aware of Elvin, his presence in dirty dishes, a skillet of grease, beer cans, banana peels, an empty Jim Beam bottle. It looked as if Hector had given up; decided, why bother? She walked through the dining room to the center hall and stopped to listen, looking up the stairway. The house was silent.

There was an odor of grass in the room with glittery wallpaper, the den. Kathy opened the sliding glass door and looked out at the patio again: at the lounge the doctor had been lying on nude; at the rubber raft she hadn't noticed the other day—it might've been there; at the wrought-iron patio table and three chairs. Where was the fourth? Nowhere on the patio that she could see. And thought, What are you looking for? He's upstairs.

Elvin woke up having to piss and found out before opening his eyes he was hung over. Not too bad, but enough to kick in a door. Last night he was going to wait till he'd done his chores before having the Jim Beam, but had got to talking with Dr. Tommy and cracked the bottle earlier than planned. Drinking helped him think. Hung over, he tended to follow his urges. Talking about Hector, the doc wanted to know if Elvin had caused him to be mad or upset. This while the booger was still in the broom closet. Elvin said no, he hadn't made him cry since the other day. The doc got tired thinking of Hector and moved on to the judge. This was a different story and what got Elvin started on the Jim Beam. Dr. Tommy saying he was calling the deal off, forget it. So then Elvin had to give the doc a talking-to, get through to him with his head all lit up that a deal was a deal, you didn't back out of one less both parties agreed. Dr. Tommy saying then, if you're going to do it, then do it. What was he waiting for? He told the doc he was ready, had his killer instincts working and would do it tonight if the law wasn't sitting out front. They'd followed when he'd gone to see the go-go whore and would follow anyplace he went. The doc saying he didn't care. Do it by the end of this week or no deal. Four days. And kept saying it in his rocked-out state, this week or forget it. The thing was, Elvin believed he did have to do it soon, else the doc might stuff himself with enough crack to o.d. on him or turn his brain to oatmeal. There was always something trying to fuck up your life.

He'd even thought he might drown for a minute there last night, waves coming in high as he took the booger out to sea, Hector riding the raft taped to a patio chair.

Elvin worked his way out of the bed. He saw he had his socks on. He needed to piss and needed a couple of cold beers right after to settle him down, calm his nerves.

Taking care of the first matter, standing at the toilet, his eyes watering with the relief of it, he started thinking: What if there was a way to slip out while the house was being watched and get it done? Slip back in, they never knowing he was gone, and he'd be free and clear. Who me? You crazy? You been watching the house? Wasn't I here all the time?

Like if Hector was still around . . . Sneak out at night afoot, Hector picks him up, takes him out to the judge's place . . . Except that would only have worked if the booger could lose the tail they'd have on him. He wasn't around anyway so, shit, think of something else. The beers might help.

Elvin went back to the bedroom, sat down in his shorts to pull his boots on. How about if he sneaked out and got a taxicab, took it over to West Palm and went in a mall. That could work. Swipe a car from the parking lot and drive out to the judge's. Do it at night.

That didn't sound too hard. No, for being hung over, usually a mean state of mind, he was calm and thinking pretty good. Couple of beers, he'd have this deal worked out.

He went along the hall to the stairway in his underwear and boots, working his mouth to get that awful taste out of it, reached the turn in the stairs and couldn't believe his eyes.

Ms. Touchy standing at the bottom looking up at him. She said, "Elvin?"

In that way she had, meaning business. Looking fresh and bright this morning making her calls. No doubt her car keys in that purse hanging from her shoulder. No doubt whatsoever, and her VW parked in the drive.

She saw a bare white body in striped underwear, boots to his calves—he looked soft but ten feet tall up there. Grinning at her, shaking his head.

"Man, you sure took me by surprise. You come to see me or Dr. Tommy?"

"Both of you," Kathy said. "Is he awake?"

"I haven't heard a peep, and I'm the early bird around here."

"What about Hector?"

"Hector, he left."

"You mean he quit?"

"I guess. He ain't here."

She'd save Hector till the doctor came down. "You going to put some clothes on?"

"I'll be right back," Elvin said. "Don't go 'way."

She asked herself, Are you afraid of that? Watching him go up the stairs in his boots and undershorts, and answered, You bet I am. Holding on to her shoulder bag.

Kathy went back to the kitchen wondering about Hector. Down a hall past the laundry room she found the door to the garage. Two cars in there, a Lincoln and a Jag. She could imagine an argument with Dr. Tommy and Hector driving off in a snit. Maybe to stay with his mother or a friend, if he had one. Wait for the doctor to call. What she couldn't imagine was Hector walking away from all this. Unless he was forced to. She would have to wait and talk to Dr. Tommy. Have Elvin bring him down. Make sure with clothes on.

She returned to the front hall to walk past the doctor's abstract art, a painting done in silver she saw as hard smoke, a sculpture that could be a woman's body with a hole in it, or it might be a doughnut. Something to think about. Decide if it made any difference . . . Kathy turned with the sound of heels clicking on the terrazzo floor.

Cowboy boots. Elvin, wearing a bright blue suit and his big straw, putting on a pair of sunglasses.

Kathy waited for him. "You going somewhere?"

He came toward her nodding. "We are. You're gonna drive me."

28

Leanne said, "Big, what I have to do first is remove all the psychic dirt that's crusted on your body, built up there over the years."

He asked her, "Will it hurt?"

"You're an old scaredy-cat, aren't you? No, it won't hurt and you'll feel lighter after, your body free of all that old static full of negative thoughts and emotions."

He wondered if by "negative" she meant what were considered by some, dirty thoughts. Like having that little girl from the *Port St. Lucie Shopping News* in his mind, but no chance of it happening in real life, Leanne back in the house. They were on the screened porch this morning, seven A.M., Leanne in a white leotard and white hose, looking like an egg with arms and legs; the judge in a T-shirt and pants from his seersucker suit, both cotton, Leanne insisting he had to wear natural-fiber clothes for the cleansing or it wouldn't work. He didn't argue, still in shock from her homecoming.

"Once I clean you up," Leanne said, "we'll go outside

and I'll show you how to exchange energy with nature. It'll do you good."

Wasn't that what he did growing orchids? "I communicate with it all the time."

"I'm not knocking it, Big. I think it's the only thing that has kept you whole. Oh," she said, thinking of something else. "Please don't tell me you've had a drink this morning."

"Not yet I haven't."

"It doesn't work if there's alcohol in you."

He wished he did, standing with his feet eighteen inches apart, knees slightly bent, the way Leanne had positioned him. She was behind him now.

"I'm hoping my body heat won't interfere. I have to get close if I'm going to give you a good scraping."

"You have to use the Epsom salts?"

A bowl of it sat on the table within reach.

"What I do after each scraping," Leanne said, "is brush the psychic dirt from my hands into the bowl to be absorbed. Salt has been used for cleansing since the beginning of time. Maybe even longer, they're not sure."

He felt the side of her hand scraping down his back as she told him, "I have to be careful I don't get any of your energy on me. See? I scrape my hand each time into the Epsom salts."

"You gonna clean all my parts? I know one's got rusty from not having been used."

Leanne said, "Shhhhh."

It was true. He could count on one hand the times he'd scored since Stephanie left. Well, maybe two. But, boy, he missed her. They had a routine, he'd walk up to her at the Helen Wilkes or wherever they were meeting and whisper in her ear, "What do you say to a little fuck?"

And Steph would turn to him and say, "Hi, you little fuck." She was a big one. Outweighed him nearly twenty pounds. Ms. Bacar now, she was more his size.

Leanne said, "Your friend Kathy—"

And he jumped like she'd goosed him.

"What's wrong?"

"You hit a tender spot there."

This woman was spooky the way she seemed to read your mind. Like some little part of her otherworld airy-fairyness was real.

"I call her my messenger," Leanne said, scraping away. "One that comes with glad tidings."

Wesley blew his horn as they pulled out of the drive and turned north, away from him. Wesley letting her know he was alert, on the job. Elvin might have wondered about it, hunched down on the backseat, but didn't say anything. He became talkative once they were heading west on Southern Boulevard, Elvin sitting up now, his face and part of his hat in the rearview mirror.

"Nice day, huh?"

Kathy didn't answer.

"Yes, it is," Elvin said. "I hope it don't get too hot."

She saw his face staring at the back of her head.

"Aren't you curious why I want to see the judge?" He waited. "Or do you already know?"

About the only thing she wasn't sure of this trip, how he was going to get back after.

"That was too bad what happened to your boyfriend. I wonder who done it."

Her bag was on the seat next to her, the snap open. He'd had no reason to search her, knowing probation officers were unarmed. Ordinarily.

"I said I wonder who done it."

She thought, Why antagonize him? Stared at the road thinking, Why not? And said, "I'm surprised you didn't shoot him in the back."

That was done.

She glanced at the mirror to see him moving, getting comfortable, fooling with his hat. It didn't antagonize him. It made him happy that she knew.

"Why you think it was me?"

That was it. No more.

" 'Cause you know I have the nerve?"

She kept quiet. It was hard.

"I ain't *say*ing it was me, you understand. You can think what you want. The thing I can't figure is what you saw in that dink. A hair puller? Shit, you can do better'n that." He waited a few moments. "Don't care to talk about it?"

She stared straight ahead, eyes on the road: light traffic in this direction, most of it coming in toward West Palm.

"You're prob'ly thinking I done Hector too."

She almost looked at the mirror to ask him why. But that was what he wanted.

"Me and Hector went swimming last night. I ain't seen him since."

They passed the Polo Lounge off to the right.

"I could use a cold one, but I don't expect they're open this early. I get cranky I don't have my beer in the morning. Maybe the judge'll have one for me. I know he drinks Beam, I saw it there. You happen to know he keeps beer in the house?"

He was telling her, whether he knew it or not, he had been there. For whatever that was worth.

"I wish you'd talk to me." They passed beneath the Florida Turnpike and he said, "Man, that road brings back memories. Go left at the next light. Case you forgot how to get there."

Kathy made the turn before looking at the mirror again. She said, "How're you going to get back?"

He didn't answer right away. They were on the road through woods now, thick vegetation on both sides. She kept looking at his face in the mirror, his eyes, his hand fooling with the hat brim. He said, "You're gonna drive me, aren't you?"

Because he couldn't say he was going to kill her. She felt it looking at him. But he would have to. He wasn't going to leave a witness. Anyone who was there . . . She knew this from the beginning, from the moment he told her where they were going, but there was nothing she could do about it until maybe now, getting close to the house and thinking, He's going to kill you. Concentrating on that fact alone. He's going to kill both of you. She stared at the road again, empty, the way it was the other day, and thought, He's going to kill all three of you.

Remembering the judge's wife was home.

Elvin said, "Turn left and then left again."

She needed time. Five seconds to reach in her bag and get turned around before he could grab her or pull his gun. He hadn't shown a gun yet but would have one, it was what he used.

She made the turns, saw the canal extending along the left side of the road and it was in her mind to aim for it, grab her bag, dive out of the car . . . But it was too close, there wouldn't be time. So she took the other way—mashed the accelerator and swerved away from the bank to bounce over a ditch, Elvin yelling "Jesus Christ!" as the

VW plowed through scrub to scrape past trees and nose to a stop in thick brush. Before she could touch her bag Elvin's hand was in her hair, yanking her head back hard against the seat. He hunched in close to say, "Hon, on second thought, I don't think you'll be driving me back."

One thing about Leanne he always liked was how she called him Big. "Now we'll go outside, Big, and I'll show you how to draw energy from nature. But you have to be barefoot." Well, naturally. So he took his shoes off and she brought him out to one of the petticoat palms where she told him to stand facing away from it, but close enough to reach back and touch it gently with his hands. She said, "You're giving to the tree, Big, and it's giving to you." He tried it. She said, "Now don't you feel better?" What he felt was stupid, but went along, telling her, yeah, he did, he felt his bodily juices flowing. She told him to swap energies with some of the other trees while she went in to change out of her leotards, her cleaning outfit, and put breakfast on.

He was doing a laurel oak now thinking how she smelled pretty nice; had baby powder on. Before, when she was scraping psychic dirt off the front of him, he felt himself getting a hard-on. She felt it too and looked at him in a way he hadn't seen since she wore a lamé tail and smiled underwater. It was funny, he'd always meant to ask how you did that, smiled without taking in water, but never had. He wondered if he ought to slip in there now while she was changing and ask her. Take his clothes off, too, tell her he was full of sap from swapping energies with trees and would like to prove it to her.

He walked out of shade into sunlight and stopped.

* * *

Elvin had her by the arm coming around from the other side of the house. As soon as he saw the judge he let go and Kathy moved away from him, working her hand into the bag hanging from her shoulder. It was old leather, soft, in shades of brown. She felt her wallet and wanted to take it out, put it in her pocket. Elvin and the judge were staring at each other. Now the judge was looking this way.

He said to her, "What's going on?"

Kathy wasn't sure how to tell him. Now Elvin glanced at her and motioned with his hand.

"Get over there with him."

She started to but stopped when Elvin looked at the judge again. Now she edged away, not knowing what kind of gun Elvin had and wanting some distance between them. Thirty feet would be about right—if she could get her hand on the .38 wedged down in the bag. She felt her ID case and a pack of gum.

Elvin said to her, "Where you going?" Then looked away as the judge spoke to him.

"I've seen you before."

"When you sentenced me to ten years," Elvin said, and gave his name.

"I know who you are," Gibbs said. "I want you out of here. If you're in trouble, get a lawyer."

Elvin said, "I'm not in trouble, Judge, you are," and brought the gun out of his coat pocket.

A Walther, Kathy was pretty sure, but couldn't tell what caliber. Not that it mattered, as close as he was. Twenty feet from the judge, less than that from her. She brought her wallet out of the bag, dropped it on the ground and felt inside the bag again. This time her fingers touched the checkered grip of the .38. She got her hand around it, finger on the trigger, ready to fire through the bag as Elvin raised the Walther toward Gibbs, and a woman's voice stopped both of them.

"Big?" Coming from the screened porch.

Kathy watched Elvin turn enough to look that way and still hold the Walther on Gibbs. She heard Leanne again.

"Big?"

And another voice she recognized.

"You bes' go out there now."

The screen door opened and Leanne came out in a loose white dress that reached to the ground. She seemed to barely move but was in the yard now, arms at her sides.

Elvin said, "I heard somebody else in there. A colored girl."

"Look if you want," Leanne said, staring at him, watching as he walked over and opened the screen door.

"Where'd she go?"

Leanne stood with her hands enveloped in the folds of her skirt—Kathy saw a priestess—a motionless figure in pure white. She said to Elvin, "I know why you're here. I can tell, even though your energy is vibrating at a very low frequency. You must be caked with dirt. What's that you have on?"

Elvin was squinting at her. "My suit?"

"It's polyester, isn't it? Yet I can feel your emotions, your purpose." Her eyelids began to flutter.

Kathy saw it. Leanne seemed about to speak, then clamped her jaw shut, gritting her teeth, and her hand came out of the folds of her skirt with a revolver, firing it —firing again as Elvin swung the Walther from Gibbs to put it on her and this time she hit him. Elvin stumbled back, left hand going to his hip, caught himself planting his feet apart and was taking aim at Leanne as Kathy brought the .38 out of her bag and shot him, saw him look at her and shot him again and saw him go down.

She moved toward him—Elvin sprawled on his back, eyes open, arms outstretched, the Walther lying close by—and kicked it away, not sure if there was life in him until she stood close and looked. She had shot a man. Twice through the heart or close to it. She began to think, This is what it's like . . . But this one's different. You wanted to. And looked away to keep from thinking about it. At least for now.

She saw the judge with Leanne, taking the revolver from her, saying something Kathy couldn't hear as he put his arm around his wife. Now she saw Leanne give him a vague, where-am-I kind of look and say, "What don't you believe?"

The judge was patting her shoulder. "See you come out of the house with my gun? Do what you did?"

Leanne looked surprised now. She said, "I didn't shoot him, Big. Wanda did."

Kathy stood at the window by the sink. Gibbs had said, "Let's wait before making the call," and left her there. She had this time to stare at Elvin lying in the yard and go over it again, taking it apart. See Elvin turning as she shot him. Hear the sound of it and feel the gun jump in her hand. See him looking at her as she shot him again, concentrating, taking time to aim, doing it right her first time . . . And thought, Wait a minute, you didn't mean that. *Your first time.* That was like Wesley saying, *Not yet.* Expecting it to happen. She wasn't like that and it bothered her, the feeling, to know she could shoot someone if she had to.

You're *not* like that. You don't *want* to.

No, but there it was. She could do it.

The judge came in the kitchen and got out the Jim Beam and a glass, not bothering with ice this morning. "She's on the porch staring at one of her rocks. You need a drink?"

Kathy said, "No thanks," turning from the window, and said, "I keep expecting him to move." Maybe to minimize what she had done, or to sound innocent; she wasn't sure.

"The holes you put in him," Gibbs said, "it would be a second coming if he even twitched."

"Leanne shot him too."

"No, she didn't."

"I mean Wanda."

"She didn't either," Gibbs said. "Can you imagine Leanne at the coroner's hearing? Talking to news people after? Saying a colored girl who died a hundred and thirty-five years ago shot him? Did it 'cause if I passed over now I'd have an awful time adjusting?"

"I like Leanne," Kathy said, knowing what he was leading up to.

"Then don't let her become an object of ridicule. You shot him twice. I shot him once. Okay? Can you live with that?"

"I suppose."

"We'll get our pictures in the paper and it won't hurt either of us one bit."

"I'm going to get fired for packing a gun."

"Don't worry about it. I'll speak to Corrections."

"I'm ready to leave anyway," Kathy said. "I'm thinking of going into something else."

"It's time you did," Gibbs said. "You know what you'd

be good at? Law enforcement. I could work it for you, too. All the friends I have at the Sheriff's Office? You'd be an investigator in no time. Listen, have supper with me this evening and we'll talk it over. What do you say?"